Also by Roger Zelazny

CREATURES OF LIGHT AND DARKNESS	03525	.75
LORD OF LIGHT	05652	.95
NINE PRINCES IN AMBER	04291	.75

Where better paperbacks are sold, or directly from the publisher. Include 15¢ per copy for mailing; allow three weeks for delivery.

Avon Books, Mail Order Dept., 250 West 55th Street, New York, N. Y. 10019

THE DOORS OF HIS FACE, THE LAMPS OF HIS MOUTH

AND OTHER STORIES

ROGER ZELAZNY

AVON
PUBLISHERS OF BARD, CAMELOT, DISCUS, EQUINOX AND FLARE BOOKS

To Alan Huff

CONTENTS

THE DOORS OF HIS FACE, THE LAMPS OF HIS MOUTH

AND OTHER STORIES

1.

The Doors
of His Face,
The Lamps of His Mouth

I'M A BAITMAN. No one is born a baitman, except in a
French novel where everyone is. (In fact, I think that's
the title, *We are All Bait,* Pfft!) How I got that way is
barely worth telling and has nothing to do with neo-exes,
but the days of the beast deserve a few words, so here
they are.

The Lowlands of Venus lie between the thumb and forefinger of the continent known as Hand. When you break
into Cloud Alley it swings its silverblack bowling ball
toward you without a warning. You jump then, inside that
firetailed tenpin they ride you down in, but the straps keep
you from making a fool of yourself. You generally
chuckle afterwards, but you always jump first.

Next, you study Hand to lay its illusion and the two
middle fingers become dozen-ringed archipelagoes as the
outers resolve into greengray peninsulas; the thumb is too
short, and curls like the embryo tail of Cape Horn.

You suck pure oxygen, sigh possibly, and begin the
long topple to the Lowlands.

There, you are caught like an infield fly at the Lifeline
landing area—so named because of its nearness to the
great delta in the Eastern Bay—located between the first

11

peninsula and "thumb." For a minute it seems as if you're
going to miss Lifeline and wind up as canned seafood, but
afterwards—shaking off the metaphors—you descend to
scorched concrete and present your middle-sized telephone directory of authorizations to the short, fat man in
the gray cap. The papers show that you are not subject to
mysterious inner rottings and etcetera. He then smiles you
a short, fat, gray smile and motions you toward the bus
which hauls you to the Reception Area. At the R.A. you
spend three days proving that, indeed, you are not subject
to mysterious inner rottings and etcetera.

Boredom, however, is another rot. When your three
days are up, you generally hit Lifeline hard, and it returns
the compliment as a matter of reflex. The effects of alcohol in variant atmospheres is a subject on which the con-
noisseurs have written numerous volumes, so I will con-
fine my remarks to noting that a good binge is worthy of
at least a week's time and often warrants a lifetime study.

I had been a student of exceptional promise (strictly
undergraduate) for going on two years when the *Bright
Water* fell through our marble ceiling and poured its people like targets into the city.

Pause. The Worlds Almanac re Lifeline: ". . . Port city
on the eastern coast of Hand. Employees of the Agency
for Non-terrestrial Research compromise approximately
85% of its 100,000 population (2010 Census). Its other
residents are primarily personnel maintained by several
industrial corporations engaged in basic research. Indepen-
dent marine biologists, wealthy fishing enthusiasts, and
waterfront entrepreneurs make up the remainder of its
inhabitants."

I turned to Mike Dabis, a fellow entrepreneur, and
commented on the lousy state of basic research.

"Not if the mumbled truth be known."

He paused behind his glass before continuing the slow
swallowing process calculated to obtain my interest and a
few oaths, before he continued.

"Carl," he finally observed, poker playing, "they're
shaping Ten-square."

I could have hit him. I might have refilled his glass with
sulfuric acid and looked on with glee as his lips blackened
and cracked. Instead, I grunted a noncommittal.

"Who's fool enough to shell out fifty grand a day? ANR?"

He shook his head.

"Jean Luharich," he said, "the girl with the violet contacts and fifty or sixty perfect teeth. I understand her eyes are really brown."

"Isn't she selling enough face cream these days?"

He shrugged.

"Publicity makes the wheels go 'round. Luharich Enterprises jumped sixteen points when she picked up the Sun Trophy. You ever play golf on Mercury?"

I had, but I overlooked it and continued to press.

"So she's coming here with a blank check and a fishhook?"

"*Bright Water*, today," he nodded. "Should be down by now. Lots of cameras. She wants an Ikky, bad."

"Hmm," I hmmed. "How bad?"

"Sixty day contract, Tensquare. Indefinite extension clause. Million and a half deposit," he recited.

"You seem to know a lot about it."

"I'm Personal Recruitment. Luharich Enterprises approached me last month. It helps to drink in the right places."

"Or own them." He smirked, after a moment.

I looked away, sipping my bitter brew. After awhile I swallowed several things and asked Mike what he expected to be asked, leaving myself open for his monthly temperance lecture.

"They told me to try getting you," he mentioned. "When's the last time you sailed?"

"Month and a half ago. The *Corning*."

"Small stuff," he snorted. "When have you been under, yourself?"

"It's been awhile."

"It's been over a year, hasn't it? That time you got cut by the screw, under the *Dolphin*?"

I turned to him.

"I was in the river last week, up at Angleford where the currents are strong. I can still get around."

"Sober," he added.

"I'd stay that way," I said, "on a job like this."

A doubting nod.

"Straight union rates. Triple time for extraordinary circumstances," he narrated. "Be at Hangar Sixteen with your gear, Friday morning, five hundred hours. We push off Saturday, daybreak."

"You're sailing?"

"I'm sailing."

"How come?"

"Money."

"Ikky guano."

"The bar isn't doing so well and baby needs new minks."

"I repeat—"

". . . And I want to get away from baby, renew my contact with basics—fresh air, exercise, make cash. . . ."

"All right, sorry I asked."

I poured him a drink, concentrating on H_2SO_4, but it didn't transmute. Finally I got him soused and went out into the night to walk and think things over.

Around a dozen serious attempts to land *Ichthyform Leviosaurus Levianthus,* generally known as "Ikky," had been made over the past five years. When Ikky was first sighted, whaling techniques were employed. These proved either fruitless or disastrous, and a new procedure was inaugurated. Tensquare was constructed by a wealthy sportsman named Michael Jandt, who blew his entire roll on the project.

After a year on the Eastern Ocean, he returned to file bankruptcy. Carlton Davits, a playboy fishing enthusiast, then purchased the huge raft and laid a wake for Ikky's spawning grounds. On the nineteenth day out he had a strike and lost one hundred and fifty bills' worth of untested gear, along with one *Ichthyform Levianthus.* Twelve days later, using tripled lines, he hooked, narcotized, and began to hoist the huge beast. It awakened then, destroyed a control tower, killed six men, and worked general hell over five square blocks of Tensquare. Carlton was left with partial hemiplegia and a bankruptcy suit of his own. He faded into waterfront atmosphere and Tensquare changed hands four more times, with less spectacular but equally expensive results.

Finally, the big raft, built only for one purpose, was purchased at auction by ANR for "marine research."

Lloyd's still won't insure it, and the only marine research it has ever seen is an occasional rental at fifty bills a day— to people anxious to tell Leviathan fish stories. I've been baitman on three of the voyages, and I've been close enough to count Ikky's fangs on two occasions. I want one of them to show my grandchildren, for personal reasons.

I faced the direction of the landing area and resolved a resolve.

"You want me for local coloring, gal. It'll look nice on the feature page and all that. But clear this—If anyone gets you an Ikky, it'll be me. I promise."

I stood in the empty Square. The foggy towers of Lifeline shared their mists.

Shoreline a couple eras ago, the western slope above Lifeline stretches as far as forty miles inland in some places. Its angle of rising is not a great one, but it achieves an elevation of several thousand feet before it meets the mountain range which separates us from the Highlands. About four miles inland and five hundred feet higher than Lifeline are set most of the surface airstrips and privately owned hangars. Hangar Sixteen houses Cal's Contract Cab, hop service, shore to ship. I do not like Cal, but he wasn't around when I climbed from the bus and waved to a mechanic.

Two of the hoppers tugged at the concrete, impatient beneath flywing haloes. The one on which Steve was working belched deep within its barrel carburetor and shuddered spasmodically.

"Bellyache?" I inquired.

"Yeah, gas pains and heartburn."

He twisted setscrews until it settled into an even keening, and turned to me.

"You're for out?"

I nodded.

"Tensquare. Cosmetics. Monsters. Stuff like that."

He blinked into the beacons and wiped his freckles. The temperature was about twenty, but the big overhead spots served a double purpose.

"Luharich," he muttered. "Then you *are* the one. There's some people want to see you."

"What about?"

"Cameras. Microphones. Stuff like that."

"I'd better stow my gear. Which one am I riding?"

He poked the screwdriver at the other hopper.

"That one. You're on video tape now, by the way. They wanted to get you arriving."

He turned to the hangar, turned back.

"Say 'cheese.' They'll shoot the close-ups later."

I said something other than "cheese." They must have been using telelens and been able to read my lips, because that part of the tape was never shown.

I threw my junk in the back, climbed into a passenger seat, and lit a cigarette. Five minutes later, Cal himself emerged from the office Quonset, looking cold. He came over and pounded on the side of the hopper. He jerked a thumb back at the hangar.

"They want you in there!" he called through cupped hands. "Interview!"

"The show's over!" I yelled back. "Either that, or they can get themselves another baitman!"

His rustbrown eyes became nailheads under blond brows and his glare a spike before he jerked about and stalked off. I wondered how much they had paid him to be able to squat in his hangar and suck juice from his generator.

Enough, I guess, knowing Cal. I never liked the guy, anyway.

Venus at night is a field of sable waters. On the coasts, you can never tell where the sea ends and the sky begins. Dawn is like dumping milk into an inkwell. First, there are erratic curdles of white, then streamers. Shade the bottle for a gray colloid, then watch it whiten a little more. All of a sudden you've got day. Then start heating the mixture.

I had to shed my jacket as we flashed out over the bay. To our rear, the skyline could have been under water for the way it waved and rippled in the heatfall. A hopper can accommodate four people (five, if you want to bend Regs and underestimate weight), or three passengers with the sort of gear a baitman uses. I was the only fare, though, and the pilot was like his machine. He hummed and made no unnecessary noises. Lifeline turned a somersault and evaporated in the rear mirror at about the same time Tensquare broke the fore-horizon. The pilot stopped humming and shook his head.

I leaned forward. Feelings played flopdoodle in my guts. I knew every bloody inch of the big raft, but the feelings you once took for granted change when their source is out of reach. Truthfully, I'd had my doubts I'd ever board the hulk again. But now, now I could almost believe in predestination. There it was!

A tensquare football field of a ship. A-powered. Flat as a pancake, except for the plastic blisters in the middle and the "Rooks" fore and aft, port and starboard.

The Rook towers were named for their corner positions —and any two can work together to hoist, co-powering the graffles between them. The graffles—half gaff, half grapple—can raise enormous weights to near water level; their designer had only one thing in mind, though, which accounts for the gaff half. At water level, the Slider has to implement elevation for six to eight feet before the graffles are in a position to push upward, rather than pulling.

The Slider, essentially, is a mobile room—a big box capable of moving in any of Tensquare's crisscross groovings and "anchoring" on the strike side by means of a powerful electromagnetic bond. Its winches could hoist a battleship the necessary distance, and the whole craft would tilt, rather than the Slider come loose, if you want any idea of the strength of that bond.

The Slider houses a section operated control indicator which is the most sophisticated "reel" ever designed. Drawing broadcast power from the generator beside the center blister, it is connected by shortwave with the sonar room, where the movements of the quarry are recorded and repeated to the angler seated before the section control.

The fisherman might play his "lines" for hours, days even, without seeing any more than metal and an outline on the screen. Only when the beast is graffled and the extensor shelf, located twelve feet below waterline, slides out for support and begins to aid the winches, only then does the fisherman see his catch rising before him like a

fallen Seraph. Then, as Davits learned, one looks into the
Abyss itself and is required to act. He didn't, and a hundred meters of unimaginable tonnage, undernarcotized
and hurting, broke the cables of the winch, snapped a
graffle, and took a half-minute walk across Tensquare.

We circled till the mechanical flag took notice and
waved us on down. We touched beside the personnel
hatch and I jettisoned my gear and jumped to the deck.

"Luck," called the pilot as the door was sliding shut.
Then he danced into the air and the flag clicked blank.

I shouldered my stuff and went below.

Signing in with Malvern, the de facto captain, I learned
that most of the others wouldn't arrive for a good eight
hours. They had wanted me alone at Cal's so they could
pattern the pub footage along twentieth-century cinema
lines.

Open: landing strip, dark. One mechanic prodding a
contrary hopper. Stark-o-vision shot of slow bus pulling
in. Heavily dressed baitman descends, looks about, limps
across field. Close-up: he grins. Move in for words: "Do
you think this is the time? The time he *will* be landed?"
Embarrassment, taciturnity, a shrug. Dub something—
"I see. And why do you think Miss Luharich has a better
chance than any of the others? It is because she's better
equipped? [Grin.] Because more is known now about the
creature's habits than when you were out before? Or is it
because of her will to win, to be a champion? Is it any
one of these things, or is it all of them?" Reply: "Yeah,
all of them." "—Is that why you signed on with her?
Because your instincts say, 'This one will be it'?" Answer:
"She pays union rates. I couldn't rent that damned thing
myself. And I want in." Erase. Dub something else. Fade-
out as he moves toward hopper, etcetera.

"Cheese," I said, or something like that, and took a
walk around Tensquare, by myself.

I mounted each Rook, checking out the controls and
the underwater video eyes. Then I raised the main lift.

Malvern had no objections to my testing things this
way. In fact, he encouraged it. We had sailed together
before and our positions had even been reversed upon a
time. So I wasn't surprised when I stepped off the lift into
the Hopkins Locker and found him waiting. For the next

ten minutes we inspected the big room in silence, walking through its copper coil chambers soon to be Arctic.

Finally, he slapped a wall.

"Well, will we fill it?"

I shook my head.

"I'd like to, but I doubt it. I don't give two hoots and a damn who gets credit for the catch, so long as I have a part in it. But it won't happen. That gal's an egomaniac. She'll want to operate the Slider, and she can't."

"You ever meet her?"

"Yeah."

"How long ago?"

"Four, five years."

"She was a kid then. How do you know what she can do now?"

"I know. She'll have learned every switch and reading by this time. She'll be up on all theory. But do you remember one time we were together in the starboard Rook, forward, when Ikky broke water like a porpoise?"

"How could I forget?"

"Well?"

He rubbed his emery chin.

"Maybe she can do it, Carl. She's raced torch ships and she's scubaed in bad waters back home." He glanced in the direction of invisible Hand. "And she's hunted in the Highlands. She might be wild enough to pull that horror into her lap without flinching.

". . . For John Hopkins to foot the bill and shell out seven figures for the corpus," he added. "That's money, even to a Luharich."

I ducked through a hatchway.

"Maybe you're right, but she was a rich witch when I knew her.

"And she wasn't blonde," I added, meanly.

He yawned.

"Let's find breakfast."

We did that.

When I was young I thought that being born a sea creature was the finest choice Nature could make for anyone. I grew up on the Pacific coast and spent my summers on the Gulf or the Mediterranean. I lived months of my life negotiating coral, photographing trench dwellers, and playing tag with dolphins. I fished everywhere there are fish, resenting the fact that they can go places I can't. When I grew older I wanted bigger fish, and there was nothing living that I knew of, excepting a Sequoia, that came any bigger than Ikky. That's part of it. . . .

I jammed a couple of extra rolls into a paper bag and filled a thermos with coffee. Excusing myself, I left the galley and made my way to the Slider berth. It was just the way I remembered it. I threw a few switches and the shortwave hummed.

"That you, Carl?"

"That's right, Mike. Let me have some juice down here, you double-crossing rat."

He thought it over, then I felt the hull vibrate as the generators cut in. I poured my third cup of coffee and found a cigarette.

"So why am I a double-crossing rat this time?" came his voice again.

"You knew about the cameramen at Hangar Sixteen?"

"Yes."

"Then you're a double-crossing rat. The last thing I want is publicity. 'He who fouled up so often before is ready to try it, nobly once more.' I can read it now."

"You're wrong. The spotlight's only big enough for one, and she's prettier than you."

My next comment was cut off as I threw the elevator switch and the elephant ears flapped above me. I rose, settling flush with the deck. Retracting the lateral rail, I cut forward into the groove. Amidships, I stopped at a juncture, dropped the lateral, and retracted the longitudinal rail.

I slid starboard, midway between the Rooks, halted, and threw on the coupler.

I hadn't spilled a drop of coffee.

"Show me pictures."

The screen glowed. I adjusted and got outlines of the bottom.

"Okay."

I threw a Status Blue switch and he matched it. The light went on. The winch unlocked. I aimed out over the waters, extended the arm, and fired a cast.

"Clean one," he commented.

"Status Red. Call strike." I threw a switch.

"Status Red."

The baitman would be on his way with this, to make the barbs tempting.

It's not exactly a fishhook. The cables bear hollow tubes; the tubes convey enough dope for any army of hopheads; Ikky takes the bait, dangled before him by remote control, and the fisherman rams the barbs home.

My hands moved over the console, making the necessary adjustments. I checked the narco-tank reading. Empty. Good, they hadn't been filled yet. I thumbed the Inject button.

"In the gullet," Mike murmured.

I released the cables. I played the beast imagined. I let him run, swinging the winch to stimulate his sweep.

I had an air conditioner on and my shirt off and it was still uncomfortably hot, which is how I knew that morning had gone over into noon. I was dimly aware of the arrivals and departures of the hoppers. Some of the crew sat in the "shade" of the doors I had left open, watching the operation. I didn't see Jean arrive or I would have ended the session and gotten below.

She broke my concentration by slamming the door hard enough to shake the bond.

"Mind telling me who authorized you to bring up the Slider?" she asked.

"No one," I replied. "I'll take it below now."

"Just move aside."

I did, and she took my seat. She was wearing brown slacks and a baggy shirt and she had her hair pulled back in a practical manner. Her cheeks were flushed, but not necessarily from the heat. She attacked the panel with a nearly amusing intensity that I found disquieting.

"Status Blue," she snapped, breaking a violet fingernail on the toggle.

I forced a yawn and buttoned my shirt slowly. She threw a side glance my way, checked the registers, and fired a cast.

I monitored the lead on the screen. She turned to me for a second.

"Status Red," she said levelly.

I nodded my agreement.

She worked the winch sideways to show she knew how. I didn't doubt she knew how and she didn't doubt that I didn't doubt, but then—

"In case you're wondering," she said, "you're not going to be anywhere near this thing. You were hired as a baitman, remember? Not a Slider operator! A baitman! Your duties consist of swimming out and setting the table for our friend the monster. It's dangerous, but you're getting well paid for it. Any questions?"

She squashed the Inject button and I rubbed my throat.

"Nope," I smiled, "but I am qualified to run that thingamajigger—and if you need me I'll be available, at union rates."

"Mister Davits," she said, "I don't want a loser operating this panel."

"Miss Luharich, there has never been a winner at this game."

She started reeling in the cable and broke the bond at the same time, so that the whole Slider shook as the big yo-yo returned. We skidded a couple of feet backward. She raised the laterals and we shot back along the groove. Slowing, she transferred rails and we jolted to a clanging halt, then shot off at a right angle. The crew scrambled away from the hatch as we skidded onto the elevator.

"In the future, Mister Davits, do not enter the Slider without being ordered," she told me.

"Don't worry. I won't even step inside if I am ordered," I answered. "I signed on as a baitman. Remember? If you want me in here, you'll have to *ask* me."

"That'll be the day," she smiled.

I agreed, as the doors closed above us. We dropped the subject and headed in our different directions after the Slider came to a halt in its berth. She did say "good day," though, which I thought showed breeding as well as determination, in reply to my chuckle.

Later that night Mike and I stoked our pipes in Malvern's cabin. The winds were shuffling waves, and a steady spattering of rain and hail overhead turned the deck into a tin roof.

"Nasty," suggested Malvern.

I nodded. After two bourbons the room had become a familiar woodcut, with its mahogany furnishings (which I had transported from Earth long ago on a whim) and the dark walls, the seasoned face of Malvern, and the perpetually puzzled expression of Dabis set between the big pools of shadow that lay behind chairs and splashed in cornets, all cast by the tiny table light and seen through a glass, brownly.

"Glad I'm in here."

"What's it like underneath on a night like this?"

I puffed, thinking of my light cutting through insides of a black diamond, shaken slightly. The meteor-dart of a suddenly illuminated fish, the swaying of grotesque ferns, like nebulae—shadow, then green, then gone—swam in a moment through my mind. I guess it's like a spaceship would feel, if a spaceship could feel, crossing between worlds—and quiet, uncannily, preternaturally quiet; and peaceful as sleep.

"Dark," I said, "and not real choppy below a few fathoms."

"Another eight hours and we shove off," commented Mike.

"Ten, twelve days, we should be there," noted Malvern.

"What do you thing Ikky's doing?"

"Sleeping on the bottom with Mrs. Ikky if he has any brains."

"He hasn't. I've seen ANR's skeletal extrapolation from the bones that have washed up—"

"Hasn't everyone?"

". . . Fully fleshed, he'd be over a hundred meters long. That right, Carl?"

I agreed.

". . . Not much of a brain box, though, for his bulk."

"Smart enough to stay out of our locker."

Chuckles, because nothing exists but this room, really. The world outside is an empty, sleet drummed deck. We lean back and make clouds.

"Boss lady does not approve of unauthorized fly fishing."

"Boss lady can walk north till her hat floats."

"What did she say in there?"

"She told me that my place, with fish manure, is on the bottom."

"You don't Slide?"

"I bait."

"We'll see."

"That's all I do. If she wants a Slideman she's going to have to ask nicely."

"You think she'll have to?"

"I think she'll have to."

"And if she does, can you do it?"

"A fair question," I puffed. "I don't know the answer, though."

I'd incorporate my soul and trade forty percent of the stock for the answer. I'd give a couple years off my life for the answer. But there doesn't seem to be a lineup of supernatural takers, because no one knows. Supposing when we get out there, luck being with us, we find ourselves an Ikky? Supposing we succeed in baiting him and get lines on him. What then? If we get him shipside, will she hold on or crack up? What if she's made of sterner stuff than Davits, who used to hunt sharks with poison-darted air pistols? Supposing she lands him and Davits has to stand there like a video extra.

Worse yet, supposing she asks for Davits and he still stands there like a video extra or something else—say, some yellowbellied embodiment named Cringe?

It was when I got him up above the eight-foot horizon of steel and looked out at all that body, sloping on and on till it dropped out of sight like a green mountain range . . . And that head. Small for the body, but still immense. Fat, craggy, with lidless roulettes that had spun black and red since before my forefathers decided to try the New Continent. And swaying.

Fresh narco-tanks had been connected. It needed another shot, fast. But I was paralyzed.

It had made a noise like God playing a Hammond organ. . . .

And looked at me!

I don't know if seeing is even the same process in eyes like those. I doubt it. Maybe I was just a gray blur behind a black rock, with the plexi-reflected sky hurting its pupils. But it fixed on me. Perhaps the snake doesn't really paralyze the rabbit, perhaps it's just that rabbits are cowards by constitution. But it began to struggle and I still couldn't move, fascinated.

Fascinated by all that power, by those eyes, they found me there fifteen minutes later, a little broken about the head and shoulders, the Inject still unpushed.

And I dream about those eyes. I want to face them once more, even if their finding takes forever. I've got to know if there's something inside me that sets me apart from a rabbit, from notched plates of reflexes and instincts that always fall apart in exactly the same way whenever the proper combination is spun.

Looking down, I noticed that my hand was shaking. Glancing up, I noticed that no one else was noticing.

I finished my drink and emptied my pipe. It was late and no songbirds were singing.

I sat whittling, my legs hanging over the aft edge, the chips spinning down into the furrow of our wake. Three days out. No action.

"You!"

"Me?"

"You."

Hair like the end of the rainbow, eyes like nothing in nature, fine teeth.

"Hello."

"There's a safety rule against what you're doing, you know."

"I know. I've been worrying about it all morning."

A delicate curl climbed my knife then drifted out behind us. It settled into the foam and was plowed under. I watched her reflection in my blade, taking a secret pleasure in its distortion.

"Are you baiting me?" she finally asked.

I heard her laugh then, and turned, knowing it had been intentional.

"What, me?"

"I could push you off from here, very easily."

"I'd make it back."

"Would you push me off, then—some dark night, perhaps?"

"They're all dark, Miss Luharich. No, I'd rather make you a gift of my carving."

She seated herself beside me then, and I couldn't help but notice the dimples in her knees. She wore white shorts and a halter and still had an offworld tan to her which was awfully appealing. I almost felt a twinge of guilt at having planned the whole scene, but my right hand still blocked her view of the wooden animal.

"Okay, I'll bite. What have you got for me?"

"Just a second. It's almost finished."

Solemnly, I passed her the wooden jackass I had been carving. I felt a little sorry and slightly jackass-ish myself, but I had to follow through. I always do. The mouth was split into a braying grin. The ears were upright.

She didn't smile and she didn't frown. She just studied it.

"It's very good," she finally said, "like most things you do—and appropriate, perhaps."

"Give it to me." I extended a palm.

She handed it back and I tossed it out over the water. It missed the white water and bobbed for awhile like a pigmy seahorse.

"Why did you do that?"

"It was a poor joke. I'm sorry."

"Maybe you are right, though. Perhaps this time I've bitten off a little too much."

I snorted.

"Then why not do something safer, like another race?"

She shook her end of the rainbow.

"No. It has to be an Ikky."

"Why?"

"Why did you want one so badly that you threw away a fortune?"

"Many reasons," I said. "An unfrocked analyst who held black therapy sessions in his basement once told me, 'Mister Davits, you need to reinforce the image of your masculinity by catching one of every kind of fish in existence.' Fish are a very ancient masculinity symbol, you know. So I set out to do it. I have one more to go. Why do you want to reinforce *your* masculinity?"

"I don't," she said. "I don't want to reinforce anything but Luharich Enterprises. My chief statistician once said, 'Miss Luharich, sell all the cold cream and face powder in the System and you'll be a happy girl. Rich, too.' And he was right. I am the proof. I can look the way I do and

do anything, and I sell most of the lipstick and face powder in the System—but I have to be *able* to do anything."

"You do look cool and efficient," I observed.

"I don't feel cool," she said, rising. "Let's go for a
swim."

"May I point out that we are making pretty good
time?"

"If you want to indicate the obvious, you may. You
said you could make it back to the ship, unassisted. Change
your mind?"

"No."

"Then get us two scuba outfits and I'll race you under
Tensquare.

"I'll win, too," she added.

I stood and looked down at her, because that usually
makes me feel superior to women.

"Daughter of Lir, eyes of Picasso," I said, "you've got
yourself a race. Meet me at the forward Rook, starboard,
in ten minutes."

"Ten minutes," she agreed.

And ten minutes it was. From the center blister to the
Rook took maybe two of them, with the load I was carrying. My sandals grew very hot and I was glad to shuck
them for flippers when I reached the comparative cool
of the corner.

We slid into harnesses and adjusted our gear. She had
changed into a trim one-piece green job that made me
shade my eyes and look away, then look back again.

I fastened a rope ladder and kicked it over the side.
Then I pounded on the wall of the Rook.

"Yeah?"

"You talk to the port Rook, aft?" I called.

"They're all set up," came the answer. "There's ladders
and drag-lines all over that end."

"You sure you want to do this?" asked the sunburnt
little gink who was her publicity man, Anderson yclept.

He sat beside the Rook in a deckchair, sipping lemonade
through a straw.

"It might be dangerous," he observed, sunken-mouthed.
(His teeth were beside him, in another glass.)

"That's right," she smiled. "It *will* be dangerous. Not
overly, though."

"Then why don't you let me get some pictures? We'd have them back to Lifeline in an hour. They'd be in New York by tonight. Good copy."

"No," she said, and turned away from both of us.

She raised her hands to her eyes.

"Here, keep these for me."

She passed him a box full of her unseeing, and when she turned back to me they were the same brown that I remembered.

"Ready?"

"No," I said, tautly. "Listen carefully, Jean. If you're going to play this game there are a few rules. First," I counted, "we're going to be directly beneath the hull, so we have to start low and keep moving. If we bump the bottom, we could rupture an air tank. . . ."

She began to protest that any moron knew that and I cut her down.

"Second," I went on, "there won't be much light, so we'll stay close together, and we will *both* carry torches."

Her wet eyes flashed.

"I dragged you out of Govino without—"

Then she stopped and turned away. She picked up a lamp.

"Okay. Torches. Sorry."

". . . And watch out for the drive-screws," I finished. "There'll be strong currents for at least fifty meters behind them."

She wiped her eyes again and adjusted the mask.

"All right, let's go."

We went.

She led the way, at my insistence. The surface layer was pleasantly warm. At two fathoms the water was bracing; at five it was nice and cold. At eight we let go the swinging stairway and struck out. Tensquare sped forward and we raced in the opposite direction, tattooing the hull yellow at ten-second intervals.

The hull stayed where it belonged, but we raced on like two darkside satellites. Periodically, I tickled her frog feet with my light and traced her antennae of bubbles. About a five meter lead was fine; I'd beat her in the home stretch, but I couldn't let her drop behind yet.

Beneath us, black. Immense. Deep. The Mindanao of

Venus, where eternity might eventually pass the dead to a rest in cities of unnamed fishes. I twisted my head away and touched the hull with a feeler of light; it told me we were about a quarter of the way along.

I increased my beat to match her stepped-up stroke, and narrowed the distance which she had suddenly opened by a couple meters. She sped up again and I did, too. I spotted her with my beam.

She turned and it caught on her mask. I never knew whether she'd been smiling. Probably. She raised two fingers in a V-for-Victory and then cut ahead at full speed.

I should have known. I should have felt it coming. It was just a race to her, something else to win. Damn the torpedoes!

So I leaned into it, hard. I don't shake in the water. Or, if I do it doesn't matter and I don't notice it. I began to close the gap again.

She looked back, sped on, looked back. Each time she looked it was nearer, until I'd narrowed it down to the original five meters.

Then she hit the jatoes.

That's what I had been fearing. We were about halfway under and she shouldn't have done it. The powerful jets of compressed air could easily rocket her upward into the hull, or tear something loose if she allowed her body to twist. Their main use is in tearing free from marine plants or fighting bad currents. I had wanted them along as a safety measure, because of the big suck-and-pull windmills behind.

She shot ahead like a meteorite, and I could feel a sudden tingle of perspiration leaping to meet and mix with the churning waters.

I swept ahead, not wanting to use my own guns, and she tripled, quadrupled the margin.

The jets died and she was still on course. Okay, I was an old fuddyduddy. She *could* have messed up and headed toward the top.

I plowed the sea and began to gather back my yardage, a foot at a time. I wouldn't be able to catch her or beat her now, but I'd be on the ropes before she hit deck.

Then the spinning magnets began their insistence and

she wavered. It was an awfully powerful drag, even at this
distance. The call of the meat grinder.

I'd been scratched up by one once, under the *Dolphin,*
a fishing boat of the middle-class. I *had* been drinking, but
it was also a rough day, and the thing had been turned
on prematurely. Fortunately, it was turned off in time,
also, and a tendon-stapler made everything good as new,
except in the log, where it only mentioned that I'd been
drinking. Nothing about it being off-hours when I had a
right to do as I damn well pleased.

She had slowed to half her speed, but she was still
moving crosswise, toward the port, aft corner. I began to
feel the pull myself and had to slow down. She'd made it
past the main one, but she seemed too far back. It's hard
to gauge distances under water, but each red beat of time
told me I was right. She was out of danger from the main
one, but the smaller port screw, located about eighty meters in, was no longer a threat but a certainty.

She had turned and was pulling away from it now.
Twenty meters separated us. She was standing still. Fifteen.

Slowly, she began a backward drifting. I hit my jatoes,
aiming two meters behind her and about twenty back of
the blades.

Straightline! Thankgod! Catching, softbelly, leadpipe on
shoulder SWIMLIKEHELL! maskcracked, not broke though
AND UP!

We caught a line and I remember brandy.

Into the cradle endlessly rocking I spit, pacing. Insomnia
tonight and left shoulder sore again, so let it rain on me—
they can cure rheumatism. Stupid as hell. What I said. In
blankets and shivering. She: "Carl, I can't say it." Me:
"Then call it square for that night in Govino, Miss
Luharich. Huh?" She: nothing. Me: "Any more of that
brandy?" She: "Give me another, too." Me: sounds of
sipping. It had only lasted three months. No alimony.
Many $ on both sides. Not sure whether they were happy
or not. Wine-dark Aegean. Good fishing. Maybe he should
have spent more time on shore. Or perhaps she shouldn't
have. Good swimmer, though. Dragged him all the way to
Vido to wring out his lungs. Young. Both. Strong. Both.
Rich and spoiled as hell. Ditto. Corfu should have brought

them closer. Didn't. I think that mental cruelty was a
trout. He wanted to go to Canada. She: "Go to hell if you
want!" He: "Will you go along?" She: "No." But she did,
anyhow. Many hells. Expensive. He lost a monster or two.
She inherited a couple. Lot of lightning tonight. Stupid as
hell. Civility's the coffin of a conned soul. By whom?—
Sounds like a bloody neo-ex. . . . But I hate you, Anderson,
with your glass full of teeth and her new eyes. . . . Can't
keep this pipe lit, keep sucking tobacco. Spit again!

Seven days out and the scope showed Ikky.

Bells jangled, feet pounded, and some optimist set the
thermostat in the Hopkins. Malvern wanted me to sit out,
but I slipped into my harness and waited for whatever
came. The bruise looked worse than it felt. I had exercised
every day and the shoulder hadn't stiffened on me.

A thousand meters ahead and thirty fathoms deep, it
tunneled our path. Nothing showed on the surface.

"Will we chase him?" asked an excited crewman.

"Not unless she feels like using money for fuel." I
shrugged.

Soon the scope was clear, and it stayed that way. We
remained on alert and held our course.

I hadn't said over a dozen words to my boss since the
last time we went drowning together, so I decided to raise
the score.

"Good afternoon," I approached. "What's new?"

"He's going north-northeast. We'll have to let this one
go. A few more days and we can afford some chasing. Not
yet."

Sleek head . . .

I nodded. "No telling where this one's headed."

"How's your shoulder?"

"All right. How about you?"

Daughter of Lir . . .

"Fine. By the way, you're down for a nice bonus."

Eyes of perdition!

"Don't mention it," I told her back.

Later that afternoon, and appropriately, a storm shattered. (I prefer "shattered" to "broke." It gives a more
accurate idea of the behavior of tropical storms on Venus
and saves lots of words.) Remember that inkwell I men-

tioned earlier? Now take it between thumb and forefinger and hit its side with a hammer. Watch your self! Don't get splashed or cut—

Dry, then drenched. The sky one million bright fractures as the hammer falls. And sounds of breaking.

"Everyone below?" suggested loudspeakers to the already scurrying crew.

Where was I? Who do you think was doing the loud-speaking?

Everything loose went overboard when the water got to walking, but by then no people were loose. The Slider was the first thing below decks. Then the big lifts lowered their shacks.

I had hit it for the nearest Rook with a yell the moment I recognized the pre-brightening of the holocaust. From there I cut in the speakers and spent half a minute coaching the track team.

Minor injuries had occurred, Mike told me over the radio, but nothing serious. I, however, was marooned for the duration. The Rooks do not lead anywhere; they're set too far out over the hull to provide entry downwards, what with the extensor shelves below.

So I undressed myself of the tanks which I had worn for the past several hours, crossed my flippers on the table, and leaned back to watch the hurricane. The top was black as the bottom and we were in between, and somewhat illuminated because of all that flat, shiny space. The waters above didn't rain down—they just sort of got together and dropped.

The Rooks were secure enough—they'd weathered any number of these onslaughts—it's just that their positions gave them a greater arc of rise and descent when Ten-square makes like the rocker of a very nervous grandma. I had used the belts from my rig to strap myself into the bolted-down chair, and I removed several years in purgatory from the soul of whoever left a pack of cigarettes in the table drawer.

I watched the water make teepees and mountains and hands and trees until I started seeing faces and people. So I called Mike.

"What are you doing down there?"

"Wondering what you're doing up there," he replied. "What's it like?"

"You're from the Midwest, aren't you?"

"Yeah."

"Get bad storms out there?"

"Sometimes."

"Try to think of the worst one you were ever in. Got a slide rule handy?"

"Right here."

"Then put a one under it, imagine a zero or two following after, and multiply the thing out."

"I can't imagine the zeros."

"Then retain the multiplicand—that's all you can do."

"So what are you doing up there?"

"I've strapped myself in the chair. I'm watching things roll around the floor right now."

I looked up and out again. I saw one darker shadow in the forest.

"Are you praying or swearing?"

"Damned if I know. But if this were the Slider—if only this were the Slider!"

"He's out there?"

I nodded, forgetting that he couldn't see me.

Big, as I remembered him. He'd only broken surface for a few moments, to look around. *There is no power on Earth that can be compared with him who was made to fear no one.* I dropped my cigarette. It was the same as before. Paralysis and an unborn scream.

"You all right, Carl?"

He had looked at me again. Or seemed to. Perhaps that mindless brute had been waiting half a millenium to ruin the life of a member of the most highly developed species in business. . . .

"You okay?"

. . . Or perhaps it had been ruined already, long before their encounter, and theirs was just a meeting of beasts, the stronger bumping the weaker aside, body to psyche. . . .

"Carl, dammit! Say something!"

He broke again, this time nearer. Did you ever see the trunk of a tornado? It seems like something alive, moving around in all that dark. Nothing has a right to be so big, so strong, and moving. It's a sickening sensation.

"Please answer me."

He was gone and did not come back that day. I finally made a couple of wisecracks at Mike, but I held my next cigarette in my right hand.

The next seventy or eighty thousand waves broke by with a monotonous similarity. The five days that held them were also without distinction. The morning of the thirteenth day out, though, our luck began to rise. The bells broke our coffee-drenched lethargy into small pieces, and we dashed from the galley without hearing what might have been Mike's finest punchline.

"Aft!" cried someone. "Five hundred meters!"

I stripped to my trunks and started buckling. My stuff is always within grabbing distance.

I flipflopped across the deck, girding myself with a deflated squiggler.

"Five hundred meters, twenty fathoms!" boomed the speakers.

The big traps banged upward and the Slider grew to its full height, m'lady at the console. It rattled past me and took root ahead. Its one arm rose and lengthened.

I breasted the Slider as the speakers called, "Foureighty, twenty!"

"Status Red!"

A belch like an emerging champagne cork and the line arced high over the waters.

"Four-eighty, twenty!" it repeated, all Malvern and static. "Baitman, attend!"

I adjusted my mask and hand-over-handed it down the side. Then warm, then cool, then away.

Green, vast, down. Fast. This is the place where I am equal to a squiggler. If something big decides a baitman looks tastier than what he's carrying, then irony colors his title as well as the water about it.

I caught sight of the drifting cables and followed them down. Green to dark green to black. It had been a long cast, too long. I'd never had to follow one this far down before. I didn't want to switch on my torch.

But I had to.

Bad! I still had a long way to go. I clenched my teeth and stuffed my imagination into a straightjacket.

Finally the line came to an end.

I wrapped one arm about it and unfastened the squiggler. I attached it, working as fast as I could, and plugged in the little insulated connections which are the reason it can't be fired with the line. Ikky could break them, but by then it wouldn't matter.

My mechanical eel hooked up, I pulled its section plugs and watched it grow. I had been dragged deeper during this operation, which took about a minute and a half. I was near—too near—to where I never wanted to be.

Loathe as I had been to turn on my light, I was suddenly afraid to turn it off. Panic gripped me and I seized the cable with both hands. The squiggler began to glow, pinkly. It started to twist. It was twice as big as I am and doubtless twice as attractive to pink squiggler-eaters. I told myself this until I believed it, then I switched off my light and started up.

If I bumped into something enormous and steel-hided my heart had orders to stop beating immediately and release me—to dart fitfully forever along Acheron, and gibbering.

Ungibbering, I made it to green water and fled back to the nest.

As soon as they hauled me aboard I made my mask a necklace, shaded my eyes, and monitored for surface turbulence. My first question, of course, was: "Where is he?"

"Nowhere," said a crewman; "we lost him right after you went over. Can't pick him up on the scope now. Musta dived."

"Too bad."

The squiggler stayed down, enjoying its bath. My job ended for the time being, I headed back to warm my coffee with rum.

From behind me, a whisper: "Could you laugh like that afterwards?"

Perceptive Answer: "Depends on what he's laughing at."

Still chuckling, I made my way into the center blister with two cupfuls.

"Still hell and gone?"

Mike nodded. His big hands were shaking, and mine were steady as a surgeon's when I set down the cups.

He jumped as I shrugged off the tanks and looked for a bench.

"Don't drip on that panel! You want to kill yourself and blow expensive fuses?"

I toweled down, then settled down to watching the unfilled eye on the wall. I yawned happily; my shoulder seemed good as new.

The little box that people talk through wanted to say something, so Mike lifted the switch and told it to go ahead.

"Is Carl there, Mister Dabis?"

"Yes, ma'am."

"Then let me talk to him."

Mike motioned and I moved.

"Talk," I said.

"Are you all right?"

"Yes, thanks. Shouldn't I be?"

"That was a long swim. I—I guess I overshot my cast."

"I'm happy," I said. "More triple-time for me. I really clean up on that hazardous duty clause."

"I'll be more careful next time," she apologized. "I guess I was too eager. Sorry—" Something happened to the sentence, so she ended it there, leaving me with half a bagful of replies I'd been saving.

I lifted the cigarette from behind Mike's ear and got a light from the one in the ashtray.

"Carl, she was being nice," he said, after turning to study the panels.

"I know," I told him. "I wasn't."

"I mean, she's an awfully pretty kid, pleasant. Headstrong and all that. But what's she done to you?"

"Lately?" I asked.

He looked at me, then dropped his eyes to his cup.

"I know it's none of my bus—" he began.

"Cream and sugar?"

Ikky didn't return that day, or that night. We picked up some Dixieland out of Lifeline and let the muskrat ramble while Jean had her supper sent to the Slider. Later she had a bunk assembled inside. I piped in "Deep Water Blues" when it came over the air and waited for her to call up and cuss us out. She didn't, though, so I decided she was sleeping.

Then I got Mike interested in a game of chess that went on until daylight. It limited conversation to several "checks," one "checkmate," and a "damn!" Since he's a poor loser it also effectively sabotaged subsequent talk, which was fine with me. I had a steak and fried potatoes for breakfast and went to bed.

Ten hours later someone shook me awake and I propped myself on one elbow, refusing to open my eyes.

"Whassamadder?"

"I'm sorry to get you up," said one of the younger crewmen, "but Miss Luharich wants you to disconnect the squiggler so we can move on."

I knuckled open one eye, still deciding whether I should be amused.

"Have it hauled to the side. Anyone can disconnect it."

"It's at the side now, sir. But she said it's in your contract and we'd better do things right."

"That's very considerate of her. I'm sure my Local appreciates her remembering."

"Uh, she also said to tell you to change your trunks and comb your hair, and shave, too. Mister Anderson's going to film it."

"Okay. Run along; tell her I'm on my way—and ask if she has some toenail polish I can borrow."

I'll save on details. It took three minutes in all, and I played it properly, even pardoning myself when I slipped and bumped into Anderson's white tropicals with the wet squiggler; he smiled, brushed it off; she smiled, even though Luharich Complectacolor couldn't completely mask the dark circles under her eyes; and I smiled, waving to all our fans out there in videoland. —Remember, Mrs. Universe, you, too, can look like a monster-catcher. Just use Luharich face cream.

I went below and made myself a tuna sandwich, with mayonnaise.

Two days like icebergs—bleak, blank, half-melting, all frigid, mainly out of sight, and definitely a threat to peace of mind—drifted by and were good to put behind. I experienced some old guilt feelings and had a few disturbing dreams. Then I called Lifeline and checked my bank balance.

"Going shopping?" asked Mike, who had put the call through for me.

"Going home," I answered.

"Huh?"

"I'm out of the baiting business after this one, Mike. The Devil with Ikky! The Devil with Venus and Luharich Enterprises! And the Devil with you!"

Up eyebrows.

"What brought that on?"

"I waited over a year for this job. Now that I'm here, I've decided the whole thing stinks."

"You knew what it was when you signed on. No matter what else you're doing, you're selling face cream when you work for face cream sellers."

"Oh, that's not what's biting me. I admit the commercial angle irritates me, but Tensquare has always been a publicity spot, ever since the first time it sailed."

"What, then?"

"Five or six things, all added up. The main one being that I don't care any more. Once it meant more to me than anything else to hook that critter, and now it doesn't. I went broke on what started out as a lark and I wanted blood for what it cost me. Now I realize that maybe I had it coming. I'm beginning to feel sorry for Ikky."

"And you don't want him now?"

"I'll take him if he comes peacefully, but I don't feel like sticking out my neck to make him crawl into the Hopkins."

"I'm inclined to think it's one of the four or five other things you said you added."

"Such as?"

He scrutinized the ceiling.

I growled.

"Okay, but I won't say it, not just to make you happy you guessed right."

He, smirking: "That look she wears isn't just for Ikky."

"No good, no good." I shook my head. "We're both fission chambers by nature. You can't have jets on both ends of the rocket and expect to go anywhere—what's in the middle just gets smashed."

"That's how it *was*. None of my business, of course—"

"Say that again and you'll say it without teeth."

"Any day, big man"—he looked up—"any place . . ."

"So go ahead. Get it said!"

"She doesn't care about that bloody reptile, she came here to drag you back where you belong. You're not the baitman this trip."

"Five years is too long."

"There must be something under that cruddy hide of yours that people like," he muttered, "or I wouldn't be talking like this. Maybe you remind us humans of some really ugly dog we felt sorry for when we were kids. Anyhow, someone wants to take you home and raise you—also, something about beggars not getting menus."

"Buddy," I chuckled, "do you know what I'm going to do when I hit Lifeline?"

"I can guess."

"You're wrong. I'm torching it to Mars, and then I'll cruise back home, first class. Venus bankruptcy provisions do not apply to Martian trust funds, and I've still got a wad tucked away where moth and corruption enter not. I'm going to pick up a big old mansion on the Gulf and if you're ever looking for a job you can stop around and open bottles for me."

"You are a yellowbellied fink," he commented.

"Okay," I admitted, "but it's her I'm thinking of, too."

"I've heard the stories about you both," he said. "So you're a heel and a goofoff and she's a bitch. That's called compatibility these days. I dare you, baitman, try keeping something you catch."

I turned.

"If you ever want that job, look me up."

I closed the door quietly behind me and left him sitting there waiting for it to slam.

The day of the beast dawned like any other. Two days after my gutless flight from empty waters I went down to rebait. Nothing on the scope. I was just making things ready for the routine attempt.

I hollered a "good morning" from outside the Slider and received an answer from inside before I pushed off. I had reappraised Mike's words, sans sound, sans fury, and while

I did not approve of their sentiment or significance, I had opted for civility anyhow.

So down, under, and away. I followed a decent cast about two hundred-ninety meters out. The snaking cables burned black to my left and I paced their undulations from the yellowgreen down into the darkness. Soundless lay the wet night, and I bent my way through it like a cock-eyed comet, bright tail before.

I caught the line, slick and smooth, and began baiting. An icy world swept by me then, ankles to head. It was a draft, as if some one had opened a big door beneath me. I wasn't drifting downwards that fast either.

Which meant that something might be moving up, something big enough to displace a lot of water. I still didn't think it was Ikky. A freak current of some sort, but not Ikky. Ha!

I had finished attaching the leads and pulled the first plug when a big, rugged, black island grew beneath me. . . .

I flicked the beam downward. His mouth was opened.

I was rabbit.

Waves of the death-fear passed downward. My stomach imploded. I grew dizzy.

Only one thing, and one thing only. Left to do. I managed it, finally. I pulled the rest of the plugs.

I could count the scaly articulations ridging his eyes by then.

The squiggler grew, pinked into phosphorescence . . . squiggled!

Then my lamp. I had to kill it, leaving just the bait before him.

One glance back as I jammed the jatoes to life.

He was so near that the squiggler reflected on his teeth, in his eyes. Four meters, and I kissed his lambent jowls with two jets of backwash as I soared. Then I didn't know whether he was following or halted. I began to black out as I waited to be eaten.

The jatoes died and I kicked weakly.

Too fast, I felt a cramp coming on. One flick of the beam, cried rabbit. One second, to know . . .

Or end things up, I answered. No, rabbit, we don't dart before hunters. Stay dark.

Green waters finally, to yellowgreen, then top.

Doubling, I beat off toward Tensquare. The waves from the explosion behind pushed me on ahead. The world closed in, and a screamed, "He's alive!" in the distance.

A giant shadow and a shock wave. The line was alive, too. Happy Fishing Grounds. Maybe I did something wrong. . . .

Somewhere Hand was clenched. What's bait?

A few million years. I remember starting out as a one-celled organism and painfully becoming an amphibian, then an air-breather. From somewhere high in the treetops I heard a voice.

"He's coming around."

I evolved back into homosapience, then a step further into a hangover.

"Don't try to get up yet."

"Have we got him?" I slurred.

"Still fighting, but he's hooked. We thought he took you for an appetizer."

"So did I."

"Breathe some of this and shut up."

A funnel over my face. Good. Lift your cups and drink. . . .

"He was awfully deep. Below scope range. We didn't catch him till he started up. Too late, then."

I began to yawn.

"We'll get you inside now."

I managed to uncase my ankle knife.

"Try it and you'll be minus a thumb."

"You need rest."

"Then bring me a couple more blankets. I'm staying."

I fell back and closed my eyes.

Someone was shaking me. Gloom and cold. Spotlights bled yellow on the deck. I was in a jury-rigged bunk, bulked against the center blister. Swaddled in wool, I still shivered.

"It's been eleven hours. You're not going to see anything now."

I tasted blood.

"Drink this."

Water. I had a remark but I couldn't mouth it.

"Don't ask how I feel," I croaked. "I know that comes next, but don't ask me. Okay?"

"Okay. Want to go below now?"

"No. Just get me my jacket."

"Right here."

"What's he doing?"

"Nothing. He's deep, he's doped but he's staying down."

"How long since last time he showed?"

"Two hours, about."

"Jean?"

"She won't let anyone in the Slider. Listen, Mike says come on in. He's right behind you in the blister."

I sat up and turned. Mike was watching. He gestured; I gestured back.

I swung my feet over the edge and took a couple of deep breaths. Pains in my stomach. I got to my feet and made it into the blister.

"Howza gut?" queried Mike.

I checked the scope. No Ikky. Too deep.

"You buying?"

"Yeah, coffee."

"Not coffee."

"You're ill. Also, coffee is all that's allowed in here."

"Coffee is a brownish liquid that burns your stomach. You have some in the bottom drawer."

"No cups. You'll have to use a glass."

"Tough."

He poured.

"You do that well. Been practicing for that job?"

"What job?"

"The one I offered you—"

A bolt on the scope!

"Rising, ma'am! Rising!" he yelled into the box.

"Thanks, Mike. I've got it in here," she crackled.

"Jean!"

"Shut up! She's busy!"

"Was that Carl?"

"Yeah," I called. "Talk later," and I cut it.

Why did I do that?

"Why did you do that?"

I didn't know.

"I don't know."

Damned echoes! I got up and walked outside.

Nothing. Nothing.

Something?

Tensquare actually rocked! He must have turned when he saw the hull and started downward again. White water to my left, and boiling. An endless spaghetti of cable roared hotly into the belly of the deep.

I stood awhile, then turned and went back inside.

Two hours sick. Four, and better.

"The dope's getting to him."

"Yeah."

"What about Miss Luharich?"

"What about her?"

"She must be half dead."

"Probably."

"What are you going to do about it?"

"She signed the contract for this. She knew what might happen. It did."

"I think you could land him."

"So do I."

"So does she."

"Then let her ask me."

Ikky was drifting lethargically, at thirty fathoms.

I took another walk and happened to pass behind the Slider. She wasn't looking my way.

"Carl, come in here!"

Eyes of Picasso, that's what, and a conspiracy to make me Slide . . .

"It that an order?"

"Yes—No! Please."

I dashed inside and monitored. He was rising.

"Push or pull?"

I slammed the "wind" and he came like a kitten.

"Make up your own mind now."

He balked at ten fathoms.

"Play him?"

"No!"

She wound him upwards—five fathoms, four . . .

She hit the extensors at two, and they caught him. Then the graffles.

Cries without and a heat lightning of flashbulbs.

The crew saw Ikky.

He began to struggle. She kept the cables tight, raised the graffles . . .

Up.

Another two feet and the graffles began pushing.

Screams and fast footfalls.

Giant beanstalk in the wind, his neck, waving. The green hills of his shoulders grew.

"He's big, Carl!" she cried.

And he grew, and grew, and grew uneasy . . .

"Now!"

He looked down.

He looked down, as the god of our most ancient ancestors might have looked down. Fear, shame, and mocking laughter rang in my head. Her head, too?

"Now!"

She looked up at the nascent earthquake.

"I can't!"

It was going to be so damnably simple this time, now the rabbit had died. I reached out.

I stopped.

"Push it yourself."

"I can't. You do it. Land him, Carl!"

"No. If I do, you'll wonder for the rest of your life whether you could have. You'll throw away your soul finding out. I know you will, because we're alike, and I did it that way. Find out now!"

She stared.

I gripped her shoulders.

"Could be that's me out there," I offered. "I am a green sea serpent, a hateful, monstrous beast, and out to destroy you. I am answerable to no one. Push the Inject."

Her hand moved to the button, jerked back.

"Now!"

She pushed it.

I lowered her still form to the floor and finished things up with Ikky.

It was a good seven hours before I awakened to the steady, sea-chewing grind of Tensquare's blades.

"You're sick," commented Mike.

"How's Jean?"

"The same."

"Where's the best?"

"Here."

"Good." I rolled over. ". . . Didn't get away this time."

So that's the way it was. No one is born a baitman, I don't think, but the rings of Saturn sing epithalamium the sea-beast's dower.

2.

The Keys
to December

BORN OF MAN and woman, in accordance with Catform
Y7 requirements, Coldworld Class (modified per Alyonal),
3.2-E, G.M.I. option, Jarry Dark was not suited for existence anywhere in the universe which had guaranteed
him a niche. This was either a blessing or a curse, depending on how you looked at it.

So look at it however you would, here is the story:

It is likely that his parents could have afforded the temperature control unit, but not much more than that. (Jarry
required a temperature of at least −50°C. to be comfortable.)

It is unlikely that his parents could have provided for
the air pressure control and gas mixture equipment required to maintain his life.

Nothing could be done in the way of 3.2-E grav-
simulation, so daily medication and physiotherapy were
required. It is unlikely that his parents could have provided for this.

The much-maligned option took care of him, however.
It safeguarded his health. It provided for his education.
It assured his economic welfare and physical well-being.

It might be argued that Jarry Dark would not have
been a homeless Coldworld Catform (modified per Alyonal) had it not been for General Mining, Incorporated,
which had held the option. But then it must be borne in

46

mind that no one could have foreseen the nova which destroyed Alyonal.

When his parents had presented themselves at the Public Health Planned Parenthood Center and requested advice and medication pending offspring, they had been informed as to the available worlds and the bodyform requirements for them. They had selected Alyonal, which had recently been purchased by General Mining for purposes of mineral exploitation. Wisely, they had elected the option; that is to say, they had signed a contract on behalf of their anticipated offspring, who would be eminently qualified to inhabit that world, agreeing that he would work as an employee of General Mining until he achieved his majority, at which time he would be free to depart and seek employment wherever he might choose (though his choices would admittedly be limited). In return for this guarantee, General Mining agreed to assure his health, education and continuing welfare for so long as he remained in their employ.

When Alyonal caught fire and went away, those Coldworld Catforms covered by the option who were scattered about the crowded galaxy were, by virtue of the agreement, wards of General Mining.

This is why Jarry grew up in a hermetically sealed room containing temperature and atmosphere controls, and why he received a first-class closed circuit education, along with his physiotherapy and medicine. This is also why Jarry bore some resemblance to a large gray ocelot without a tail, had webbing between his fingers and could not go outside to watch the traffic unless he wore a pressurized refrigeration suit and took extra medication.

All over the swarming galaxy, people took the advice of Public Health Planned Parenthood Centers, and many others had chosen as had Jarry's parents. Twenty-eight thousand, five hundred sixty-six of them, to be exact. In any group of over twenty-eight thousand five hundred sixty, there are bound to be a few talented individuals. Jarry was one of them. He had a knack for making money. Most of his General Mining pension check was invested in well-chosen stocks of a speculative nature. (In fact, after a time he came to own considerable stock in General Mining.)

When the man from the Galactic Civil Liberties Union had come around, expressing concern over the pre-birth contracts involved in the option and explaining that the Alyonal Catforms would make a good test case (especially since Jarry's parents lived within jurisdiction of the 877th Circuit, where they would be assured a favorable court-room atmosphere), Jarry's parents had demurred, for fear of jeopardizing the General Mining pension. Later on, Jarry himself dismissed the notion also. A favorable decision could not make him an E-world Normform, and what else mattered? He was not vindictive. Also, he owned considerable stock in G.M. by then.

He loafed in his methane tank and purred, which meant that he was thinking. He operated his cryo-computer as he purred and thought. He was computing the total net worth of all the Catforms in the recently organized December Club.

He stopped purring and considered a sub-total, stretched, shook his head slowly. Then he returned to his calculations.

When he had finished, he dictated a message into his speech-tube, to Sanza Barati, President of December and his betrothed:

"Dearest Sanza—The funds available, as I suspected, leave much to be desired. All the more reason to begin immediately. Kindly submit the proposal to the business committee, outline my qualifications and seek immediate endorsement. I've finished drafting the general statement to the membership. (Copy attached.) From these figures, it will take me between five and ten years, if at least eighty percent of the membership backs me. So push hard, beloved. I'd like to meet you someday, in a place where the sky is purple. Yours, always, Jarry Dark, Treasurer. P.S. I'm pleased you were pleased with the ring."

Two years later, Jarry had doubled the net worth of December Incorporated.

A year and a half after that, he had doubled it again.

When he received the following letter from Sanza, he leapt onto his trampoline, bounded into the air, landed upon his feet at the opposite end of his quarters, returned to his viewer and replayed it:

Dear Jarry,

Attached are specifications and prices for five more worlds. The research staff likes the last one. So do I. What do you think? Alyonal II? If so, how about the price? When could we afford that much? The staff also says that an hundred Worldchange units could alter it to what we want in 5-6 centuries. Will forward costs of this machinery shortly.

Come live with me and be my love, in a place where there are no walls. . . .

Sanza

"One year," he replied, "and I'll buy you a world! Hurry up with the costs of machinery and transport. . . ."

When the figures arrived Jarry wept icy tears. One hundred machines, capable of altering the environment of a world, plus twenty-eight thousand coldsleep bunkers, plus transportation costs for the machinery and his people, plus . . . Too high! He did a rapid calculation.

He spoke into the speech-tube:

". . . Fifteen additional years is too long to wait, Pussy-cat. Have them figure the time-span if we were to purchase only twenty Worldchange units. Love and kisses, Jarry."

During the days which followed, he stalked above his chamber, erect at first, then on all fours as his mood deepened.

"Approximately three thousand years," came the reply. "May your coat be ever shiny—Sanza."

"Let's put it to a vote, Greeneyes," he said.

Quick, a world in 300 words or less! Picture this. . . .

One land mass, really, containing three black and brack-ish looking seas; gray plains and yellow plains and skies the color of dry sand; shallow forests with trees like mush-rooms which have been swabbed with iodine; no moun-tains, just hills brown, yellow, white, lavender; green birds with wings like parachutes, bills like sickles, feathers like oak leaves, an inside-out umbrella behind; six very distant

moons, like spots before the eyes in daytime, snowflakes
at night, drops of blood at dusk and dawn; grass like
mustard in the moister valleys; mists like white fire on
windless mornings, albino serpents when the air's astir;
radiating chasms, like fractures in frosted windowpanes;
hidden caverns, like chains of dark bubbles; seventeen
known dangerous predators, ranging from one to six meters in length, excessively furred and fanged; sudden hail-
storms, like hurled hammerheads from a clear sky; an
icecap like a blue beret at either flattened pole; nervous
bipeds a meter and a half in height, short on cerebrum,
which wander the shallow forests and prey upon the giant
caterpillar's larva, as well as the giant caterpillar, the green
bird, the blind burrower, and the offal-eating murk-beast;
seventeen mighty rivers; clouds like pregnant purple cows,
which quickly cross the land to lie-in beyond the visible
east; stands of windblasted stones like frozen music; nights
like soot, to obscure the lesser stars; valleys which flow
like the torsos of women or instruments of music; perpetual frost in places of shadow; sounds in the morning
like the cracking of ice, the trembling of tin, the snapping
of steel strands. . . .
They knew they would turn it to heaven.

The vanguard arrived, decked out in refrigeration suits,
installed ten Worldchange units in either hemisphere, began
setting up cold-sleep bunkers in several of the larger
caverns.
Then came the members of December down from the
sand-colored sky.
They came and they saw, decided it was almost heaven,
then entered their caverns and slept. Over twenty-eight
thousand Coldworld Catforms (modified per Alyonal)
came into their own world to sleep for a season in silence
the sleep of ice and of stone, to inherit the new Alyonal.
There is no dreaming in that sleep. But had there been,
their dreams might have been as the thoughts of those
yet awake.
"It is bitter, Sanza."
"Yes, but only for a time—"
". . . To have each other and our own world, and still

to go forth like divers at the bottom of the sea. To have to crawl when you want to leap. . . ."

"It is only for a short time, Jarry, as the senses will reckon it."

"But it is really three thousand years! An ice age will come to pass as we doze. Our former worlds will change so that we would not know them were we to go back for a visit—and none will remember us."

"Visit what? Our former cells? Let the rest of the worlds go by! Let us be forgotten in the lands of our birth! We are a people apart and we have found our home. What else matters?"

"True. . . . It will be but a few years, and we shall stand our tours of wakefulness and watching together."

"When is the first?"

"Two and a half centuries from now—three months of wakefulness."

"What will it be like then?"

"I don't know. Less warm. . . ."

"Then let us return and sleep. Tomorrow will be a better day."

"Yes."

"Oh! See the green bird! It drifts like a dream . . ."

When they awakened that first time, they stayed within the World-change installation at the place called Deadland. The world was already colder and the edges of the sky were tinted with pink. The metal walls of the great installation were black and rimed with frost. The atmosphere was still lethal and the temperature far too high. They remained within their special chambers for most of the time, venturing outside mainly to make necessary tests and to inspect the structure of their home.

Deadland. . . . Rocks and sand. No trees, no marks of life at all.

The time of terrible winds was still upon the land, as the world fought back against the fields of the machines. At night, great clouds of real estate smoothed and sculpted the stands of stone, and when the winds departed the desert would shimmer as if fresh-painted and the stones would stand like flames within the morning and its singing. After the sun came up into the sky and hung there for a time, the winds would begin again and a dun-colored fog would curtain the day. When the morning winds departed, Jarry and Sanza would stare out across Deadland through the east window of the installation, for that was their favorite—the one on the third floor—where the stone that looked like a gnarly Normform waved to them, and they would lie upon the green couch they had moved up from the first floor, and would sometimes make love as they listened for the winds to rise again, or Sanza would sing and Jarry would write in the log or read back through it, the scribblings of friends and unknowns through the centuries, and they would purr often but never laugh, because they did not know how.

One morning, as they watched, they saw one of the biped creatures of the iodine forests moving across the land. It fell several times, picked itself up, continued, fell once more, lay still.

"What is it doing this far from its home?" asked Sanza.

"Dying," said Jarry. "Let's go outside."

They crossed a catwalk, descended to the first floor, donned their protective suits and departed the installation.

The creature had risen to its feet and was staggering once again. It was covered with a reddish down, had dark eyes and a long wide nose, lacked a true forehead. It had four brief digits, clawed, upon each hand and foot.

When it saw them emerge from the Worldchange unit, it stopped and stared at them. Then it fell.

They moved to its side and studied it where it lay.

It continued to stare at them, its dark eyes wide, as it lay there shivering.

"It will die if we leave it here," said Sanza.

". . . And it will die if we take it inside," said Jarry.

It raised a forelimb toward them, let it fall again. Its eyes narrowed, then closed.

Jarry reached out and touched it with the toe of his boot. There was no response.

"It's dead," he said.

"What will we do?"

"Leave it here. The sands will cover it."

They returned to the installation, and Jarry entered the event in the log.

During their last month of duty, Sanza asked him, "Will everything die here but us? The green birds and the big eaters of flesh? The funny little trees and the hairy cater-pillars?"

"I hope not," said Jarry. "I've been reading back through the biologists' notes. I think life might adapt. Once it gets a start anywhere, it'll do anything it can to keep going. It's probably better for the creatures of this planet that we could afford only twenty Worldchangers. That way they have three millennia to grow more hair and learn to breathe our air and drink our water. With a hundred units we might have wiped them out and had to import coldworld creatures or breed them. This way, the ones who live here might be able to make it."

"It's funny," she said, "but the thought just occurred to me that we're doing here what was done to us. They made us for Alyonal, and a nova took it away. These creatures came to life in this place, and we're taking it away. We're turning all of life on this planet into what we were on our former worlds—misfits."

"The difference, however, is that we are taking our time," said Jarry, "and giving them a chance to get used to the new conditions."

"Still, I feel that all that—outside there"—she gestured toward the window—"is what this world is becoming: one big Deadland."

"Deadland was here before we came. We haven't created new deserts."

"All the animals are moving south. The trees are dying. When they get as far south as they can go and still the temperature drops, and the air continues to burn in their lungs—then it will be all over for them."

"By then they might have adapted. The trees are spreading, are developing thicker barks. Life will make it."

"I wonder. . . ."

"Would you prefer to sleep until it's all over?"

"No; I want to be by your side, always."

"Then you must reconcile yourself to the fact that something is always hurt by any change. If you do this, you will not be hurt yourself."

Then they listened for the winds to rise.

Three days later, in the still of sundown, between the winds of day and the winds of night, she called him to the window. He climbed to the third floor and moved to

her side. Her breasts were rose in the sundown light and
the places beneath them silver and dark. The fur of her
shoulders and haunches was like an aura of smoke. Her
face was expressionless and her wide, green eyes were not
turned toward him.

He looked out.

The first big flakes were falling, blue, through the pink
light. They drifted past the stone and gnarly Normform;
some stuck to the thick quartz windowpane; they fell
upon the desert and lay there like blossoms of cyanide;
they swirled as more of them came down and were caught
by the first puffs of the terrible winds. Dark clouds had
mustered overhead and from them, now, great cables and
nets of blue descended. Now the flakes flashed past the
window like butterflies, and the outline of Deadland flickered on and off. The pink vanished and there was only
blue, blue and darkening blue, as the first great sigh of
evening came into their ears and the billows suddenly
moved sidewise rather than downwards, becoming indigo
as they raced by.

"The machine is never silent," Jarry wrote. "Sometimes I
fancy I can hear voices in its constant humming, its occasional growling, its crackles of power. I am alone here
at the Deadland station. Five centuries have passed since
our arrival. I thought it better to let Sanza sleep out this
tour of duty, lest the prospect be too bleak. (It is.) She
will doubtless be angry. As I lay half-awake this morning,
I thought I heard my parents' voices in the next room. No
words. Just the sounds of their voices as I used to hear
them over my old intercom. They must be dead by now,
despite all geriatrics. I wonder if they thought of me much
after I left? I couldn't even shake my father's hand without my gauntlet, or kiss my mother goodbye. It is strange,
the feeling, to be this alone, with only the throb of the
machinery about me as it rearranges the molecules of the
atmosphere, refrigerates the world, here in the middle of
the blue place. Deadland. This, despite the fact that I grew
up in a steel cave. I call the other nineteen stations every
afternoon. I am afraid I am becoming something of a
nuisance. I won't call them tomorrow, or perhaps the next
day.

"I went outside without my refrig-pack this morning, for a few moments. It is still deadly hot. I gulped a mouthful of air and choked. Our day is still far off. But I can notice the difference from the last time I tried it, two and a half hundred years ago. I wonder what it will be like when we have finished? —And I, an economist! What will my function be in our new Alyonal? Whatever, so long as Sanza is happy. . . .

"The Worldchanger stutters and groans. All the land is blue for so far as I can see. The stones still, but their shapes are changed from what they were. The sky is entirely pink now, and it becomes almost maroon in the morning and the evening. I guess it's really a wine-color, but I've never seen wine, so I can't say for certain. The trees have not died. They've grown hardier. Their barks are thicker, their leaves are darker and larger. They grow much taller now, I've been told. There are no trees in Deadland.

"The caterpillars still live. They seem much larger, I understand, but it is actually because they have become woolier than they used to be. It seems that most of the animals have heavier pelts these days. Some apparently have taken to hibernating. A strange thing: Station Seven reported that they had thought the bipeds were growing heavier coats. There seem to be quite a few of them in that area, and they often see them off in the distance. They looked to be shaggier. Closer observation, however, revealed that some of them were either carrying or were wrapped in the skins of dead animals! Could it be that they are more intelligent that we have given them credit for? This hardly seems possible, since they were tested quite thoroughly by the Bio Team before we set the machines in operation. Yet, it is very strange.

"The winds are still severe. Occasionally, they darken the sky with ash. There has been considerable vulcanism southwest of here. Station Four was relocated because of this. I hear Sanza singing now, within the sounds of the machine. I will let her be awakened the next time. Things should be more settled by then. No, that is not true. It is selfishness. I want her here beside me. I feel as if I were the only living thing in the whole world. The voices on the radio are ghosts. The clock ticks loudly and the silences between the ticks are filled with the humming of the machine, which is a kind of silence, too, because it is constant. Sometimes I think is is not there; I listen for it, I strain my ears, and I do not know whether there is a humming or not. I check the indicators then, and they assure me that the machine is functioning. Or perhaps there is something wrong with the indicators. But they seem to be all right. No. It is me. And the blue of Deadland is a kind of visual silence. In the morning even the rocks are covered with blue frost. Is is beautiful or ugly? There is no response within me. It is a part of the great silence, that's all. Perhaps I shall become a mystic. Perhaps I shall develop occult powers to achieve something bright and liberating as I sit here at the center of the great silence. Perhaps I shall see visions. Already I hear voices. Are there ghosts in Deadland? No, there was never anything here to be ghosted. Except perhaps for the little biped. Why did it cross Deadland, I wonder? Why did it head for the center of destruction rather than away, as its fellows did? I shall never know. Unless perhaps I have a vision. I think it is time to suit up and take a walk. The polar icecaps are heavier. The glaciation has begun. Soon, soon things will be better. Soon the silence will end, I hope. I wonder, though, whether silence is not the true state of affairs in the universe, our little noises serving only to accentuate it, like a speck of black on a field of blue. Everything was once silence and will be so again—is now, perhaps. Will I ever hear real sounds, or only sounds out of the silence? Sanza is singing again. I wish I could wake her up now, to walk with me, out there. It is beginning to snow."

Jarry awakened again on the eve of the millennium.

Sanza smiled and took his hand in hers and stroked it, as he explained why he had let her sleep, as he apologized.

"Of course I'm not angry," she said, "considering I did the same thing to you last cycle."

Jarry stared up at her and felt the understanding begin.

"I'll not do it again," she said, "and I know you couldn't. The aloneness is almost unbearable."

"Yes," he replied.

"They warmed us both alive last time. I came around

first and told them to put you back to sleep. I was angry then, when I found out what you had done. But I got over it quickly, so often did I wish you were there."

"We will stay together," said Jarry.

"Yes, always."

They took a flier from the cavern of sleep to the World-change installation at Deadland, where they relieved the other attendants and moved the new couch up to the third floor.

The air of Deadland, while sultry, could now be breathed for short periods of time, though a headache invariably followed such experiments. The heat was still oppressive. The rock, once like an old Normform waving, had lost its distinctive outline. The winds were no longer so severe.

On the fourth day, they found some animal tracks which seemed to belong to one of the larger predators. This cheered Sanza, but another, later occurrence produced only puzzlement.

One morning they went forth to walk in Deadland.

Less than a hundred paces from the installation, they came upon three of the giant caterpillars, dead. They were stiff, as though dried out rather than frozen, and they were surrounded by rows of markings within the snow. The footprints which led to the scene and away from it were rough of outline, obscure.

"What does it mean?" she asked.

"I don't know, but I think we had better photograph this," said Jarry.

They did. When Jarry spoke to Station Eleven that afternoon, he learned that similar occurrences had occasionally been noted by attendants of other installations. These were not too frequent, however.

"I don't understand," said Sanza.

"I don't want to," said Jarry.

It did not happen again during their tour of duty. Jarry entered it into the log and wrote a report. Then they abandoned themselves to lovemaking, monitoring, and occasional nights of drunkenness. Two hundred years previously, a biochemist had devoted his tour of duty to experimenting with compounds which would produce the same reactions in Catforms as the legendary whiskey did

in Normforms. He had been successful, had spent four
weeks on a colossal binge, neglected his duty and been
relieved of it, was then retired to his coldbunk for the
balance of the Wait. His basically simple formula had
circulated, however, and Jarry and Sanza found a well-
stocked bar in the storeroom and a hand-written manual
explaining its use and a variety of drinks which might be
compounded. The author of the document had expressed
the hope that each tour of attendance might result in the
discovery of a new mixture, so that when he returned for
his next cycle the manual would have grown to a size
proportionate to his desire. Jarry and Sanza worked at it
conscientiously, and satisfied the request with a Snow-
flower Punch which warmed their bellies and made their
purring turn into giggles, so that they discovered laughter
also. They celebrated the millennium with an entire bowl
of it, and Sanza insisted on calling all the other installations and giving them the formula, right then, on the
graveyard watch, so that everyone could share in their joy.
It is quite possible that everyone did, for the recipe was
well-received. And always, even after that bowl was but
a memory, they kept the laughter. Thus are the first
simple lines of tradition sometimes sketched.

"The green birds are dying," said Sanza, putting aside a
report she had been reading.

"Oh?" said Jarry.

"Apparently they've done all the adapting they're able
to," she told him.

"Pity," said Jarry.

"It seems less than a year since we came here. Actually,
it's a thousand."

"Time flies," said Jarry.

"I'm afraid," she said.

"Of what?"

"I don't know. Just afraid."

"Why?"

"Living the way we've been living, I guess. Leaving
little pieces of ourselves in different centuries. Just a few
months ago, as my memory works, this place was a desert.
Now it's an ice field. Chasms open and close. Canyons
appear and disappear. Rivers dry up and new ones spring

forth. Everything seems so very transitory. Things look solid, but I'm getting afraid to touch things now. They might go away. They might turn into smoke, and my hand will keep on reaching through the smoke and touch—something . . . God, maybe. Or worse yet, maybe not. No one really knows what it will be like here when we've finished. We're traveling toward an unknown land and it's too late to go back. We're moving through a dream, heading toward an idea. . . . Sometimes I miss my cell . . . and all the little machines that took care of me there. Maybe *I* can't adapt. Maybe I'm like the green bird . . ."

"No, Sanza. You're not. We're real. No matter what happens out there, *we* will last. Everything is changing because we want it to change. We're stronger than the world, and we'll squeeze it and paint it and poke holes in it until we've made it exactly the way we want it. Then we'll take it and cover it with cities and children. You want to see God? Go look in the mirror. God has pointed ears and green eyes. He is covered with soft gray fur. When He raises His hand there is webbing between His fingers."

"It is good that you are strong, Jarry."

"Let's get out the power sled and go for a ride."

"All right."

Up and down, that day, they drove through Deadland, where the dark stones stood like clouds in another sky.

It was twelve and a half hundred years.

Now they could breathe without respirators, for a short time.

Now they could bear the temperature, for a short time.

Now all the green birds were dead.

Now a strange and troubling thing began.

The bipeds came by night, made markings upon the snow, left dead animals in the midst of them. This happened now with much more frequency than it had in the past. They came long distances to do it, many of them with fur which was not their own upon their shoulders.

Jarry searched through the history files for all the reports on the creatures.

"This one speaks of lights in the forest," he said. "Station Seven."

"What . . . ?"

"Fire," he said. "What if they've discovered fire?"

"Then they're not really beasts!"

"But they were!"

"They wear clothing now. They make some sort of sacrifice to our machines. They're not beasts any longer."

"How could it have happened?"

"How do you think? *We* did it. Perhaps they would have remained stupid—animals—if we had not come along and forced them to get smart in order to go on living. We've accelerated their evolution. They had to adapt or die, and they adapted."

D'you think it would have happened if we hadn't come along?" he asked.

"Maybe—some day. Maybe not, too."

Jarry moved to the window, stared out across Deadland.

"I have to find out," he said. "If they are intelligent, if they are—human, like us," he said, then laughed, "then we must consider their ways."

"What do you propose?"

"Locate some of the creatures. See whether we can communicate with them."

"Hasn't it been tried?"

"Yes."

"What were the results?"

"Mixed. Some claim they have considerable understanding. Others place them far below the threshold where humanity begins."

"We may be doing a terrible thing," she said. "Creating men, then destroying them. Once, when I was feeling low, you told me that we were the gods of this world, that ours was the power to shape and to break. Ours *is* the power to shape and break, but I don't feel especially divine. What can we do? They have come this far, but do you think they can bear the change that will take us the rest of the way? What if they are like the green birds? What if they've adapted as fast and as far as they can and it is not sufficient? What would a god do?"

"Whatever he wished," said Jarry.

That day, they cruised over Deadland in the flier, but the only signs of life they saw were each other. They continued to search in the days that followed, but they did not meet with success.

Under the purple morning, however, two weeks later, it happened.

"They've been here," said Sanza.

Jarry moved to the front of the installation and stared out.

The snow was broken in several places, inscribed with the lines he had seen before, about the form of a small, dead beast.

"They can't have gone very far," he said.

"No."

"We'll search in the sled."

Now over the snow and out, across the land called Dead they went, Sanza driving and Jarry peering at the lines of footmarks in the blue.

They cruised through the occurring morning, hinting of fire and violet, and the wind went past them like a river, and all about them there came sounds like the cracking of ice, the trembling of tin, the snapping of steel strands. The bluefrosted stones stood like frozen music, and the long shadow of their sled, black as ink, raced on ahead of them. A shower of hailstones drumming upon the roof of their vehicle like a sudden visitation of demon dancers, as suddenly was gone. Deadland sloped downward, slanted up again.

Jarry placed his hand upon Sanza's shoulder.

"Ahead!"

She nodded, began to brake the sled.

They had it at bay. They were using clubs and long poles which looked to have fire-hardened points. They threw stones. They threw pieces of ice.

Then they backed away and it killed them as they went.

The Catforms had called it a bear because it was big and shaggy and could rise up onto its hind legs. . . .

This one was about three and a half meters in length, was covered with bluish fur and had a thin, hairless snout like the business end of a pair of pliers.

Five of the little creatures lay still in the snow. Each time that it swung a paw and connected, another one fell.

Jarry removed the pistol from its compartment and checked the charge.

"Cruise by slowly," he told her. "I'm going to try to burn it about the head."

His first shot missed, scoring the boulder at its back. His second singed the fur of its neck. He leapt down from the sled then, as they came abreast of the beast, thumbed the power control up to maximum, and fired the entire charge into its breast, point-blank.

The bear stiffened, swayed, fell, a gaping wound upon it, front to back.

Jarry turned and regarded the little creatures. They stared up at him.

"Hello," he said. "My name is Jarry. I dub thee Redforms—"

He was knocked from his feet by a blow from behind.

He rolled across the snow, lights dancing before his eyes, his left arm and shoulder afire with pain.

A second bear had emerged from the forest of stone.

He drew his long hunting knife with his right hand and climbed back to his feet.

As the creature lunged, he moved with the catspeed of his kind, thrusting upward, burying his knife to the hilt in its throat.

A shudder ran through it, but it cuffed him and he fell once again, the blade torn from his grasp.

The Redforms threw more stones, rushed toward it with their pointed sticks.

Then there was a thud and a crunching sound, and it rose up into the air and came down on top of him.

He awakened.

He lay on his back, hurting, and everything he looked at seemed to be pulsing, as if about to explode.

How much time had passed, he did not know.

Either he or the bear had been moved.

The little creatures crouched, watching.

Some watched the bear. Some watched him.

Some watched the broken sled. . . .

The broken sled. . . .

He struggled to his feet.

The Redforms drew back.

He crossed to the sled and looked inside.

He knew she was dead when he saw the angle of her

neck. But he did all the things a person does to be sure, anyway, before he would let himself believe it.

She had delivered the deathblow, crashing the sled into the creature, breaking its back. It had broken the sled. Herself, also.

He leaned against the wreckage, composed his first prayer, then removed her body.

The Redforms watched.

He lifted her in his arms and began walking, back toward the installation, across Deadland.

The Redforms continued to watch as he went, except for the one with the strangely high brow-ridge, who studied instead the knife that protruded from the shaggy and steaming throat of the beast.

Jarry asked the awakened executives of December: "What should we do?"

"She is the first of our race to die on this world," said Yan Turl, Vice President.

"There is no tradition," said Selda Kein, Secretary. "Shall we establish one?"

"I don't know," said Jarry. "I don't know what is right to do."

"Burial or cremation seem to be the main choices. Which would you prefer?"

"I don't— No, not the ground. Give her back to me. Give me a large flier . . . I'll burn her."

"Then let us construct a chapel."

"No. It is a thing I must do in my own way. I'd rather do it alone."

"As you wish. Draw what equipment you need, and be about it."

"Please send someone else to keep the Deadland installation. I wish to sleep again when I have finished this thing—until the next cycle."

"Very well, Jarry. We are sorry."

"Yes—we are."

Jarry nodded, gestured, turned, departed.

Thus are the heavier lines of life sometimes drawn.

At the southeastern edge of Deadland there was a blue

mountain. It stood to slightly over three thousand meters in height. When approached from the northwest, it gave the appearance of being a frozen wave in a sea too vast to imagine. Purple clouds rent themselves upon its peak. No living thing was to be found on its slopes. It had no name, save that which Jarry Dark gave it.

He anchored the flier.

He carried her body to the highest point to which a body might be carried.

He placed her there, dressed in her finest garments, a wide scarf concealing the angle of her neck, a dark veil covering her emptied features.

He was about to try a prayer when the hail began to fall. Like thrown rocks, the chunks of blue ice came down upon him, upon her.

"God damn you!" he cried and he raced back to the flier.

He climbed into the air, circled.

Her garments were flapping in the wind. The hail was a blue, beaded curtain that separated them from all but these final caresses: fire aflow from ice to ice, from clay aflow immortally through guns.

He squeezed the trigger and a doorway into the sun opened in the side of the mountain that had been nameless. She vanished within it, and he widened the doorway until he had lowered the mountain.

Then he climbed upward into the cloud, attacking the storm until his guns were empty.

He circled then above the molten mesa, there at the southeastern edge of Deadland.

He circled above the first pyre this world had seen.

Then he departed, to sleep for a season in silence the sleep of ice and of stone, to inherit the new Alyonal. There is no dreaming in that sleep.

Fifteen centuries. Almost half the Wait. Two hundred words or less. . . . Picture—

. . . Nineteen mighty rivers flowing, but the black seas rippling violet now.

. . . No shallow iodine-colored forests. Mighty shag-barked barrel trees instead, orange and lime and black and tall across the land.

. . . Great ranges of mountains in the place of hills brown, yellow, white, lavender. Black corkscrews of smoke unwinding from smoldering cones.

. . . Flowers, whose roots explore the soil twenty meters beneath their mustard petals, unfolded amidst the blue frost and the stones.

. . . Blind burrowers burrowing deeper; offal-eating murk-beasts now showing formidable incisors and great rows of ridged molars; giant caterpillars growing smaller but looking larger because of increasing coats.

. . . The contours of valleys still like the torsos of women, flowing and rolling, or perhaps like instruments of music.

. . . Gone much windblasted stone, but ever the frost.

. . . Sounds in the morning as always, harsh, brittle, metallic.

They were sure they were halfway to heaven.

Picture that.

The Deadland log told him as much as he really needed to know. But he read back through the old reports, also.

Then he mixed himself a drink and stared out the third floor window.

". . . Will die," he said, then finished his drink, outfitted himself, and abandoned his post.

It was three days before he found a camp.

He landed the flier at a distance and approached on foot. He was far to the south of Deadland, where the air was warmer and caused him to feel constantly short of breath.

They were wearing animal skins—skins which had been cut for a better fit and greater protection, skins which were tied about them. He counted sixteen lean-to arrangements and three campfires. He flinched as he regarded the fires, but he continued to advance.

When they saw him, all their little noises stopped, a brief cry went up, and then there was silence.

He entered the camp.

The creatures stood unmoving about him. He heard some bustling within the large lean-to at the end of the clearing.

He walked about the camp.

A slab of dried meat hung from the center of a tripod

of poles. Several long spears stood before each dwelling place. He advanced and studied one. A stone which had been flaked into a leaf-shaped spearhead was affixed to its end.

There was the outline of a cat carved upon a block of wood. . . .

He heard a footfall and turned.

One of the Redforms moved slowly toward him. It appeared older than the others. Its shoulders sloped; as it opened its mouth to make a series of popping noises, he saw that some of its teeth were missing; its hair was grizzled and thin. It bore something in its hands, but Jarry's attention was drawn to the hands themselves.

Each hand bore an opposing digit.

He looked about him quickly, studying the hands of the others. All of them seemed to have thumbs. He studied their appearance more closely.

They now had foreheads.

He returned his attention to the old Redform.

It placed something at his feet, and then it backed away from him.

He looked down.

A chunk of dried meat and a piece of fruit lay upon a broad leaf.

He picked up the meat, closed his eyes, bit off a piece, chewed and swallowed. He wrapped the rest in the leaf and placed it in the side pocket of his pack.

He extended his hand and the Redform drew back.

He lowered his hand, unrolled the blanket he had carried with him and spread it upon the ground. He seated himself, pointed to the Redform, then indicated a position across from him at the other end of the blanket.

The creature hesitated, then advanced and seated itself.

"We are going to learn to talk with one another," he said slowly. Then he placed his hand upon his breast and said, "Jarry."

Jarry stood before the reawakened executives of December.

"They are intelligent," he told them. "It's all in my report."

"So?" asked Yan Turl.

"I don't think they will be able to adapt. They have come very far, very rapidly. But I don't think they can go much further. I don't think they can make it all the way."

"Are you a biologist, an ecologist, a chemist?"

"No."

"Then on what do you base your opinion?"

"I observed them at close range for six weeks."

"Then it's only a feeling you have. . . ?"

"You know there are no experts on a thing like this. It's never happened before."

"Granting their intelligence—granting even that what you have said concerning their adaptability is correct—what do you suggest we do about it?"

"Slow down the change. Give them a better chance. If they can't make it the rest of the way, then stop short of our goal. It's already livable here. *We* can adapt the rest of the way."

"Slow it down? How much?"

"Supposing we took another seven or eight thousand years?"

"Impossible!"

"Entirely!"

"Too much!"

"Why?"

"Because everyone stands a three-month watch every two hundred fifty years. That's one year of personal time for every thousand. You're asking too much of everyone's time."

"But the life of an entire race may be at stake!"

"You do not know for certain."

"No, I don't. But do you feel it is something to take a chance with?"

"Do you want to put it to an executive vote?"

"No—I can see that I'll lose. I want to put it before the entire membership."

"Impossible. They're all asleep."

"Then wake them up."

"That would be quite a project."

"Don't you think that the fate of a race is worth the effort? Especially since we're the ones who forced intel-

ligence upon them? We're the ones who made them evolve,
cursed them with intellect."

"Enough! They were right at the threshhold. They
might have become intelligent had we *not* come along—"

"But you can't say for certain! You don't really know!
And it doesn't really matter how it happened. They're
here and we're here, and they think we're gods—maybe
because we do nothing for them but make them miserable.
We have some responsibility to an intelligent race though.
At least to the extent of not murdering it."

"Perhaps we could do a long-range study . . ."

"They could be dead by then. I formally move, in my
capacity as Treasurer, that we awaken the full membership and put the matter to a vote."

"I don't hear any second to your motion."

"Selda?" he said.

She looked away.

"Tarebell? Clond? Bondici?"

There was silence in the cavern that was high and wide
about him.

"All right. I can see when I'm beaten. We will be our
own serpents when we come into our Eden. I'm going
now, back to Deadland, to finish my tour of duty."

"You don't have to. In fact, it might be better if you
sleep the whole thing out . . ."

"No. If it's going to be this way, the guilt will be mine
also. I want to watch, share it fully."

"So be it," said Turl.

Two weeks later, when Installation Nineteen tried to raise
the Deadland Station on the radio, there was no response.

After a time, a flier was dispatched.

The Deadland Station was a shapeless lump of melted
metal.

Jarry Dark was nowhere to be found.

Later that afternoon, Installation Eight went dead.

A flier was immediately dispatched.

Installation Eight no longer existed. Its attendants
were found several miles away, walking. They told how
Jarry Dark had forced them from the station at gunpoint.
Then he burnt it to the ground, with the fire-cannons
mounted upon his flier.

At about the time they were telling this story, Installation Six became silent.

The order went out: MAINTAIN CONTINUOUS RADIO CONTACT WITH TWO OTHER STATIONS AT ALL TIMES.

The other order went out: GO ARMED AT ALL TIMES. TAKE ANY VISITOR PRISONER.

Jarry waited. At the bottom of a chasm, parked beneath a shelf of rock, Jarry waited. An opened bottle stood upon the control board of his flier. Next to it was a small case of white metal.

Jarry took a long, last drink from the bottle as he waited for the broadcast he knew would come.

When it did, he stretched out on the seat and took a nap.

When he awakened, the light of day was waning.

The broadcast was still going on. . . .

". . . Jarry. They will be awakened and a referendum will be held. Come back to the main cavern. This is Yan Turl. Please do not destroy any more installations. This action is not necessary. We agree with your proposal that a vote be held. Please contact us immediately. We are waiting for your reply, Jarry . . ."

He tossed the empty bottle through the window and raised the flier out of the purple shadow into the air and up.

When he descended upon the landing stage within the main cavern, of course they were waiting for him. A dozen rifles were trained upon him as he stepped from the flier.

"Remove your weapons, Jarry," came the voice of Yan Turl.

"I'm not wearing any weapons," said Jarry. "Neither is my flier," he added; and this was true, for the fire-cannons no longer rested within their mountings.

Yan Turl approached, looked up at him.

"Then you may step down."

"Thank you, but I like it right where I am."

"You are a prisoner."

"What do you intend to do with me?"

"Put you back to sleep until the end of the Wait. Come down here!"

"No. And don't try shooting—or using a stun charge or gas, either. If you do, we're all of us dead the second it hits."

"What do you mean?" asked Turl, gesturing gently to the riflemen.

"My flier," said Jarry, "is a bomb, and I'm holding the fuse in my right hand." He raised the white metal box. "So long as I keep the lever on the side of this box depressed, we live. If my grip relaxes, even for an instant, the explosion which ensues will doubless destroy this entire cavern."

"I think you're bluffing."

"You know how you can find out for certain."

"You'll die too, Jarry."

"At the moment, I don't really care. Don't try burning my hand off either, to destroy the fuse," he cautioned, "because it doesn't really matter. Even if you should succeed, it will cost you at least two installations."

"Why is that?"

"What do you think I did with the fire-cannons? I taught the Redforms how to use them. At the moment, these weapons are manned by Redforms and aimed at two installations. If I do not personally visit my gunners by dawn, they will open fire. After destroying their objectives, they will move on and try for two more."

"You trusted those beasts with laser projectors?"

"That is correct. Now, will you begin awakening the others for the voting?"

Turl crouched as if to spring at him, appeared to think better of it, relaxed.

"Why did you do it, Jarry?'" he asked. "What are they to you that you would make your own people suffer for them?"

"Since you do not feel as I feel," said Jarry, "my reasons would mean nothing to you. After all, they are only based upon my feelings, which are different than your own—for mine are based upon sorrow and loneliness. Try this one, though: I am their god. My form is to be found in their every camp. I am the Slayer of Bears from the Desert of the Dead. They have told my story for two and a half centuries, and I have been changed by it. I am powerful and wise and good, so far as they are concerned. In this capacity, I owe them some consideration. If I do not give them their lives, who will there be to honor me in snow and chant my story around the fires and cut for me the best portions of the woolly caterpillar? None, Turl. And these things are all that my life is worth now. Awaken the others. You have no choice."

"Very well," said Turl. "And if their decision should go against you?"

"Then I'll retire, and you can be god," said Jarry.

Now every day when the sun goes down out of the purple sky, Jarry Dark watches it in its passing, for he shall sleep no more the sleep of ice and of stone, wherein there is no dreaming. He has elected to live out the span of his days in a tiny instant of the Wait, never to look upon the New Alyonal of his people. Every morning, at the new Deadland installation, he is awakened by sounds like the cracking of ice, the trembling of tin, the snapping of steel strands, before they come to him with their offerings, singing and making marks upon the snow. They praise him and he smiles upon them. Sometimes he coughs.

Born of man and woman, in accordance with Catform Y7 requirements, Coldworld Class, Jarry Dark was not suited for existence anywhere in the universe which had guaranteed him a niche. This was either a blessing or a curse, depending on how you looked at it. So look at it however you would, that was the story. Thus does life repay those who would serve her fully.

3.

Devil Car

MURDOCK SPED ACROSS the Great Western Road Plain.

High above him the sun was a fiery yo-yo as he took the innumerable hillocks and rises of the Plain at better than a hundred-sixty miles an hour. He did not slow for anything, and Jenny's hidden eyes spotted all the rocks and potholes before they came to them, and she carefully adjusted their course, sometimes without his even detecting the subtle movements of the steering column beneath his hands.

Even through the dark-tinted windshield and the thick goggles he wore, the glare from the fused Plain burnt into his eyes, so that at times it seemed as if he were steering a very fast boat through night, beneath a brilliant alien moon, and that he was cutting his way across a lake of silver fire. Tall dust waves rose in his wake, hung in the air, and after a time settled once more.

"You are wearing yourself out," said the radio, "sitting there clutching the wheel that way, squinting ahead. Why don't you try to get some rest? Let me fog the shields. Go to sleep and leave the driving to me."

"No," he said. "I want it this way."

"All right," said Jenny. "I just thought I would ask."

"Thanks."

About a minute later the radio began playing—it was a soft stringy sort of music.

"Cut that out!"

"Sorry, boss. Thought it might relax you."

"When I need relaxing, *I'll* tell *you*."

"Check, Sam. Sorry."

The silence seemed oppressive after its brief interruption. She was a good car though, Murdock knew that. She was always concerned with his welfare, and she was anxious to get on with his quest.

She was made to look like a carefree Swinger sedan: bright red, gaudy, fast. But there were rockets under the bulges of her hood, and two fifty-caliber muzzles lurked just out of sight in the recesses beneth her headlamps; she wore a belt of five- and ten-second timed grenades across her belly; and in her trunk was a spray-tank containing a highly volatile naphthalic.

. . . .For his Jenny was a specially designed deathcar, built for him by the Archengineer of the Geeyem Dynasty, far to the East, and all the cunning of that great artificer had gone into her construction.

"We'll find it this time, Jenny," he said, "and I didn't mean to snap at you like I did."

"That's all right, Sam," said the delicate voice. "I am programmed to understand you."

They roared on across the Great Plain and the sun fell away to the west. All night and all day they had searched, and Murdock was tired. The last Fuel Stop/Rest Stop Fortress seemed so long ago, so far back . . .

Murdock leaned forward and his eyes closed.

The windows slowly darkened into complete opacity. The seat belt crept higher and drew him back away from the wheel. Then the seat gradually leaned backwards until he was reclining on a level plane. The heater came on as the night approached, later.

The seat shook him awake a little before five in the morning.

"Wake up, Sam! Wake up!"

"What is it?" he mumbled.

"I picked up a broadcast twenty minutes ago. There was a recent car-raid out this way. I changed course immediately, and we are almost there."

"Why didn't you get me up right away?"

"You needed the sleep, and there was nothing you could do but get tense and nervous."

"Okay, you're probably right. Tell me about the raid."

"Six vehicles, proceeding westward, were apparently ambushed by an undetermined number of wild cars some-time last night. The Patrol Copter was reporting it from above the scene and I listened in. All the vehicles were stripped and drained and their brains were smashed, and their passengers were all apparently killed too. There were no signs of movement."

"How far is it now?"

"Another two or three minutes."

The windshields came clear once more, and Murdock stared as far ahead through the night as the powerful lamps could cut.

"I see something," he said, after a few moments.

"This is the place," said Jenny, and she began to slow down.

They drew up beside the ravaged cars. His seat belt unsnapped and the door sprang open on his side.

"Circle around, Jenny," he said, "and look for heat tracks. I won't be long."

The door slammed and Jenny moved away from him. He snapped on his pocket torch and moved toward the wrecked vehicles.

The Plain was like a sand-strewn dance floor—hard and gritty—beneath his feet. There were many skid-marks, and a spaghetti-work of tire tracks lay about the area.

A dead man sat behind the wheel of the first car. His neck was obviously broken. The smashed watch on his wrist said 2:24. There were three persons—two women and a young man—lying about forty feet away. They had been run down as they tried to flee from their assaulted vehicles.

Murdock moved on, inspected the others. All six cars were upright. Most of the damage was to their bodies. The tires and wheels had been removed from all of them, as well as essential portions of their engines; the gas tanks stood open, siphoned empty; the spare tires were gone from the sprung trunks. There were no living passengers.

Jenny pulled up beside him and her door opened.

"Sam," she said, "pull the brain leads on that blue car, the third one back. It's still drawing some energy from an auxiliary battery, and I can hear it broadcasting."

"Okay."

Murdock went back and tore the leads free. He returned to Jenny and climbed into the driver's seat.

"Did you find anything?"

"Some traces, heading northwest."

"Follow them."

The door slammed and Jenny turned in that direction.

They drove for about five minutes in silence. Then Jenny said: "There were eight cars in that convoy."

"What?"

"I just heard it on the news. Apparently two of the cars communicated with the wild ones on an off-band. They threw in with them. They gave away their location and turned on the others at the time of the attack."

"What about their passengers?"

"They probably monoed them before they joined the pack."

Murdock lit a cigarette, his hands shaking.

"Jenny, what makes a car run wild?" he asked. "Never knowing where it will get its next fueling—or being sure of finding spare parts for its auto-repair unit? Why do they do it?"

"I do not know, Sam. I have never thought about it."

"Ten years ago the Devil Car, their leader, killed my brother in a raid on his Gas Fortress," said Murdock, "and I've hunted that black Caddy ever since. I've searched for it from the air and I've searched on foot. I've used other cars. I've carried heat trackers and missiles. I even laid mines. But always it's been to fast or too smart or too strong for me. Then I had you built."

"I knew you hated it very much. I always wondered why," Jenny said.

Murdock drew on his cigarette.

"I had you specially programmed and armored and armed to be the toughest, fastest, smartest thing on wheels, Jenny. You're the Scarlet Lady. You're the one car can take the Caddy and his whole pack. You've got fangs and claws of the kind they've never met before. This time I'm going to get them."

"You could have stayed home, Sam, and let me do the hunting."

"No. I know I could have, but I want to be there. I want to give the orders, to press some of the buttons myself, to watch that Devil Car burn away to a metal skeleton. How many people, how many cars has it smashed? We've lost count. I've got to get it, Jenny!"

"I'll find it for you, Sam."

They sped on, at around two hundred miles an hour.

"How's the fuel level, Jenny?"

"Plenty there, and I have not yet drawn upon the auxiliary tanks. Do not worry.

"—The track is getting stronger," she added.

"Good. How's the weapons system?"

"Red light, all around. Ready to go."

Murdock snubbed out his cigarette and lit another.

". . . Some of them carry dead people strapped inside," said Murdock, "so they'll look like decent cars with passengers. The black Caddy does it all the time, and it changes them pretty regularly. It keeps its interior refrigerated—so they'll last."

"You know a lot about it, Sam."

"It fooled my brother with phoney passengers and phoney plates. Got him to open his Gas Fortress to it that way. Then the whole pack attacked. It's painted itself red and green and blue and white, on different occasions, but it always goes back to black, sooner or later. It doesn't like yellow or brown or two-tone. I've a list of almost every phoney plate it's ever used. It's even driven the big freeways right into towns and fueled up at regular gas stops. They often get its number as it tears away from them, just as the attendant goes up on the driver's side for his money. It can fake dozens of human voices. They can never catch it afterwards though, because its souped itself up too well. It always makes it back here to the Plain and loses them. It's even raided used car lots—"

Jenny turned sharply in her course.

"Sam! The trail is quite strong now. *This* way! It goes off in the direction of those mountains."

"Follow!" said Murdock.

For a long time then Murdock was silent. The first inklings of morning began in the east. The pale morning star was a white thumbtack on a blueboard behind them. They began to climb a gentle slope.

"Get it, Jenny. Go get it," urged Murdock.

"I think we will," she said.

The angle of the slope increased. Jenny slowed her pace to match the terrain, which was becoming somewhat bumpy.

"What's the matter?" asked Murdock.

"It's harder going here," she said, "also, the trail is getting more difficult to follow."

"Why is that?"

"There is still a lot of background radiation in these parts," she told him, "and it is throwing off my tracking system."

"Keep trying, Jenny."

"The track seems to go straight toward the mountains."

"Follow it, follow it!"

They slowed some more.

"I am all fouled up now, Sam," she said. "I have just lost the trail."

"It must have a stronghold somewhere around here— a cave or something like that—where it can be sheltered overhead. It's the only way it could have escaped aerial detection all these years."

"What should I do?"

"Go as far forward as you can and scan for low openings in the rock. Be wary. Be ready to attack in an instant."

They climbed into the low foothills. Jenny's aerial rose high into the air, and the moths of steel cheesecloth unfolded their wings and danced and spun about it, bright there in the morning light.

"Nothing yet," said Jenny, "and we can't go much further."

"Then we'll cruise along the length of it and keep scanning."

"To the right or to the left?"

"I don't know. Which way would you go if you were a renegade car on the lam?"

"I do not know."

"Pick one. It doesn't matter."

"To the right, then," she said, and they turned in that direction.

After half an hour the night was dropping away behind the mountains. To his right morning was exploding at the far end of the Plain, fracturing the sky into all the colors of autumn trees. Murdock drew a squeeze bottle of hot coffee, of the kind spacers had once used, from beneath the dashboard.

"Sam, I think I have found something."

"What? Where?"

"Ahead, to the left of that big boulder, a declivity with some kind of opening at its end."

"Okay, baby, make for it. Rockets ready."

They pulled abreast of the boulder, circled around its far side, headed downhill.

"A cave, or a tunnel," he said. "Go slow—"

"Heat! Heat!" she said. "I'm tracking again!"

"I can even see tire marks, lots of them!" said Murdock. "This is it!"

They moved toward the opening.

"Go in, but go slowly," he ordered. "Blast the first thing that moves."

They entered the rocky portal, moving on sand now. Jenny turned off her visible lights and switched to infra-red. An i-r lens rose before the windshield, and Murdock studied the cave. It was about twenty feet high and wide enough to accommodate perhaps three cars going abreast. The floor changed from sand to rock, but it was smooth and fairly level. After a time it sloped upward.

"There's some light ahead," he whispered.

"I know."

"A piece of the sky, I think."

They crept toward it, Jenny's engine but the barest sigh within the great chambers of rock.

They stopped at the threshold to the light. The i-r shield dropped again.

It was a sand-and-shale canyon that he looked upon. Huge slantings and overhangs of rock hid all but the far end from any eye in the sky. The light was pale at the far end, and there was nothing unusual beneath it.

But nearer . . .

Murdock blinked.

Nearer, in the dim light of morning and in the shadows, stood the greatest junkheap Murdock had ever seen in his life.

Pieces of cars, of every make and model, were heaped into a small mountain before him. There were batteries and tires and cables and shock absorbers; there were fenders and bumpers and headlamps and headlamp housings; there were doors and windshields and cylinders and pistons, carburetors, voltage regulators, and oil pumps.

Murdock stared.

"Jenny," he whispered, "we've found the graveyard of the autos!"

A very old car, which Murdock had not even distinguished from the junk during that first glance, jerked several feet in their direction and stopped as suddenly. The sound of rivet heads scoring ancient brake drums screeched in his ears. Its tires were completely bald, and the left front one was badly in need of air. Its right front headlamp was broken and there was a crack in its windshield. It stood there before the heap, its awakened engine making a terrible rattling noise.

"What's happening?" asked Murdock. "What is it?"

"He is talking to me," said Jenny. "He is very old. His speedometer has been all the way around so many times that he forgets the number of miles he has seen. He hates people, whom he says have abused him whenever they could. He is the guardian of the graveyard. He is too old to go raiding any more, so he has stood guard over the spare parts heap for many years. He is not the sort who can repair himself, as the younger ones do, so he must rely on their charity and their auto-repair units. He wants to know what I want here."

"Ask him where the others are."

But as he said it, Murdock heard the sound of many engines turning over, until the valley was filled with the thunder of their horsepower.

"They are parked on the other side of the heap," she said. "They are coming now."

"Hold back until I tell you to fire," said Murdock, as the first car—a sleek yellow Chrysler—nosed around the heap.

Murdock lowered his head to the steering wheel, but kept his eyes open behind his goggles.

"Tell them that you came here to join the pack and that you've monoed your driver. Try to get the black Caddy to come into range."

"He will not do it," she said. "I am talking with him now. He can broadcast just as easily from the other side of the pile, and he says he is sending the six biggest members of his pack to guard me while he decides what to do. He has ordered me to leave the tunnel and pull ahead into the valley."

"Go ahead then—slowly."

They crept forward.

Two Lincolns, a powerful-looking Pontiac, and two Mercs joined the Chrysler—three on each side of them, in position to ram.

"Has he given you any idea how many there are on the other side?"

"No. I asked, but he will not tell me."

"Well, we'll just have to wait then."

He stayed slumped, pretending to be dead. After a time, his already tired shoulders began to ache. Finally, Jenny spoke:

"He wants me to pull around the far end of the pile," she said, "now that they have cleared the way, and to head into a gap in the rock which he will indicate. He wants to have his auto-mech go over me."

"We can't have that," said Murdock, "but head around the pile. I'll tell you what to do when I've gotten a glimpse of the other side."

The two Mercs and the Big Chief drew aside and Jenny crept past them. Murdock stared upwards from the corner of his eye, up at the towering mound of junk they were passing. A couple of well-placed rockets on either end could topple it, but the auto-mech would probably clear it eventually.

They rounded the lefthand end of the pile.

Something like forty-five cars were facing them at about a hundred-twenty yards' distance, to the right and ahead. They had fanned out. They were blocking the exit around the other end of the pile, and the six guards in back of him now blocked the way behind Murdock.

On the far side of the farthest rank of the most distant cars an ancient black Caddy was parked.

It had been beaten forth from assembly during a year when the apprentice-engineers were indeed thinking big. Huge it was, and shiny, and a skeleton's face smiled from behind its wheel. Black it was, and gleaming chromium, and its headlamps were like dusky jewels or the eyes of insects. Every plane and curve shimmered with power, and its great fishtailed rear end seemed ready to slap at the sea of shadows behind it on an instant's notice, as it sprang forward for its kill.

"That's it!" whispered Murdock. "The Devil Car!"

"He is big!" said Jenny. "I have never seen a car that big!"

They continued to move forward.

"He wants me to head into that opening and park," she said.

"Head toward it, slowly. But don't go into it," said Murdock.

They turned and inched toward the opening. The other cars stood, the sounds of their engines rising and falling.

"Check all weapons systems."

"Red, all around."

The opening was twenty-five feet away.

"When I say 'now', go into neutral steer and turn one hundred-eighty degrees—fast. They can't be expecting that. They don't have it themselves. Then open up with the fifty-calibers and fire your rockets at the Caddy, turn at a right angle and start back the way we came, and spray the naphtha as we go, and fire on the six guards . . ."

"Now!" he cried, leaping up in his seat.

He was slammed back as they spun, and he heard the chattering of her guns before his head cleared. By then, flames were leaping up in the distance.

Jenny's guns were extruded now and turning on their mounts, spraying the line of vehicles with hundreds of leaden hammers. She shook, twice, as she discharged two rockets from beneath her partly opened hood. Then they

were moving forward, and eight or nine of the cars were
rushing downhill toward them.

She turned again in neutral steer and sprang back in the
direction from which they had come, around the southeast corner of the pile. Her guns were hammering at the
now retreating guards, and in the wide rear view mirror
Murdock could see that a wall of flame was towering high
behind them.

"You missed it!" he cried. "You missed the black
Caddy! Your rockets hit the cars in front of it and it
backed off!"

"I know! I'm sorry!"

"You had a clear shot!"

"I know! I missed!"

They rounded the pile just as two of the guard cars
vanished into the tunnel. Three more lay in smoking ruin.
The sixth had evidently preceded the other two out through
the passage.

"Here it comes now!" cried Murdock. "Around the
other end of the pile! Kill it! Kill it!"

The ancient guardian of the graveyard—it looked like
a Ford, but he couldn't be sure—moved forward with a
dreadful chattering sound and interposed itself in the line
of fire.

"My range is blocked."

"Smash that junkheap and cover the tunnel! Don't let
the Caddy escape!"

"I can't!" she said.

"Why not?"

"I just *can't!*"

"That's an order! Smash it and cover the tunnel!"

Her guns swivelled and she shot out the tires beneath
the ancient car.

The Caddy shot past and into the passageway.

"You let it get by!" he screamed. "Get after it!"

"All right, Sam! I'm doing it! Don't yell. *Please don't
yell!*"

She headed for the tunnel. Inside, he could hear the
sound of a giant engine racing away, growing softer in the
distance.

"Don't fire here in the tunnel! If you hit it we may be bottled in!"

"I know. I won't."

"Drop a couple ten-second grenades and step on the gas. Maybe we can seal in whatever's left moving back there."

Suddenly they shot ahead and emerged into daylight. There was no sign of any other vehicle about.

"Find its track," he said, "and start chasing it."

There was an explosion up the hill behind him, within the mountain. The ground trembled, then it was still once more.

"There are so many tracks . . ." she said.

"You know the one I want. The biggest, the widest, the hottest! Find it! Run it down!"

"I think I have it, Sam."

"Okay. Proceed as rapidly as possible for this terrain."

Murdock found a squeeze bottle of bourbon and took three gulps. Then he lit a cigarette and glared into the distance.

"Why did you miss it?" he asked softly. "Why did you miss it, Jenny?"

She did not answer immediately. He waited.

Finally, "Because he is not an 'it' to me," she said. "He has done much damage to cars and people, and that is terrible. But there is something about him, something— noble. The way he has fought the whole world for his freedom, Sam, keeping that pack of vicious machines in line, stopping at nothing to maintain himself that way— without a master—for as long as he can remain un-smashed, unbeaten—Sam, for a moment back there I wanted to join his pack, to run with him across the Great Road Plains, to use my rockets against the gates of the Gas Forts for him . . . But I could not mono you, Sam. I was built for you. I am too domesticated. I am too weak. I could not shoot him though, and I misfired the rockets on purpose. But I could never mono you, Sam, really."

"Thanks," he said, "you over-programmed ashcan. Thanks a lot!"

"I am sorry, Sam."

"Shut up— No, don't, not yet. First tell me what you're going to do if we find 'him'."

"I don't know."

"Well think it over fast. You see that dust cloud ahead as well as I do, and you'd better speed up."

They shot forward.

"Wait till I call Detroit. They'll laugh themselves silly, till I claim the refund."

"I am *not* of inferior construction or design. You know that. I am just more . . ."

" 'Emotional'," supplied Murdock.

". . . Than I thought I would be," she finished. "I had not really met many cars, except for young ones, before I was shipped to you. I did not know what a wild car was like, and I had never smashed *any* cars before—just targets and things like that. I was young and . . ."

" 'Innocent'," said Murdock. "Yeah. Very touching. Get ready to kill the next car we meet. If it happens to be your boyfriend and you hold your fire, then he'll kill us."

"I will try, Sam."

The car ahead had stopped. It was the yellow Chrysler. Two of its tires had gone flat and it was parked, lopsided, waiting.

"Leave it!" snarled Murdock, as the hood clicked open. "Save the ammo for something that might fight back."

They sped past it.

"Did it say anything?"

"Machine profanity," she said. "I've only heard it once or twice, and it would be meaningless to you."

He chuckled. "Cars actually swear at each other?"

"Occasionally," she said. "I imagine the lower sort indulge in it more frequently, especially on freeways and turnpikes when they become congested."

"Let me hear a machine swear-word."

"I will not. What kind of car do you think I am, anyway?"

"I'm sorry," said Murdock. "You're a lady. I forgot."

There was an audible click within the radio.

They raced forward on the level ground that lay before the foot of the mountains. Murdock took another drink, then switched to coffee.

"Ten years," he muttered, "ten years . . ."

The trail swung in a wide curve as the mountains jogged back and the foothills sprang up high beside them.

It was over almost before he knew it.

As they passed a huge, orange-colored stone massif, sculpted like an upside-down toadstool by the wind, there was a clearing to the right.

It shot forward at them—the Devil Car. It had lain in ambush, seeing that it could not outrun the Scarlet Lady, and it rushed toward a final collision with its hunter.

Jenny skidded sideways as her brakes caught with a scream and a smell of smoke, and her fifty-calibers were firing, and her hood sprang open and her front wheels rose up off the ground as the rockets leapt wailing ahead, and she spun around three times, her rear bumper scraping the saltsand plain, and the third and last time she fired her remaining rockets into the smouldering wreckage on the hillside, and she came to a rest on all four wheels; and her fifty-calibers kept firing until they were emptied, and then a steady clicking sound came from them for a full minute afterwards, and then all lapsed into silence.

Murdock sat there shaking, watching the gutted, twisted wreck blaze against the morning sky.

"You did it, Jenny. You killed him. You killed me the Devil Car," he said.

But she did not answer him. Her engine started once more and she turned toward the southeast and headed for the Fuel Stop/Rest Stop Fortress that lay in that civilized direction.

For two hours they drove in silence, and Murdock drank all his bourbon and all his coffee and smoked all his cigarettes.

"Jenny, say something," he said. "What's the matter? Tell me."

There was a click, and her voice was very soft:

"Sam—he talked to me as he came down the hill . . ." she said.

Murdock waited, but she did not say anything else.

"Well, what did he say?" he asked.

"He said, 'Say you will mono your passenger and I will swerve by you'," she told him. "He said, 'I want you,

Scarlet Lady—to run with me, to raid with me. Together they will never catch us', and I killed him."

Murdock was silent.

"He only said that to delay my firing though, did he not? He said that to stop me, so that he could smash us both when he went smash himself, did he not? He could not have meant it, could he, Sam?"

"Of course not," said Murdock, "of course not. It was too late for him to swerve."

"Yes, I suppose it was—do you think though, that he really wanted me to run with him, to raid with him—before everything, I mean—back there?"

"Probably, baby. You're pretty well-equipped."

"Thanks," she said, and turned off again.

Before she did though, he heard a strange mechanical sound, falling into the rhythms of profanity or prayer.

Then he shook his head and lowered it, softly patting the seat beside him with his still unsteady hand.

4.

A Rose
for Ecclesiastes

I

I WAS BUSY translating one of my *Madrigals Macabre* into
Martian on the morning I was found acceptable. The intercom had buzzed briefly, and I dropped my pencil and
flipped on the toggle in a single motion.

"Mister G," piped Morton's youthful contralto, "the old
man says I should 'get hold of that damned conceited
rhymer' right away, and send him to his cabin. Since
there's only one damned conceited rhymer . . ."

"Let not ambition mock thy useful toil." I cut him off.

So, the Martians had finally made up their minds! I
knocked an inch and a half of ash from a smoldering
butt, and took my first drag since I had lit it. The entire
month's anticipation tried hard to crowd itself into the
moment, but could not quite make it. I was frightened
to walk those forty feet and hear Emory say the words
I already knew he would say; and that feeling elbowed
the other one into the background.

So I finished the stanza I was translating before I got up.

It took only a moment to reach Emory's door. I knocked
twice and opened it, just as he growled, "Come in."

"You wanted to see me?" I sat down quickly to save
him the trouble of offering me a seat.

"That was fast. What did you do, run?"

I regarded his paternal discontent:

Little fatty flecks beneath pale eyes, thinning hair, and an Irish nose; a voice a decibel louder than anyone else's. . . .

Hamlet to Claudius: "I was working."

"Hah!" he snorted. "Come off it. No one's ever seen you do any of that stuff."

I shrugged my shoulders and started to rise.

"If that's what you called me down here—"

"Sit down!"

He stood up. He walked around his desk. He hovered above me and glared down. (A hard trick, even when I'm in a low chair.)

"You are undoubtedly the most antagonistic bastard I've ever had to work with!" he bellowed, like a belly-stung buffalo. "Why the hell don't you act like a human being sometime and surprise everybody? I'm willing to admit you're smart, maybe even a genius, but—oh, hell!" He made a heaving gesture with both hands and walked back to his chair.

"Betty has finally talked them into letting you go in." His voice was normal again. "They'll receive you this afternoon. Draw one of the jeepsters after lunch, and get down there."

"Okay," I said.

"That's all, then."

I nodded, got to my feet. My hand was on the door-knob when he said:

"I don't have to tell you how important this is. Don't treat them the way you treat us."

I closed the door behind me.

I don't remember what I had for lunch. I was nervous, but I knew instinctively that I wouldn't muff it. My Boston publishers expected a Martian Idyll, or at least a Saint-Exupéry job on space flight. The National Science Association wanted a complete report on the Rise and Fall of the Martian Empire.

They would both be pleased. I knew.

That's the reason everyone is jealous—why they hate

me. I always come through, and I can come through better than anyone else.

I shoveled in a final anthill of slop, and made my way to our car barn. I drew one jeepster and headed it toward Tirellian.

Flames of sand, lousy with iron oxide, set fire to the buggy. They swarmed over the open top and bit through my scarf; they set to work pitting my goggles.

The jeepster, swaying and panting like a little donkey I once rode through the Himalayas, kept kicking me in the seat of the pants. The Mountains of Tirellian shuffled their feet and moved toward me at a cockeyed angle.

Suddenly I was heading uphill, and I shifted gears to accommodate the engine's braying. Not like Gobi, not like the Great Southwestern Desert, I mused. Just red, just dead . . . without even a cactus.

I reached the crest of the hill, but I had raised too much dust to see what was ahead. It didn't matter, though; I have a head full of maps. I bore to the left and downhill, adjusting the throttle. A crosswind and solid ground beat down the fires. I felt like Ulysses in Malebolge—with a terza-rima speech in one hand and an eye out for Dante.

I rounded a rock pagoda and arrived.

Betty waved as I crunched to a halt, then jumped down.

"Hi," I choked, unwinding my scarf and shaking out a pound and a half of grit. "Like, where do I go and who do I see?"

She permitted herself a brief Germanic giggle—more at my starting a sentence with "like" than at my discomfort—then she started talking. (She is a top linguist, so a word from the Village Idiom still tickles her!)

I appreciate her precise, furry talk; informational, and all that. I had enough in the way of social pleasantries before me to last at least the rest of my life. I looked at her chocolate-bar eyes and perfect teeth, at her sun-bleached hair, close-cropped to the head (I hate blondes!), and decided that she was in love with me.

"Mr. Gallinger, the Matriarch is waiting inside to be introduced. She has consented to open the Temple records for your study." She paused here to pat her hair and squirm a little. Did my gaze make her nervous?

"They are religious documents, as well as their only

history," she continued, "sort of like the Mahabharata. She expects you to observe certain rituals in handling them, like repeating the sacred words when you turn pages—she will teach you the system."

I nodded quickly, several times.

"Fine, let's go in."

"Uh—" She paused. "Do not forget their Eleven Forms of Politeness and Degree. They take matters of form quite seriously—and do not get into any discussions over the equality of the sexes—"

"I know all about their taboos," I broke in. "Don't worry. I've lived in the Orient, remember?"

She dropped her eyes and seized my hand. I almost jerked it away.

"It will look better if I enter leading you."

I swallowed my comments, and followed her, like Samson in Gaza.

Inside, my last thought met with a strange correspondence. The Matriarch's quarters were a rather abstract version of what I imagine the tents of the tribes of Israel to have been like. Abstract, I say, because it was all frescoed brick, peaked like a huge tent, with animal-skin representations like gray-blue scars, that looked as if they had been laid on the walls with a palette knife.

The Matriarch, M'Cwyie, was short, white-haired, fifty-ish, and dressed like a Gypsy queen. With her rainbow of voluminous skirts she looked like an inverted punch bowl set atop a cushion.

Accepting my obeisances, she regarded me as an owl might a rabbit. The lids of those black, black eyes jumped upwards as she discovered my perfect accent. —The tape recorder Betty had carried on her interviews had done its part, and I knew the language reports from the first two expeditions, verbatim. I'm all hell when it comes to picking up accents.

"You are the poet?"

"Yes," I replied.

"Recite one of your poems, please."

"I'm sorry, but nothing short of a thorough translating job would do justice to your language and my poetry, and I don't know enough of your language yet."

"Oh?"

"But I've been making such translations for my own amusement, as an exercise in grammar," I continued. "I'd be honored to bring a few of them along one of the times that I come here."

"Yes. Do so."

Score one for me!

She turned to Betty.

"You may go now."

Betty muttered the parting formalities, gave me a strange sidewise look, and was gone. She apparently had expected to stay and "assist" me. She wanted a piece of the glory, like everyone else. But I was the Schliemann at this Troy, and there would be only one name on the Association report!

M'Cwyie rose, and I noticed that she gained very little height by standing. But then I'm six-six and look like a poplar in October: thin, bright red on top, and towering above everyone else.

"Our records are very, very old," she began. "Betty says that your word for their age is 'millennia.'"

I nodded appreciatively.

"I'm very eager to see them."

"They are not here. We will have to go into the Temple —they may not be removed."

I was suddenly wary.

"You have no objections to my copying them, do you?"

"No. I see that you respect them, or your desire would not be so great."

"Excellent."

She seemed amused. I asked her what was funny.

"The High Tongue may not be so easy for a foreigner to learn."

It came through fast.

No one on the first expedition had gotten this close. I had had no way of knowing that this was a double-language deal—a classical as well as a vulgar. I knew some of their Prakrit, now I had to learn all their Sanskrit.

"Ouch and damn!"

"Pardon, please?"

"It's non-translatable, M'Cwyie. But imagine yourself

having to learn the High Tongue in a hurry, and you can guess at the sentiment."

She seemed amused again, and told me to remove my shoes.

She guided me through an alcove . . .

. . . and into a burst of Byzantine brilliance!

No Earthman had ever been in this room before, or I would have heard about it. Carter, the first expedition's linguist, with the help of one Mary Allen, M.D., had learned all the grammar and vocabulary that I knew while sitting cross-legged in the antechamber.

We had had no idea this existed. Greedily, I cast my eyes about. A highly sophisticated system of esthetics lay behind the decor. We would have to revise our entire estimation of Martian culture.

For one thing, the ceiling was vaulted and corbeled; for another, there were side-columns with reverse flutings; for another—oh hell! The place was big. Posh. You could never have guessed it from the shaggy outsides.

I bent forward to study the gilt filigree on a ceremonial table. M'Cwyie seemed a bit smug at my intentness, but I'd still have hated to play poker with her.

The table was loaded with books.

With my toe, I traced a mosaic on the floor.

"Is your entire city within this one building?"

"Yes, it goes far back into the mountain."

"I see," I said, seeing nothing.

I couldn't ask her for a conducted tour, yet.

She moved to a small stool by the table.

"Shall we begin your friendship with the High Tongue?"

I was trying to photograph the hall with my eyes, knowing I would have to get a camera in here, somehow, sooner or later. I tore my gaze from a statuette and nodded, hard.

"Yes, introduce me."

I sat down.

For the next three weeks alphabet-bugs chased each other behind my eyelids whenever I tried to sleep. The sky was an unclouded pool of turquoise that rippled calligraphies whenever I swept my eyes across it. I drank quarts of coffee while I worked and mixed cocktails of Benzedrine and champagne for my coffee breaks.

M'Cwyie tutored me two hours every morning, and occasionally for another two in the evening. I spent an additional fourteen hours a day on my own, once I had gotten up sufficient momentum to go ahead alone.

And at night the elevator of time dropped me to its bottom floors. . . .

I was six again, learning my Hebrew, Greek, Latin, and Aramaic. I was ten, sneaking peeks at the *Iliad*. When Daddy wasn't spreading hellfire brimstone, and brotherly love, he was teaching me to dig the Word, like in the original.

Lord! There are so many originals and so *many* words! When I was twelve I started pointing out the little differences between what he was preaching and what I was reading.

The fundamentalist vigor of his reply brooked no debate. It was worse than any beating. I kept my mouth shut after that and learned to appreciate Old Testament poetry.

—Lord, I am sorry! Daddy—Sir—I am sorry! —It couldn't be! It couldn't be. . . .

On the day the boy graduated from high school, with the French, German, Spanish, and Latin awards, Dad Gallinger had told his fourteen-year-old, six-foot scarecrow of a son that he wanted him to enter the ministry. I remember how his son was evasive:

"Sir," he had said, "I'd sort of like to study on my own for a year or so, and then take pre-theology courses at some liberal arts university. I feel I'm still sort of young to try a seminary, straight off."

The Voice of God: "But you have the gift of tongues, my son. You can preach the Gospel in all the lands of Babel. You were born to be a missionary. You say you are young, but time is rushing by you like a whirlwind. Start early, and you will enjoy added years of service."

The added years of service were so many added tails to the cat repeatedly laid on my back. I can't see his face now; I never can. Maybe it is because I was always afraid to look at it then.

And years later, when he was dead, and laid out, in black, amidst bouquets, amidst weeping congregationalists, amidst prayers, red faces, handkerchiefs, hands patting your shoulders, solemn faced comforters . . . I looked at him and did not recognize him.

We had met nine months before my birth, this stranger and I. He had never been cruel—stern, demanding, with contempt for everyone's shortcomings—but never cruel. He was also all that I had had of a mother. And brothers. And sisters. He had tolerated my three years at St. John's, possibly because of its name, never knowing how liberal and delightful a place it really was.

But I never knew him, and the man atop the catafalque demanded nothing now; I was free not to preach the Word. But now I wanted to, in a different way. I wanted to preach a word that I could never have voiced while he lived.

I did not return for my senior year in the fall. I had a small inheritance coming, and a bit of trouble getting control of it, since I was still under eighteen. But I managed.

It was Greenwich Village I finally settled upon.

Not telling any well-meaning parishioners my new address, I entered into a daily routine of writing poetry and teaching myself Japanese and Hindustani. I grew a fiery beard, drank espresso, and learned to play chess. I wanted to try a couple of the other paths to salvation.

After that, it was two years in India with the Old Peace Corps—which broke me of my Buddhism, and gave me my *Pipes of Krishna* lyrics and the Pulitzer they deserved.

Then back to the States for my degree, grad work in linguistics, and more prizes.

Then one day a ship went to Mars. The vessel settling in its New Mexico nest of fires contained a new language. —It was fantastic, exotic, and esthetically overpowering. After I had learned all there was to know about it, and written my book, I was famous in new circles:

"Go, Gallinger. Dip your bucket in the well, and bring up a drink of Mars. Go, learn another world—but remain aloof, rail at it gently like Auden—and hand us its soul in iambics."

And I came to the land where the sun is a tarnished penny, where the wind is a whip, where two moons play at hot rod games, and a hell of sand gives you the incendiary itches whenever you look at it.

I rose from my twistings on the bunk and crossed the

darkened cabin to a port. The desert was a carpet of endless orange, bulging from the sweepings of centuries beneath it.

"I a stranger, unafraid—This is the land—I've got it
made!"

I laughed.

I had the High Tongue by the tail already—or the roots,
if you want your puns anatomical, as well as correct.

The High and Low Tongues were not so dissimilar as
they had first seemed. I had enough of the one to get me
through the murkier parts of the other. I had the grammar
and all the commoner irregular verbs down cold; the dic-
tionary I was constructing grew by the day, like a tulip,
and would bloom shortly. Every time I played the tapes
the stem lengthened.

Now was the time to tax my ingenuity, to really drive
the lessons home. I had purposely refrained from plunging
into the major texts until I could do justice to them. I had
been reading minor commentaries, bits of verse, fragments
of history. And one thing had impressed me strongly in
all that I read.

They wrote about concrete things: rock, sand, water,
winds; and the tenor couched within these elemental sym-
bols was fiercely pessimistic. It reminded me of some Bud-
hist texts, but even more so, I realized from my recent
recherches, it was like parts of the Old Testament. Spe-
cifically, it reminded me of the Book of Ecclesiastes.

That, then, would be it. The sentiment, as well as the
vocabulary, was so similar that it would be a perfect exercise. Like putting Poe into French. I would never be a
convert to the Way of Malann, but I would show them
that an Earthman had once thought the same thoughts,
felt similarly.

I switched on my desk lamp and sought King James
amidst my books.

*Vanity of vanities, saith the Preacher, vanity of vanities;
all is vanity. What profit hath a man . . .*

My progress seemed to startle M'Cwyie. She peered at me,
like Sartre's Other, across the tabletop. I ran through a
chapter in the Book of Locar. I didn't look up, but I could

feel the tight net her eyes were working about my head, shoulders, and rapid hands. I turned another page.

Was she weighing the net, judging the size of the catch? And what for? The books said nothing of fishers on Mars. Especially of men. They said that some god named Malann had spat, or had done something disgusting (depending on the version you read), and that life had gotten underway as a disease in inorganic matter. They said that movement was its first law, its first law, and that the dance was the only legitimate reply to the inorganic . . . the dance's quality its justification,—fication . . . and love is a disease in organic matter—Inorganic matter?

I shook my head. I had almost been asleep.

"M'narra."

I stood and stretched. Her eyes outlined me greedily now. So I met them, and they dropped.

"I grow tired. I want to rest awhile. I didn't sleep much last night."

She nodded, Earth's shorthand for "yes," as she had learned from me.

"You wish to relax, and see the explicitness of the doctrine of Locar in its fullness?"

"Pardon me?"

"You wish to see a Dance of Locar?"

"Oh." Their damned circuits of form and periphrasis here ran worse than the Korean! "Yes. Surely. Any time it's going to be done I'd be happy to watch."

I continued, "In the meantime, I've been meaning to ask you whether I might take some pictures—"

"Now is the time. Sit down. Rest. I will call the musicians."

She bustled out through a door I had never been past.

Well now, the dance was the highest art, according to Locar, not to mention Havelock Ellis, and I was about to see how their centuries-dead philosopher felt it should be conducted. I rubbed my eyes and snapped over, touching my toes a few times.

The blood began pounding in my head, and I sucked in a couple deep breaths. I bent again and there was a flurry of motion at the door.

To the trio who entered with M'Cwyie I must have looked as if I were searching for the marbles I had just lost, bent over like that.

I grinned weakly and straightened up, my face red from more than exertion. I hadn't expected them *that* quickly.

Suddenly I thought of Havelock Ellis again in his area of greatest popularity.

The little redheaded doll, wearing, sari-like, a diaphanous piece of Martian sky, looked up in wonder—as a child at some colorful flag on a high pole.

"Hello," I said, or its equivalent.

She bowed before replying. Evidently I had been promoted in status.

"I shall dance," said the red wound in that pale, pale cameo, her face. Eyes, the color of dream and her dress, pulled away from mine.

She drifted to the center of the room.

Standing there, like a figure in an Etruscan frieze, she was either meditating or regarding the design on the floor.

Was the mosaic symbolic of something? I studied it. If it was, it eluded me; it would make an attractive bathroom floor or patio, but I couldn't see much in it beyond that.

The other two were paint-spattered sparrows like M'Cwyie, in their middle years. One settled to the floor with a triple-stringed instrument faintly resembling a *samisen*. The other held a simple woodblock and two drumsticks.

M'Cwyie disdained her stool and was seated upon the floor before I realized it. I followed suit.

The *samisen* player was still tuning it up, so I leaned toward M'Cwyie.

"What is the dancer's name?"

"Braxa," she replied, without looking at me, and raised her left hand, slowly, which meant yes, and go ahead, and let it begin.

The stringed-thing throbbed like a toothache, and a tick-tocking, like ghosts of all the clocks they had never invented, sprang from the block.

Braxa was a statue, both hands raised to her face, elbows high and outspread.

The music became a metaphor for fire.

Crackle, purr, snap . . .

She did not move.

The hissing altered to splashes. The cadence slowed. It was water now, the most precious thing in the world, gurgling clear then green over mossy rocks.

Still she did not move.

Glassandos. A pause.

Then, so faint I could hardly be sure at first, the tremble of the winds began. Softly, gently, sighing and halting, uncertain. A pause, a sob, then a repetition of the first statement, only louder.

Were my eyes completely bugged from my reading, or was Braxa actually trembling, all over, head to foot?

She was.

She began a microscopic swaying. A fraction of an inch right, then left. Her fingers opened like the petals of a flower, and I could see that her eyes were closed.

Her eyes opened. They were distant, glassy, looking through me and the walls. Her swaying became pronounced, merged with the beat.

The wind was sweeping in from the desert now, falling against Tirellian like waves on a dike. Her fingers moved, they were the gusts. Her arms, slow pendulums, descended, began a counter-movement.

The gale was coming now. She began an axial movement and her hands caught up with the rest of her body, only now her shoulders commenced to writhe out a figure-eight.

The wind! The wind, I say. O wild, enigmatic! O muse of St. John Perse!

The cyclone was twisting around those eyes, its still center. Her head was thrown back, but I knew there was no ceiling between her gaze, passive as Buddha's, and the unchanging skies. Only the two moons, perhaps, interrupted their slumber in that elemental Nirvana of uninhabited turquoise.

Years ago, I had seen the Devadasis in India, the street-dancers, spinning their colorful webs, drawing in the male insect. But Braxa was more than this: she was a Ramadjany, like those votaries of Rama, incarnation of Vishnu, who had given the dance to man: the sacred dancers.

The clicking was monotonously steady now; the whine of the strings made me think of the stinging rays of the sun, their heat stolen by the wind's halations; the blue was Sarasvati and Mary, and a girl named Laura. I heard a sitar from somewhere, watched this statue come to life, and inhaled a divine afflatus.

I was again Rimbaud with his hashish, Baudelaire with his laudanum, Poe, De Quincy, Wilde, Mallarme and Aleister Crowley. I was, for a fleeting second, my father in his dark pulpit and darker suit, the hymns and the organ's wheeze transmuted to bright wind.

She was a spun weather vane, a feathered crucifix hovering in the air, a clothes-line holding one bright garment lashed parallel to the ground. Her shoulder was bare now, and her right breast moved up and down like a moon in the sky, its red nipple appearing momently above a fold and vanishing again. The music was as formal as Job's argument with God. Her dance was God's reply.

The music slowed, settled; it had been met, matched, answered. Her garment, as if alive, crept back into the more sedate folds it originally held.

She dropped low, lower, to the floor. Her head fell upon her raised knees. She did not move.

There was silence.

I realized, from the ache across my shoulders, how tensely I had been sitting. My armpits were wet. Rivulets had been running down my sides. What did one do now? Applaud?

I sought M'Cwyie from the corner of my eye. She raised her right hand.

As if by telepathy the girl shuddered all over and stood. The musicians also rose. So did M'Cwyie.

I got to my feet, with a charley horse in my left leg, and said, "It was beautiful," inane as that sounds.

I received three different High Forms of "thank you."

There was a flurry of color and I was alone again with M'Cwyie.

"That is the one hundred-seventeenth of the two thousand, two hundred-twenty-four dances of Locar."

I looked down at her.

"Whether Locar was right or wrong, he worked out a fine reply to the inorganic."

She smiled.

"Are the dances of your world like this?"

"Some of them are similar. I was reminded of them as

I watched Braxa—but I've never seen anything exactly like hers."

"She is good," M'Cwyie said. "She knows all the dances."

A hint of her earlier expression which had troubled me . . .

It was gone in an instant.

"I must tend my duties now." She moved to the table and closed the books. "M'narra."

"Good-bye." I slipped into my boots.

"Good-bye, Gallinger."

I walked out the door, mounted the jeepster, and roared across the evening into night, my wings of risen desert flapping slowly behind me.

II

I had just closed the door behind Betty, after a brief grammar session, when I heard the voices in the hall. My vent was opened a fraction, so I stood there and eaves-dropped:

Morton's fruity treble: "Guess what? He said 'hello' to me awhile ago."

"Hmmph!" Emory's elephant lungs exploded. "Either he's slipping, or you were standing in his way and he wanted you to move."

"Probably didn't recognize me. I don't think he sleeps any more, now he has that language to play with. I had night watch last week, and every night I passed his door at 0300—I always heard that recorder going. At 0500 when I got off, he was still at it."

"The guy *is* working hard," Emory admitted, grudgingly. "In fact, I think he's taking some kind of dope to keep awake. He looks sort of glassy-eyed these days. Maybe that's natural for a poet, though."

Betty had been standing there, because she broke in then:

"Regardless of what you think of him, it's going to take me at least a year to learn what he's picked up in three weeks. And I'm just a linguist, not a poet."

Morton must have been nursing a crush on her bovine

charms. It's the only reason I can think of for his dropping his guns to say what he did.

"I took a course in modern poetry when I was back at the university," he began. "We read six authors—Yeats, Pound, Eliot, Crane, Stevens, and Gallinger—and on the last day of the semester, when the prof was feeling a little rhetorical, he said, 'These six names are written on the century, and all the gates of criticism and hell shall not prevail against them.'

"Myself," he continued, "I thought his *Pipes of Krishna* and his *Madrigals* were great. I was honored to be chosen for an expedition he was going on.

"I think he's spoken two dozen words to me since I met him," he finished.

The Defense: "Did it ever occur to you," Betty said, "that he might be tremendously self-conscious about his appearance? He was also a precocious child, and probably never even had school friends. He's sensitive and very introverted."

"Sensitive? Self-conscious?" Emory choked and gagged. "The man is as proud as Lucifer, and he's a walking insult machine. You press a button like 'Hello' or 'Nice day' and he thumbs his nose at you. He's got it down to a reflex."

They muttered a few other pleasantries and drifted away.

Well bless you, Morton boy. You little pimple-faced, Ivy-bred connoisseur! I've never taken a course in my poetry, but I'm glad someone said that. The Gates of Hell. Well now! Maybe Daddy's prayers got heard somewhere, and I am a missionary, after all!

Only . . .

. . . Only a missionary needs something to convert people *to*. I have my private system of ethics, and I suppose it oozes an ethical by-product somewhere. But if I ever had anything to preach, really, even in my poems, I wouldn't care to preach it to such low-lifes as you. If you think I'm a slob, I'm also a snob, and there's no room for you in my Heaven—it's a private place, where Swift, Shaw, and Petronius Arbiter come to dinner.

And oh, the feasts we have! The Trimalchio's, the Emory's we dissect!

We finish you with the soup, Morton!

I turned and settled at my desk. I wanted to write something. Ecclesiastes could take a night off. I wanted to write a poem, a poem about the one hundred-seventeenth dance of Locar; about a rose following the light, traced by the wind, sick, like Blake's rose, dying. . . .

I found a pencil and began.

When I had finished I was pleased. It wasn't great—at least, it was no greater than it needed to be—High Martian not being my strongest tongue. I groped, and put it into English, with partial rhymes. Maybe I'd stick it in my next book. I called it *Braxa:*

> *In a land of wind and red, where the icy evening of Time freezes milk in the breasts of Life, as two moons overhead—cat and dog in alleyways of dream—scratch and scramble agelessly my flight . . .*
>
> *This final flower turns a burning head.*

I put it away and found some phenobarbitol. I was suddenly tired.

When I showed my poem to M'Cwyie the next day, she read it through several times, very slowly.

"It is lovely," she said. "But you used three words from your own language. 'Cat' and 'dog,' I assume, are two small animals with a hereditary hatred for one another. But what is 'flower?' "

"Oh," I said. "I've never come across your word for 'flower,' but I was actually thinking of an Earth flower, the rose."

"What is it like?"

"Well, its petals are generally bright red. That's what I meant, on one level, by 'burning heads.' I also wanted it to imply fever, though, and red hair, and the fire of life. The rose, itself, has a thorny stem, green leaves, and a distinct, pleasing aroma."

"I wish I could see one."

"I suppose it could be arranged. I'll check."

"Do it, please. You are a—" She used the word for

"prophet," or religious poet, like Isaias or Locar. "—and your poem is inspired. I shall tell Baxa of it."

I declined the nomination, but felt flattered.

This, then, I decided, was the strategic day, the day on which to ask whether I might bring in the microfilm machine and the camera. I wanted to copy all their texts, I explained, and I couldn't write fast enough to do it.

She surprised me by agreeing immediately. But she bowled me over with her invitation.

"Would you like to come and stay here while you do this thing? Then you can work night and day, any time you want—except when the Temple is being used, of course."

I bowed.

"I should be honored."

"Good. Bring your machines when you want, and I will show you a room."

"Will this afternoon be all right?"

"Certainly."

"Then I will go now and get things ready. Until this afternoon . . ."

"Good-bye."

I anticipated a little trouble from Emory, but not much. Everyone back at the ship was anxious to see the Martians, poke needles in the Martians, ask them about Martian climate, diseases, soil chemistry, politics, and mushrooms (our botanist was a fungus nut, but a reasonably good guy)—and only four or five had actually gotten to see them. The crew had been spending most of its time excavating dead cities and their acropolises. We played the game by strict rules, and the natives were as fiercely insular as the nineteenth-century Japanese. I figured I would meet with little resistance, and I figured right.

In fact, I got the distinct impression that everyone was happy to see me move out.

I stopped in the hydrophonics room to speak with our mushroom master.

"Hi, Kane. Grow any toadstools in the sand yet?"

He sniffed. He always sniffs. Maybe he's allergic to plants.

"Hello, Gallinger. No, I haven't had any success with

toadstools, but look behind the car barn next time you're out there. I've got a few cacti going."

"Great," I observed. Doc Kane was about my only friend aboard, not counting Betty.

"Say, I came down to ask you a favor."

"Name it."

"I want a rose."

"A what?"

"A rose. You know, a nice red American Beauty job—thorns, pretty smelling—"

"I don't think it will take in this soil. *Sniff, sniff.*"

"No, you don't understand. I don't want to plant it, I just want the flower."

"I'd have to use the tanks." He scratched his hairline dome. "It would take at least three months to get you flowers, even under forced growth."

"Will you do it?"

"Sure, if you don't mind the wait."

"Not at all. In fact, three months will just make it before we leave." I looked about at the pools of crawling slime, at the trays of shoots. "—I'm moving up to Tirellian today, but I'll be in and out all the time. I'll be here when it blooms."

"Moving up there, eh? Moore said they're an in-group."

"I guess I'm 'in' then."

"Looks that way—I still don't see how you learned their language, though. Of course, I had trouble with French and German for my Ph.D., but last week I heard Betty demonstrate it at lunch. It just sounds like a lot of weird noises. She says speaking it is like working a *Times* crossword and trying to imitate birdcalls at the same time."

I laughed, and took the cigarette he offered me.

"It's complicated," I acknowledged. "But, well, it's as if you suddenly came across a whole new class of mycetae here—you'd dream about it at night."

His eyes were gleaming.

"Wouldn't that be something! I might, yet, you know."

"Maybe you will."

He chuckled as we walked to the door.

"I'll start your roses tonight. Take it easy down there."

"You bet. Thanks."

Like I said, a fungus nut, but a fairly good guy.

My quarters in the Citadel of Tirellian were directly adjacent to the Temple, on the inward side and slightly to the left. They were a considerable improvement over my cramped cabin, and I was pleased that Martian culture had progressed sufficiently to discover the desirability of the mattress over the pallet. Also, the bed was long enough to accommodate me, which was surprising.

So I unpacked and took sixteen 35 mm. shots of the Temple, before starting on the books.

I took 'stats until I was sick of turning pages without knowing what they said. So I started translating a work of history.

"Lo. In the thirty-seventh year of the Process of Cillen the rains came, which gave rise to rejoicing, for it was a rare and untoward occurrence, and commonly construed a blessing.

"But it was not the life-giving semen of Malann which fell from the heavens. It was the blood of the universe, spurting from an artery. And the last days were upon us. The final dance was to begin.

"The rains brought the plague that does not kill, and the last passes of Locar began with their drumming. . . ."

I asked myself what the hell Tamur meant, for he was an historian and supposedly committed to fact. This was not their Apocalypse.

Unless they could be one and the same . . . ?

Why not? I mused. Tirellian's handful of people were the remnant of what had obviously once been a highly developed culture. They had had wars, but no holocausts; science, but little technology. A plague that did not kill . . . ? Could that have done it? How, if it wasn't fatal?

I read on, but the nature of the plague was not discussed. I turned pages, skipped ahead, and drew a blank.

M'Cwyie! M'Cwyie! When I want to question you most, you are not around!

Would it be a *faux pas* to go looking for her? Yes, I decided. I was restricted to the rooms I had been shown, that had been an implicit understanding. I would have to wait to find out.

So I cursed long and loud, in many languages, doubtless burning Malann's sacred ears, there in his Temple.

He did not see fit to strike me dead, so I decided to call it a day and hit the sack.

I must have been asleep for several hours when Braxa entered my room with a tiny lamp. She dragged me awake by tugging at my pajama sleeve.

I said hello. Thinking back, there is not much else I could have said.

"Hello."

"I have come," she said, "to hear the poem."

"What poem?"

"Yours."

"Oh."

I yawned, sat up, and did things people usually do when awakened in the middle of the night to read poetry.

"That is very kind of you, but isn't the hour a trifle awkward?"

"I don't mind," she said.

Someday I am going to write an article for the *Journal of Semantics,* called "Tone of Voice: An Insufficient Vehicle for Irony."

However, I was awake, so I grabbed my robe.

"What sort of animal is that?" she asked, pointing at the silk dragon on my lapel.

"Mythical," I replied. "Now look, it's late. I am tired. I have much to do in the morning. And M'Cwyie just might get the wrong idea if she learns you were here."

"Wrong idea?"

"You know damned well what I mean!" It was the first time I had had an opportunity to use Martian profanity, and it failed.

"No," she said, "I do not know."

She seemed frightened, like a puppy being scolded without knowing what it has done wrong.

I softened. Her red cloak matched her hair and lips so perfectly, and those lips were trembling.

"Here now, I didn't mean to upset you. On my world there are certain, uh, mores, concerning people of different sex alone together in bedrooms, and not allied by marriage. . . . Um, I mean, you see what I mean?"

"No."

They were jade, her eyes.

"Well, it's sort of . . . Well, it's sex, that's what it is."

A light was switched on in those jade lamps.

"Oh, you mean having children!"

"Yes. That's it! Exactly."

She laughed. It was the first time I had heard laughter in Tirellian. It sounded like a violinist striking his high strings with the bow, in short little chops. It was not an altogether pleasant thing to hear, especially because she laughed too long.

When she had finished she moved closer.

"I remember, now," she said. "We used to have such rules. Half a Process ago, when I was a child, we had such rules. But"—she looked as if she were ready to laugh again—"there is no need for them now."

My mind moved like a tape recorder played at triple speed.

Half a Process! HalfaProcessa-ProcessaProcess! No! Yes! Half a Process was two hundred-forty-three years, roughly speaking!

—Time enough to learn the 2224 dances of Locar.

—Time enough to grow old, if you were human.

—Earth-style human, I mean.

I looked at her again, pale as the white queen in an ivory chess set.

She was human, I'd stake my soul—alive, normal, healthy. I'd stake my life—woman, my body . . .

But she was two and a half centuries old, which made M'Cwyie Methuselah's grandma. It flattered me to think of their repeated complimenting of my skills, as linguist, as poet. These superior beings!

But what did she mean "there is no such need for them now"? Why the near-hysteria? Why all those funny looks I'd been getting from M'Cwyie?

I suddenly knew I was close to something important, besides a beautiful girl.

"Tell me," I said, in my Casual Voice, "did it have anything to do with 'the plague that does not kill,' of which Tamur wrote?"

"Yes," she replied, "the children born after the Rains could have no children of their own, and—"

"And what?" I was leaning forward, memory set at "record."

"—and the men had no desire to get any."

I sagged backward against the bedpost. Racial sterility, masculine impotence, following phenomenal weather. Had some vagabond cloud of radioactive junk from God knows where penetrated their weak atmosphere one day? One day long before Shiaparelli saw the canals, mythical as my dragon, before those "canals" had given rise to some correct guesses for all the wrong reasons, had Braxa been alive, dancing, here—damned in the womb since blind Milton had written of another paradise, equally lost?

I found a cigarette. Good thing I had thought to bring ashtrays. Mars had never had a tobacco industry either. Or booze. The ascetics I had met in India had been Dionysiac compared to this.

"What is that tube of fire?"

"A cigarette. Want one?"

"Yes, please."

She sat beside me, and I lighted it for her.

"It irritates the nose."

"Yes. Draw some into your lungs, hold it there, and exhale."

A moment passed.

"Ooh," she said.

A pause, then, "Is it sacred?"

"No, it's nicotine," I answered, "a very *ersatz* form of divinity."

Another pause.

"Please don't ask me to translate 'ersatz.' "

"I won't. I get this feeling sometimes when I dance."

"It will pass in a moment."

"Tell me your poem now."

An idea hit me.

"Wait a minute," I said; "I may have something better."

I got up and rummaged through my notebooks, then I returned and sat beside her.

"These are the first three chapters of the Book of Ecclesiastes," I explained. "It is very similar to your own sacred books."

I started reading.

I got through eleven verses before she cried out, "Please don't read that! Tell me one of yours!"

I stopped and tossed the notebook onto a nearby table.

She was shaking, not as she had quivered that day she danced as the wind, but with the jitter of unshed tears. She held her cigarette awkwardly, like a pencil. Clumsily, I put my arm about her shoulders.

"He is so sad," she said, "like all the others."

So I twisted my mind like a bright ribbon, folded it, and tied the crazy Christmas knots I love so well. From German to Martian, with love, I did an impromptu paraphrasal of a poem about a Spanish dancer. I thought it would please her. I was right.

"Ooh," she said again. "Did you write that?"

"No, it's by a better man than I."

"I don't believe you. You wrote it."

"No, a man named Rilke did."

"But you brought it across to my language. Light another match, so I can see how she danced."

I did.

"The fires of forever," she mused, "and she stamped them out, 'with small, firm feet.' I wish I could dance like that."

"You're better than any Gypsy," I laughed, blowing it out.

"No, I'm not. I couldn't do that."

"Do you want me to dance for you?"

Her cigarette was burning down, so I removed it from her fingers and put it out, along with my own.

"No," I said. "Go to bed."

She smiled, and before I realized it, had unclasped the fold of red at her shoulder.

And everything fell away.

And I swallowed, with some difficulty.

"All right," she said.

So I kissed her, as the breath of fallen cloth extinguished the lamp.

III

The days were like Shelley's leaves: yellow, red, brown, whipped in bright gusts by the west wind. They swirled past me with the rattle of microfilm. Almost all the books were recorded now. It would take scholars years to get through them, to properly assess their value. Mars was locked in my desk.

Ecclesiastes, abandoned and returned to a dozen times, was almost ready to speak in the High Tongue.

I whistled when I wasn't in the Temple. I wrote reams of poetry I would have been ashamed of before. Evenings I would walk with Braxa, across the dunes or up into the mountains. Sometimes she would dance for me; and I would read something long, and in dactylic hexameter. She still thought I was Rilke, and I almost kidded myself into believing it. Here I was, staying at the Castle Duino, writing his *Elegies*.

> *. . . It is strange to inhabit the Earth no more,*
> *to use no longer customs scarce acquired,*
> *nor interpret roses . . .*

No! Never interpret roses! Don't Smell them (sniff, Kane!), pick them, enjoy them. Live in the moment. Hold to it tightly. But charge not the gods to explain. So fast the leaves go by, are blown . . .

And no one ever noticed us. Or cared.

Laura. Laura and Braxa. They rhyme, you know, with a bit of a clash. Tall, cool, and blonde was she (I hate blondes!), and Daddy had turned me inside out, like a pocket, and I thought she could fill me again. But the big, beat word-slinger, with Judas-beard and dog-trust in his eyes, oh, he had been a fine decoration at her parties. And that was all.

How the machine cursed me in the Temple! It blasphemed Malann and Gallinger. And the wild west wind went by and something was not far behind.

The last days were upon us.

A day went by and I did not see Braxa, and a night.

And a second. A third.

I was half-mad. I hadn't realized how close we had become, how important she had been. With a dumb assurance of presence, I had fought against questioning roses.

I had to ask. I didn't want to, but I had no choice.

"Where is she, M'Cwyie? Where is Braxa?"

"She is gone," she said.

"Where?"

"I do not know."

I looked at those devil-bird eyes. Anathema maranatha rose to my lips.

"I must know."

She looked through me.

"She has left us. She is gone. Up into the hills, I suppose. Or the desert. It does not matter. What does anything matter? The dance draws to a close. The Temple will soon be empty."

"Why? Why did she leave?"

"I do not know."

"I must see her again. We lift off in a matter of days."

"I am sorry, Gallinger."

"So am I," I said, and slammed shut a book without saying "m'narra."

I stood up.

"I will find her."

I left the Temple. M'Cwyie was a seated statue. My boots were still where I had left them.

All day I roared up and down the dunes, going nowhere. To the crew of the *Aspic* I must have looked like a sandstorm, all by myself. Finally, I had to return for more fuel.

Emory came stalking out.

"Okay, make it good. You look like the abominable dust man. Why the rodeo?"

"Why, I, uh, lost something."

"In the middle of the desert? Was it one of your sonnets? They're the only thing I can think of that you'd make such a fuss over."

"No, dammit! It was something personal."

George had finished filling the tank. I started to mount the jeepster again.

"Hold on there!" he grabbed my arm.

"You're not going back until you tell me what this is all about."

I could have broken his grip, but then he could order me dragged back by the heels, and quite a few people would enjoy doing the dragging. So I forced myself to speak slowly, softly:

"It's simply that I lost my watch. My mother gave it to me and it's a family heirloom. I want to find it before we leave."

"You sure its not in your cabin, or down in Tirellian?"

"I've already checked."

"Maybe somebody hid it to irritate you. You know you're not the most popular guy around."

I shook my head.

"I thought of that. But I always carry it in my right pocket. I think it might have bounced out going over the dunes."

He narrowed his eyes.

"I remember reading on a book jacket that your mother died when you were born."

"That's right," I said, biting my tongue. "The watch belonged to her father and she wanted me to have it. My father kept it for me."

"Hmph!" he snorted. "That's a pretty strange way to look for a watch, riding up and down in a jeepster."

"I could see the light shining off it that way," I offered, lamely.

"Well, it's starting to get dark," he observed. "No sense looking any more today.

"Throw a dust sheet over the jeepster," he directed a mechanic.

He patted my arm.

"Come on in and get a shower, and something to eat. You look as if you could use both."

Little fatty flecks beneath pale eyes, thinning hair, and an Irish nose; a voice a decibel louder than anyone else's. . . .

His only qualification for leadership!

I stood there, hating him. Claudius! If only this were the fifth act!

But suddenly the idea of a shower, and food, came through to me. I could use both badly. If I insisted on hurrying back immediately I might arouse more suspicion.

So I brushed some sand from my sleeve.

"You're right. That sounds like a good idea."

"Come on, we'll eat in my cabin."

The shower was a blessing, clean khakis were the grace of God, and the food smelled like Heaven.

"Smells pretty good," I said.

We hacked up our steaks in silence. When we got to the dessert and coffee he suggested:

"Why don't you take the night off? Stay here and get some sleep."

I shook my head.

"I'm pretty busy. Finishing up. There's not much time left."

"A couple of days ago you said you were almost finished."

"Almost, but not quite."

"You also said they'll be holding a service in the Temple tonight."

"That's right. I'm going to work in my room."

He shrugged his shoulders.

Finally, he said, "Gallinger," and I looked up because my name means trouble.

"It shouldn't be any of my business," he said, "but it is. Betty says you have a girl down there."

There was no question mark. It was a statement hanging in the air. Waiting.

Betty, you're a bitch. You're a cow and a bitch. And a jealous one, at that. Why didn't you keep your nose where it belonged, shut your eyes? Your mouth?

"So?" I said, a statement with a question mark.

"So," he answered it, "it is my duty, as head of this expedition, to see that relations with the natives are carried on in a friendly, and diplomatic, manner."

"You speak of them," I said, "as though they are aborigines. Nothing could be further from the truth."

I rose.

"When my papers are published everyone on Earth will know that truth. I'll tell them things Doctor Moore never even guessed at. I'll tell the tragedy of a doomed race, waiting for death, resigned and disinterested. I'll tell why, and it will break hard, scholarly hearts. I'll write about it, and they will give me more prizes, and this time I won't want them.

"My God!" I exclaimed. "They had a culture when our ancestors were clubbing the saber-tooth and finding out how fire works!"

"*Do* you have a girl down there?"

"Yes!" I said. Yes, *Claudius! Yes, Daddy! Yes, Emory!*
"I do. But I'm going to let you in on a scholarly scoop
now. They're already dead. They're sterile. In one more
generation there won't be any Martians."

I paused, then added, "Except in my papers, except on
a few pieces of microfilm and tape. And in some poems,
about a girl who did give a damn and could only bitch
about the unfairness of it all by dancing."

"Oh," he said.

After awhile:

"You *have* been behaving differently these past couple
months. You've even been downright civil on occasion,
you know. I couldn't help wondering what was happening.
I didn't know anything mattered that strongly to you."

I bowed my head.

"Is she the reason you were racing around the desert?"

I nodded.

"Why?"

I looked up.

"Because she's out there, somewhere. I don't know
where, or why. And I've got to find her before we go."

"Oh," he said again.

Then he leaned back, opened a drawer, and took out
something wrapped in a towel. He unwound it. A framed
photo of a woman lay on the table.

"My wife," he said.

It was an attractive face, with big, almond eyes.

"I'm a Navy man, you know," he began. "Young officer
once. Met her in Japan.

"Where I come from it wasn't considered right to marry
into another race, so we never did. But she was my wife.
When she died I was on the other side of the world. They
took my children, and I've never seen them since. I
couldn't learn what orphanage, what home, they were put
into. That was long ago. Very few people know about it."

"I'm sorry," I said.

"Don't be. Forget it. But"—he shifted in his chair and
looked at me—"if you do want to take her back with you
—do it. It'll mean my neck, but I'm too old to ever head
another expedition like this one. So go ahead."

He gulped his cold coffee.

"Get your jeepster."

He swiveled the chair around.

I tried to say "thank you" twice, but I couldn't. So I got up and walked out.

"Sayonara, and all that," he muttered behind me.

"Here it is, Gallinger!" I heard a shout.

I turned on my heel and looked back up the ramp.

"Kane!"

He was limned in the port, shadow against light, but I had heard him sniff.

I returned the few steps.

"Here what is?"

"Your rose."

He produced a plastic container, divided internally. The lower half was filled with liquid. The stem ran down into it. The other half, a glass of claret in this horrible night, was a large, newly opened rose.

"Thank you," I said, tucking it into my jacket.

"Going back to Tirellian, eh?"

"Yes."

"I saw you come aboard, so I got it ready. Just missed you at the Captain's cabin. He was busy. Hollered out that I could catch you at the barns."

"Thanks again."

"It's chemically treated. It will stay in bloom for weeks."

I nodded. I was gone.

Up into the mountains now. Far. Far. The sky was a bucket of ice in which no moons floated. The going became steeper, and the little donkey protested. I whipped him with the throttle and went on. Up. Up. I spotted a green, unwinking star, and felt a lump in my throat. The encased rose beat against my chest like an extra heart. The donkey brayed, long and loudly, then began to cough. I lashed him some more and he died.

I threw the emergency brake on and got out. I began to walk.

So cold, so cold it grows. Up here. At night? Why? Why did she do it? Why flee the campfire when night comes on?

And I was up, down, around, and through every chasm,

gorge, and pass, with my long-legged strides and an ease of movement never known on Earth.

Barely two days remain, my love, and thou hast forsaken me. Why?

I crawled under overhangs. I leaped over ridges. I scraped my knees, an elbow. I heard my jacket tear.

No answer, Malann? Do you really hate your people this much? Then I'll try someone else. Vishnu, you're the Preserver. Preserve her, please! Let me find her.

Jehovah?

Adonis? Osiris? Thammuz? Manitou? Legba? Where is she?

I ranged far and high, and I slipped.

Stones ground underfoot and I dangled over an edge. My fingers so cold. It was hard to grip the rock.

I looked down.

Twelve feet or so. I let go and dropped, landed rolling.

Then I heard her scream.

I lay there, not moving, looking up. Against the night, above, she called.

"Gallinger!"

I lay still.

"Gallinger!"

And she was gone.

I heard stones rattle and knew she was coming down some path to the right of me.

I jumped up and ducked into the shadow of a boulder.

She rounded a cut-off, and picked her way, uncertainly, through the stones.

"Gallinger?"

I stepped out and seized her shoulders.

"Braxa."

She screamed again, then began to cry, crowding against me. It was the first time I had ever heard her cry.

"Why?" I asked. "Why?"

But she only clung to me and sobbed.

Finally, "I thought you had killed yourself."

"Maybe I would have," I said. "Why did you leave Tirellian? And me?"

"Didn't M'Cwyie tell you? Didn't you guess?"

"I didn't guess, and M'Cwyie said she didn't know."

"Then she lied. She knows."

"What? What is it she knows?"

She shook all over, then was silent for a long time. I realized suddenly that she was wearing only her flimsy dancer's costume. I pushed her from me, took off my jacket, and put it about her shoulders.

"Great Malann!" I cried. "You'll freeze to death!"

"No," she said, "I won't."

I was transferring the rose-case to my pocket.

"What is that?" she asked.

"A rose," I answered. "You can't make it out much in the dark. I once compared you to one. Remember?"

"Ye-Yes. May I carry it?"

"Sure." I stuck it in the jacket pocket.

"Well? I'm still waiting for an explanation."

"You really don't know?" she asked.

"No!"

"When the Rains came," she said, "apparently only our men were affected, which was enough. . . . Because I—wasn't—affected—apparently—"

"Oh," I said. "Oh."

We stood there, and I thought.

"Well, why did you run? What's wrong with being pregnant on Mars? Tamur was mistaken. Your people can live again."

She laughed, again that wild violin played by a Paginini gone mad. I stopped her before it went too far.

"How?" she finally asked, rubbing her cheek.

"Your people live longer than ours. If our child is normal it will mean our races can intermarry. There must still be other fertile women of your race. Why not?"

"You have read the Book of Locar," she said, "and yet you ask me that? Death was decided, voted upon, and passed, shortly after it appeared in this form. But long before, the followers of Locar knew. They decided it long ago. 'We have done all things,' they said, 'we have seen all things, we have heard and felt all things. The dance was good. Now let it end'."

"You can't believe that."

"What I believe does not matter," she replied. "M'Cwyie and the Mothers have decided we must die. Their very title is now a mockery, but their decisions will be upheld.

There is only one prophecy left, and it is mistaken. We will die."

"No," I said.

"What, then?"

"Come back with me, to Earth."

"No."

"All right, then. Come with me now."

"Where?"

"Back to Tirellian. I'm going to talk to the Mothers."

"You can't! There is a Ceremony tonight!"

I laughed.

"A ceremony for a god who knocks you down, and then kicks you in the teeth?"

"He is still Malann," she answered. "We are still his people."

"You and my father would have gotten along fine," I snarled. "But I am going, and you are coming with me, even if I have to carry you—and I'm bigger than you are."

"But you are not bigger than Ontro."

"Who the hell is Ontro?"

"He will stop you, Gallinger. He is the Fist of Malann."

IV

I scudded the jeepster to a halt in front of the only entrance I knew, M'Cwyie's. Braxa, who had seen the rose in a headlamp, now cradled it in her lap, like our child, and said nothing. There was a passive, lovely look on her face.

"Are they in the Temple now?" I wanted to know.

The Madonna-expression did not change. I repeated the question. She stirred.

"Yes," she said, from a distance, "but you cannot go in."

"We'll see."

I circled and helped her down.

I led her by the hand, and she moved as if in a trance. In the light of the new-risen moon, her eyes looked as they had the day I met her, when she had danced. I snapped my fingers. Nothing happened.

So I pushed the door open and led her in. The room was half-lighted.

And she screamed for the third time that evening:

"Do not harm him, Ontro! It is Gallinger!"

I had never seen a Martian man before, only women. So I had no way of knowing whether he was a freak, though I suspected it strongly.

I looked up at him.

His half-naked body was covered with moles and swellings. Gland trouble, I guessed.

I had thought I was the tallest man on the planet, but he was seven feet tall and overweight. Now I knew where my giant bed had come from!

"Go back," he said. "She may enter. You may not."

"I must get my books and things."

He raised a huge left arm. I followed it. All my belongings lay neatly stacked in the corner.

"I must go in. I must talk with M'Cwyie and the Mothers."

"You may not."

"The lives of your people depend on it."

"Go back," he boomed. "Go home to *your* people, Gallinger. Leave *us!*"

My name sounded so different on his lips, like someone else's. How old was he? I wondered. Three hundred? Four? Had he been a Temple guardian all his life? Why? Who was there to guard against? I didn't like the way he moved. I had seen men who moved like that before.

"Go back," he repeated.

If they had refined their martial arts as far as they had their dances, or, worse yet, if their fighting arts were a part of the dance, I was in for trouble.

"Go on in," I said to Braxa. "Give the rose to M'Cwyie. Tell her that I sent it. Tell her I'll be there shortly."

"I will do as you ask. Remember me on Earth, Gallinger. Good-bye."

I did not answer her, and she walked past Ontro and into the next room, bearing her rose.

"Now will you leave?" he asked. "If you like, I will tell her that we fought and you almost beat me, but I knocked you unconscious and carried you back to your ship."

"No," I said, "either I go around you or go over you, but I am going through."

He dropped into a crouch, arms extended.

"It is a sin to lay hands on a holy man," he rumbled, "but I will stop you, Gallinger."

My memory was a fogged window, suddenly exposed to fresh air. Things cleared. I looked back six years.

I was a student of Oriental Languages at the University of Tokyo. It was my twice-weekly night of recreation. I stood in a thirty-foot circle in the Kodokan, the *judogi* lashed about my high hips by a brown belt. I was *Ik-kyu*, one notch below the lowest degree of expert. A brown diamond above my right breast said "Jiu-Jitsu" in Japanese, and it meant *atemiwaza*, really, because of the one striking-technique I had worked out, found unbelievably suitable to my size, and won matches with.

But I had never used it on a man, and it was five years since I had practiced. I was out of shape, I knew, but I tried hard to force my mind *tsuki no kokoro*, like the moon, reflecting the all of Ontro.

Somewhere, out of the past, a voice said, "*Hajime*, let it begin."

I snapped into my *neko-ashi-dachi* cat-stance, and his eyes burned strangely. He hurried to correct his own position—and I threw it at him!

My one trick!

My long left leg lashed up like a broken spring. Seven feet off the ground my foot connected with his jaw as he tried to leap backward.

His head snapped back and he fell. A soft moan escaped his lips. *That's all there is to it,* I thought. *Sorry, old fellow.*

And as I stepped over him, somehow, groggily, he tripped me, and I fell across his body. I couldn't believe he had strength enough to remain conscious after that blow, let alone move. I hated to punish him any more.

But he found my throat and slipped a forearm across it before I realized there was a purpose to his action.

No! Don't let it end like this!

It was a bar of steel across my windpipe, my carotids. Then I realized that he was still unconscious, and that this was a reflex instilled by countless years of training. I had seen it happen once, in *shiai*. The man died because he had been choked unconscious and still fought on, and his opponent thought he had not been applying the choke properly. He tried harder.

But it was rare, so very rare!

I jammed my elbows into his ribs and threw my head back in his face. The grip eased, but not enough. I hated to do it, but I reached up and broke his little finger.

The arm went loose and I twisted free.

He lay there panting, face contorted. My heart went out to the fallen giant, defending his people, his religion, following his orders. I cursed myself as I had never cursed before, for walking over him, instead of around.

I staggered across the room to my little heap of possessions. I sat on the projector case and lit a cigarette.

I couldn't go into the Temple until I got my breath back, until I thought of something to say.

How do you talk a race out of killing itself?

Suddenly—

—Could it happen? Would it work that way? If I read them the Book of Ecclesiastes—if I read them a greater piece of literature than any Locar ever wrote—and as somber—and as pessimistic—and showed them that our race had gone on despite one man's condemning all of life in the highest poetry—showed them that the vanity he had mocked had borne us to the Heavens—would they believe it—would they change their minds?

I ground out my cigarette on the beautiful floor, and found my notebook. A strange fury rose within me as I stood.

And I walked into the Temple to preach the Black Gospel according to Gallinger, from the Book of Life.

There was silence all about me.

M'Cwyie had been reading Locar, the rose set at her right hand, target of all eyes.

Until I entered.

Hundreds of people were seated on the floor, barefoot. The few men were as small as the women, I noted.

I had my boots on.

Go all the way, I figured. *You either lose or you win— everything!*

A dozen crones sat in a semicircle behind M'Cwyie. The Mothers.

The barren earth, the dry wombs, the fire-touched.
I moved to the table.

"Dying yourselves, you would condemn your people," I addressed them, "that they may not know the life you have known—the joys, the sorrows, the fullness. —But it is not true that you all must die." I addressed the multitude now. "Those who say this lie. Braxa knows, for she will bear a child—"

They sat there, like rows of Buddhas. M'Cwyie drew back into the semicircle.

"—my child!" I continued, wondering what my father would have thought of this sermon.

". . . And all the women young enough may bear children. It is only your men who are sterile.—And if you permit the doctors of the next expedition to examine you, perhaps even the men may be helped. But if they cannot, you can mate with the men of Earth.

"And ours is not an insignificant people, an insignificant place," I went on. "Thousands of years ago, the Locar of our world wrote a book saying that it was. He spoke as Locar did, but we did not lie down, despite plagues, wars, and famines. We did not die. One by one we beat down the diseases, we fed the hungry, we fought the wars, and, recently, have gone a long time without them. We may finally have conquered them. I do not know.

"But we have crossed millions of miles of nothingness. We have visited another world. And our Locar had said, 'Why bother? What is the worth of it? It is all vanity, anyhow.'

"And the secret is," I lowered my voice, as at a poetry reading, "he was right! It *is* vanity; it *is* pride! It is the hubris of rationalism to always attack the prophet, the mystic, the god. It is our blasphemy which has made us great, and will sustain us, and which the gods secretly admire in us. —And the truly sacred names of God are blasphemous things to speak!"

I was working up a sweat. I paused dizzily.

"Here is the Book of Ecclesiastes," I announced, and began:

" 'Vanity of vanities, saith the Preacher, vanity of vanities; all is vanity. What profit hath a man . . .' "

I spotted Braxa in the back, mute, rapt.

I wondered what she was thinking.

And I wound the hours of night about me, like black thread on a spool.

Oh it was late! I had spoken till day came, and still I spoke. I finished Ecclesiastes and continued Gallinger.

And when I finished there was still only a silence.

The Buddhas, all in a row, had not stirred through the night. And after a long while M'Cwyie raised her right hand. One by one the Mothers did the same.

And I knew what that meant.

It meant no, do not, cease, and stop.

It meant that I had failed.

I walked slowly from the room and slumped beside my baggage.

Ontro was gone. Good that I had not killed him. . . .

After a thousand years M'Cwyie entered.

She said, "Your job is finished."

I did not move.

"The prophecy is fulfilled," she said. "My people are rejoicing. You have won, holy man. Now leave us quickly."

My mind was a deflated balloon. I pumped a little air back into it.

"I'm not a holy man," I said, "just a second-rate poet with a bad case of hubris."

I lit my last cigarette.

Finally, "All right, what prophecy?"

"The Promise of Locar," she replied, as though the explaining were unnecessary, "that a holy man would come from the Heavens to save us in our last hours, if all the dances of Locar were completed. He would defeat the Fist of Malann and bring us life."

"How?"

"As with Braxa, and as the example in the Temple."

"Example?"

"You read us his words, as great as Locar's. You read to us how there is 'nothing new under the sun.' And you mocked his words as you read them—showing us a new thing.

"There has never been a flower on Mars," she said, "but we will learn to grow them.

"You are the Sacred Scoffer," she finished. "He-Who-Must-Mock-in-the-Temple—you go shod on holy ground."

"But you voted 'no,' " I said.

"I voted not to carry out our original plan, and to let Braxa's child live instead."

"Oh." The cigarette fell from my fingers. How close it had been! How little I had known!

"And Braxa?"

"She was chosen half a Process ago to do the dances—to wait for you."

"But she said that Ontro would stop me."

M'Cwyie stood there for a long time.

"She had never believed the prophecy herself. Things are not well with her now. She ran away, fearing it was true. When you completed it and we voted, she knew."

"Then she does not love me? Never did?"

"I am sorry, Gallinger. It was the one part of her duty she never managed."

"Duty," I said flatly. . . . Dutydutyduty! Tra-la!

"She has said good-bye; she does not wish to see you again.

". . . and we will never forget your teachings," she added.

"Don't," I said, automatically, suddenly knowing the great paradox which lies at the heart of all miracles. I did not believe a word of my own gospel, never had.

I stood, like a drunken man, and muttered "M'narra."

I went outside, into my last day on Mars.

I have conquered thee, Malann—and the victory is thine! Rest easy on thy starry bed. God damned!

I left the jeepster there and walked back to the *Aspic*, leaving the burden of life so many footsteps behind me. I went to my cabin, locked the door, and took forty-four sleeping pills.

But when I awakened I was in the dispensary, and alive.

I felt the throb of engines as I slowly stood up and somehow made it to the port.

Blurred Mars hung like a swollen belly above me, until it dissolved, brimmed over, and streamed down my face.

5.

The Monster
and the Maiden

A GREAT UNREST was among the people, for the time of decision was again at hand. The Elders voted upon the candidates and the sacrifice was affirmed over the objections of Ryllik, the oldest.

"It is wrong to capitulate thus," he argued.

But they did not answer him, and the young virgin was taken to the grotto of smokes and fed the leaves of drowsiness.

Ryllik watched with disapproval.

"It should not be so," he stated. "It is wrong."

"It has always been so," said the others, "in the spring of the year, and in the fall. It has always been so." And they cast worried glances down the trail to where the sun was pouring morning upon the world.

The god was already traveling through the great-leafed forest.

"Let us go now," they said.

"Did you ever think of staying? Of watching to see what the monster god does?" asked Ryllik bitterly.

"Enough of your blasphemies! Come along!"

Ryllik followed them.

"We grow fewer every year," he said. "One day we shall no longer have any sacrifices to offer."

"Then that day we die," said the others.

"So why prolong it?" he asked. "Let us fight them—now, before we are no more!"

But the others shook their heads, a summary of that resignation Ryllik had watched grow as the centuries passed. They all respected Ryllik's age, but they did not approve of his thoughts. They cast one last look back, just as the sun caught the clanking god upon his gilt-caparisoned mount, his death-lance slung at his side. Within the place where the smokes were born the maiden thrashed her tail from side to side, rolling wild eyes beneath her youthful brow-plates. She sensed the divine presence and began to bellow.

They turned away and lumbered across the plains.

As they neared the forest Ryllik paused and raised a scaley fore-limb, groping after a thought. Finally, he spoke:

"I seem to have memory," said he, "of a time when things were different."

6.

Collector's Fever

"WHAT ARE YOU doing there, human?"

"It's a long story."

"Good, I like long stories. Sit down and talk. No—not on me!"

"Sorry. Well, it's all because of my uncle, the fabulously wealthy—"

"Stop. What does 'wealthy' mean?"

"Well, like rich."

"And 'rich'?"

"Hm. Lots of money."

"What's money?"

"You want to hear this story or don't you?"

"Yes, but I'd like to understand it too."

"Sorry, Rock, I'm afraid I don't understand it all myself."

"The name is Stone."

"Okay, Stone. My uncle, who is a very important man, was supposed to send me to the Space Academy, but he didn't. He decided a liberal education was a better thing. So he sent me to his old spinster alma mater to major in nonhuman humanities. You with me, so far?"

"No, but understanding is not necessarily an adjunct to appreciation."

"That's what I say. I'll never understand Uncle Sidney,

127

but I appreciate his outrageous tastes, his magpie instinct
and his gross meddling in other people's affairs. I appreciate them till I'm sick to the stomach. There's nothing
else I can do. He's a carnivorous old family monument,
and fond of having his own way. Unfortunately, he also
has all the money in the family—so it follows, like a *xxt*
after a *zzn*, that he always *does* have his own way."

"This money must be pretty important stuff."

"Important enough to send me across ten thousand
light-years to an unnamed world which, incidentally, I've
just named Dunghill."

"The low-flying *zatt* is a heavy eater, which accounts
for its low flying . . ."

"So I've noted. That *is* moss though, isn't it?"

"Yes."

"Good, then crating will be less of a problem."

"What's 'crating'?"

"It means to put something in a box to take it somewhere else."

"Like moving around?"

"Yes."

"What are you planning on crating?"

"Yourself, Stone."

"I've never been the rolling sort . . ."

"Listen, Stone, my uncle is a rock collector, see? You
are the only species of intelligent mineral in the galaxy.
You are also the largest specimen I've spotted so far. Do
you follow me?"

"Yes, but I don't want to."

"Why not? You'd be lord of his rock collection. Sort of
a one-eyed man in a kingdom of the blind, if I may ven-
ture an inappropriate metaphor."

"Please don't do that, whatever it is. It sounds awful.
Tell me, how did your uncle learn of our world?"

"One of my instructors read about this place in an old
space log. *He* was an old space log collector. The log had
belonged to a Captain Fairhill, who landed here several
centuries ago and held lengthy discourses with your
people."

"Good old Foul Weather Fairhill! How is he these
days? Give him my regards—"

"He's dead."

"What?"

"Dead. Kaput. Blooey. Gone. Deeble."

"Oh my! When did it happen? I trust it was an esthetic occurrence of major import—"

"I really couldn't say. But I passed the information on to my uncle, who decided to collect you. That's why I'm here—he sent me."

"Really, as much as I appreciate the compliment, I can't accompany you. It's almost deeble time—"

"I know, I read all about deebling in the Fairhill log before I showed it to Uncle Sidney. I tore those pages out. I want him to be around when you do it. Then I can inherit his money and console myself in all manner of expensive ways for never having gone to the Space Academy. First I'll become an alcoholic, then I'll take up wenching—or maybe I'd better do it the other way around . . ."

"But I want to deeble here, among the things I've become attached to!"

"This is a crowbar. I'm going to unattach you."

"If you try it, I'll deeble right now."

"You can't. I measured your mass before we struck up this conversation. It will take at least eight months, under Earth conditions, for you to reach deebling proportions."

"Okay, I was bluffing. But have you no compassion? I've rested here for centuries, ever since I was a small pebble, as did my fathers before me. I've added so carefully to my atom collection, building up the finest molecular structure in the neighborhood. And now, to be snatched away right before deebling time, it's—it's quite unrock of you."

"It's not that bad. I promise you'll collect the finest Earth atoms available. You'll go places no other Stone has ever been before."

"Small consolation. I want my friends to see."

"I'm afraid that's out of the question."

"You are a very cruel human. I hope you're around when I deeble."

"I intend to be far away and on the eve of prodigious debaucheries when that occurs."

Under Dunghill's sub-E gravitation Stone was easily rolled

to the side of the space sedan, crated, and, with the help of a winch, installed in the compartment beside the atomic pile. The fact that it was a short-jaunt sport model sedan, customized by its owner, who had removed much of the shielding, was the reason Stone felt a sudden flush of volcanic drunkenness, rapidly added select items to his collection and deebled on the spot.

He mushroomed upwards, then swept in great waves across the plains of Dunghill. Several young Stones fell from the dusty heavens wailing their birth pains across the community band.

"Gone fission," commented a distant neighbor, above the static, "and sooner than I expected. Feel that warm afterglow!"

"An excellent deeble," agreed another. "It always pays to be a cautious collector."

7.

This Mortal
Mountain

I

I LOOKED DOWN at it and I was sick! I wondered, where
did it lead? Stars?

There were no words. I stared and I stared, and I
cursed the fact that the thing existed and that someone
had found it while I was still around.

"Well?" said Lanning, and he banked the flier so that
I could look upward.

I shook my head and shaded my already shielded eyes.

"Make it go away," I finally told him.

"Can't. It's bigger than I am."

"It's bigger than anybody," I said.

"I can make *us* go away . . ."

"Never mind. I want to take some pictures."

He brought it around, and I started to shoot.

"Can you hover—or get any closer?"

"No, the winds are too strong."

"That figures."

So I shot—through telescopic lenses and scan attach-
ment and all—as we circled it.

"I'd give a lot to see the top."

"We're at thirty thousand feet, and fifty's the ceiling on

131

this baby. The Lady, unfortunately, stands taller than the atmosphere."

"Funny," I said, "from here she doesn't strike me as the sort to breathe ether and spend all her time looking at stars."

He chuckled and lit a cigarette, and I reached us another bulb of coffee.

"How *does* the Gray Sister strike you?"

And I lit one of my own and inhaled, as the flier was buffeted by sudden gusts of something from somewhere and then ignored, and I said, "Like Our Lady of the Abattoir—right between the eyes."

We drank some coffee, and then he asked, "She too big, Whitey?" and I gnashed my teeth through caffeine, for only my friends call me Whitey, my name being Jack Summers and my hair having always been this way, and at the moment I wasn't too certain whether Henry Lanning qualified for that status—just because he'd known me for twenty years—after going out of his way to find this thing on a world with a thin atmosphere, a lot of rocks, a too-bright sky and a name like LSD pronounced backwards, after George Diesel, who had set foot in the dust and then gone away—smart fellow!

"A forty-mile-high mountain," I finally said, "is not a mountain. It is a world all by itself, which some dumb diety forgot to throw into orbit."

"I take it you're not interested?"

I looked back at the gray and lavender slopes and followed them upward once again, until all color drained away, until the silhouette was black and jagged and the top still nowhere in sight, until my eyes stung and burned behind their protective glasses; and I saw clouds bumping up against that invincible outline, like icebergs in the sky, and I heard the howling of the retreating winds which had essayed to measure its grandeur with swiftness and, of course, had failed.

"Oh, I'm interested," I said, "in an academic sort of way. Let's go back to town, where I can eat and drink and maybe break a leg if I'm lucky."

He headed the flier south, and I didn't look around as we went. I could sense her presence at my back, though, all the way: The Gray Sister, the highest mountain in the known universe. Unclimbed, of course.

She remained at my back during the days that followed, casting her shadow over everything I looked upon. For the next two days I studied the pictures I had taken and I dug up some maps and I studied them, too; and I spoke with people who told me stories of the Gray Sister, strange stories. . . .

During this time, I came across nothing really encouraging. I learned that there had been an attempt to colonize Diesel a couple centuries previously, back before faster-than-light ships were developed. A brand-new disease had colonized the first colonists, however, wiping them out to a man. The new colony was four years old, had better doctors, had beaten the plague, was on Diesel to stay and seemed proud of its poor taste when it came to worlds. Nobody, I learned, fooled around much with the Gray Sister. There had been a few abortive attempts to climb her, and some young legends that followed after.

During the day, the sky never shut up. It kept screaming into my eyes, until I took to wearing my climbing goggles whenever I went out. Mainly, though, I sat in the hotel lounge and ate and drank and studied the pictures and cross-examined anybody who happened to pass by and glance at them, spread out there on the table.

I continued to ignore all Henry's questions. I knew what he wanted, and he could damn well wait. Unfortunately, he did, and rather well, too, which irritated me. He felt I was almost hooked by the Sister, and he wanted to Be There When It Happened. He'd made a fortune on the Kasla story, and I could already see the opening sentences of this one in the smug lines around his eyes. Whenever he tried to make like a poker player, leaning on his fist and slowly turning a photo, I could see whole paragraphs. If I followed the direction of his gaze, I probably could even have seen the dust jacket.

At the end of the week, a ship came down out of the sky, and some nasty people got off and interrupted my train of thought. When they came into the lounge, I recognized them for what they were and removed my black lenses so that I could nail Henry with my basilisk gaze and turn him to stone. As it would happen, he had too much alcohol in him, and it didn't work.

"You tipped off the press," I said.

"Now, now," he said, growing smaller and stiffening as my gaze groped its way through the murk of his central nervous system and finally touched upon the edges of that tiny tumor, his forebrain. "You're well-known, and . . ."

I replaced my glasses and hunched over my drink, looking far gone, as one of the three approached and said, "Pardon me, but are you Jack Summers?"

To explain the silence which followed, Henry said, "Yes, this is Mad Jack, the man who climbed Everest at twenty-three and every other pile of rocks worth mentioning since that time. At thirty-one, he became the only man to conquer the highest mountain in the known universe—Mount Kasla on Litan—elevation 89,941 feet. My book—"

"Yes," said the reporter. "My name is Cary, and I'm with GP. My friends represent two of the other syndicates. We've heard that you are going to climb the Gray Sister."

"You've heard incorrectly," I said.

"Oh?"

The other two came up and stood beside him.

"We thought that—" one of them began.

"—you were already organizing a climbing party," said the other.

"Then you're not going to climb the Sister?" asked Cary, while one of the two looked over my pictures and the other got ready to take some of his own.

"Stop that!" I said, raising a hand at the photographer. "Bright lights hurt my eyes!"

"Sorry. I'll use the infra," he said, and he started fooling with his camera.

Cary repeated the question.

"All I said was that you've heard incorrectly," I told him. "I didn't say I was and I didn't say I wasn't. I haven't made up my mind."

"If you should decide to try it, have you any idea when it will be?"

"Sorry, I can't answer that."

Henry took the three of them over to the bar and started explaining something, with gestures. I heard the

words ". . . out of retirement after four years," and
when/if they looked to the booth again, I was gone.

I had retired, to the street which was full of dusk, and
I walked along it thinking. I trod her shadow even then,
Linda. And the Gray Sister beckoned and forbade with
her single unmoving gesture. I watched her, so far away,
yet still so large, a piece of midnight at eight o'clock. The
hours that lay between died like the distance at her feet,
and I knew that she would follow me wherever I went,
even into sleep. Especially into sleep.

So I knew, at that moment. The days that followed were
a game I enjoyed playing. Fake indecision is delicious
when people want you to do something. I looked at her
then, my last and my largest, my very own Koshtra Piv-
rarcha, and I felt that I was born to stand upon her summit. Then I could retire, probably remarry, cultivate my
mind, not worry about getting out of shape, and do all
the square things I didn't do before, the lack of which had
cost me a wife and a home, back when I had gone to
Kasla, elevation 89,941 feet, four and a half years ago, in
the days of my glory. I regarded my Gray Sister across
the eight o'clock world, and she was dark and noble and
still and waiting, as she had always been.

II

The following morning I sent the messages. Out across the
light-years like cosmic carrier pigeons they went. They
winged their ways to some persons I hadn't seen in years
and to others who had seen me off at Luna Station. Each
said, in its own way, "If you want in on the biggest climb
of them all, come to Diesel. The Gray Sister eats Kaslas
for breakfast. R.S.V.P. c/o. The Lodge, Georgetown.
Whitey."

Backwards, turn backwards. . . .

I didn't tell Henry. Nothing at all. What I had done
and where I was going, for a time, were my business only,
for that same time. I checked out well before sunrise and
left him a message at the desk:

"Out of town on business. Back in a week. Hold the
fort. Mad Jack."

I had to gauge the lower slopes, tug the hem of the

lady's skirt, so to speak, before I introduced her to my friends. They say only a madman climbs alone, but they call me what they call me for a reason.

From my pix, the northern face had looked promising. I set the rented flier down as near as I could, locked it up, shouldered my pack and started walking.

Mountains rising to my right and to my left, mountains at my back, all dark as sin now in the predawn light of a white, white day. Ahead of me, not a mountain, but an almost gentle slope which kept rising and rising and rising. Bright stars above me and cold wind past me as I walked. Straight up, though, no stars, just black. I wondered for the thousandth time what a mountain weighed. I always wonder that as I approach one. No clouds in sight. No noises but my boot sounds on the turf and the small gravel. My goggles flopped around my neck. My hands were moist within my gloves. On Diesel, the pack and I together probably weighed about the same as me alone on Earth—for which I was duly grateful. My breath burned as it came and steamed as it went. I counted a thousand steps and looked back, and I couldn't see the flier. I counted a thousand more and then looked up to watch some stars go out. About an hour after that, I had to put on my goggles. By then I could see where I was headed. And by then the wind seemd stronger.

She was so big that the eye couldn't take all of her in at once. I moved my head from side to side, leaning further and further backward. Wherever the top, it was too high. For an instant, I was seized by a crazy acrophobic notion that I was looking down rather than up, and the soles of my feet and the palms of my hands tingled, like an ape's must when, releasing one high branch to seize another, he discovers that there isn't another.

I went on for two more hours and stopped for a light meal. This was hiking, not climbing. As I ate, I wondered what could have caused a formation like the Gray Sister. There were some ten- and twelve-mile peaks within sixty miles of the place and a fifteen-mile mountain called Burke's Peak on the adjacent continent, but nothing else like the Sister. The lesser gravitation? Her composition? I couldn't say. I wondered what Doc and Kelly and Mallardi would say when they saw her.

I don't define them, though. I only climb them.

I looked up again, and a few clouds were brushing against her now. From the photos I had taken, she might be an easy ascent for a good ten or twelve miles. Like a big hill. There were certainly enough alternate routes. In fact, I thought she just might be a pushover. Feeling heartened, I repacked my utensils and proceeded. It was going to be a good day. I could tell.

And it was. I got off the slope and onto something like a trail by late afternoon. Daylight lasts about nine hours on Diesel, and I spent most of it moving. The trail was so good that I kept on for several hours after sundown and made considerable height. I was beginning to use my respiration equipment by then, and the heating unit in my suit was turned on.

The stars were big, brilliant flowers, the way was easy, the night was my friend. I came upon a broad, flat piece and made my camp under an overhang.

There I slept, and I dreamt of snowy women with breasts like the Alps, pinked by the morning sun; and they sang to me like the wind and laughed, had eyes of ice prismatic. They fled through a field of clouds.

The following day I made a lot more height. The "trail" began to narrow, and it ran out in places, but it was easy to reach for the sky until another one occurred. So far, it had all been good rock. It was still tapering as it heightened, and balance was no problem. I did a lot of plain old walking. I ran up one long zigzag and hit it up a wide chimney almost as fast as Santa Claus comes down one. The winds were strong, could be a problem if the going got difficult. I was on the respirator full time and feeling great.

I could see for an enormous distance now. There were mountains and mountains, all below me like desert dunes. The sun beat halos of heat about their peaks. In the east, I saw Lake Emerick, dark and shiny as the toe of a boot. I wound my way about a jutting crag and came upon a giant's staircase, going up for at least a thousand feet. I mounted it. At its top I hit my first real barrier: a fairly smooth, almost perpendicular face rising for about eighty-five feet.

No way around it, so I went up. It took me a good

hour, and there was a ridge at the top leading to more easy climbing. By then, though, the clouds attacked me. Even though the going was easy, I was slowed by the fog. I wanted to outclimb it and still have some daylight left, so I decided to postpone eating.

But the clouds kept coming. I made another thousand feet, and they were still about me. Somewhere below me, I heard thunder. The fog was easy on my eyes, though, so I kept pushing.

Then I tried a chimney, the top of which I could barely discern, because it looked a lot shorter than a jagged crescent to its left. This was a mistake.

The rate of condensation was greater than I'd guessed. The walls were slippery. I'm stubborn, though, and I fought with skidding boots and moist back until I was about a third of the way up, I thought, and winded.

I realized then what I had done. What I had thought was the top wasn't. I went another fifteen feet and wished I hadn't. The fog began to boil about me, and I suddenly felt drenched. I was afraid to go down and I was afraid to go up, and I couldn't stay where I was forever.

Whenever you hear a person say that he inched along, do not accuse him of a fuzzy choice of verbs. Give him the benefit of the doubt and your sympathy.

I inched my way, blind, up an unknown length of slippery chimney. If my hair hadn't already been white when I entered at the bottom. . . .

Finally, I got above the fog. Finally, I saw a piece of that bright and nasty sky, which I decided to forgive for the moment. I aimed at it, arrived on target.

When I emerged, I saw a little ledge about ten feet above me. I climbed to it and stretched out. My muscles were a bit shaky, and I made them go liquid. I took a drink of water, ate a couple of chocolate bars, took another drink.

After perhaps ten minutes, I stood up. I could no longer see the ground. Just the soft, white cottony top of a kindly old storm. I looked up.

It was amazing. She was still topless. And save for a couple spots, such as the last—which had been the fault of my own stupid overconfidence—it had almost been as easy as climbing stairs.

Now the going appeared to be somewhat rougher, how-ever. This was what I had really come to test.

I swung my pick and continued.

All the following day I limped, steadily, taking no un-necessary risks, resting periodically, drawing maps, taking wide-angle photos. The ascent eased in two spots that afternoon, and I made a quick seven thousand feet. Higher now than Everest, and still going, I. Now, though, there were places where I crawled and places where I used ropes, and there were places where I braced myself and used my pneumatic pistol to blast a toehold. (No, in case you're wondering: I could have broken my eardrums, some ribs, an arm and doubtless ultimately, my neck, if I'd tried using the gun in the chimney.)

Just near sunset, I came upon a high, easy winding way up and up and up. I debated with my more discreet self. I'd left the message that I'd be gone a week. This was the end of the third day. I wanted to make as much height as possible and start back down on the fifth day. If I followed the rocky route above me as far as it would take me I'd probably break forty thousand feet. Then, depend-ing, I might have a halfway chance of hitting near the ten-mile mark before I had to turn back. Then I'd be able to get a much better picture of what lay above.

My more discreet self lost, three to nothing, and Mad Jack went on.

The stars were so big and blazing I was afraid they'd bite. The wind was no problem. There wasn't any at that height. I had to keep stepping up the temperature controls on my suit, and I had the feeling that if I could spit around my respirator, it would freeze before it hit the trail.

I went on even further than I'd intended, and I broke forty-two thousand that night.

I found a resting place, stretched out, killed my hand beacon.

It was an odd dream that came to me.

It was all cherry fires and stood like a man, only bigger, on the slope above me. It stood in an impossible position, so I knew I had to be dreaming. Something from the other end of my life stirred, however, and I was convinced for a bitter moment that it was the Angel of Judgment. Only,

in its right hand it seemed to hold a sword of fire rather
than a trumpet. It had been standing there forever, the
tip of its blade pointed toward my breast. I could see the
stars through it. It seemed to speak.

It said: *"Go back."*

I couldn't answer, though, for my tongue clove to the
roof of my mouth. And it said it again, and yet a third
time, *"Go back."*

"Tomorrow," I thought, in my dream, and this seemed
to satisfy it. For it died down and ceased, and the blackness rolled about me.

The following day, I climbed as I hadn't climbed in years.
By late lunchtime I'd hit forty-eight thousand feet. The
cloud cover down below had broken. I could see what lay
beneath me once more. The ground was a dark and light
patchwork. Above, the stars didn't go away.

The going was rough, but I was feeling fine. I knew I
couldn't make ten miles, because I could see that the way
was pretty much the same for quite a distance, before it
got even worse. My good spirits stayed, and they continued to rise as I did.

When it attacked, it came on with a speed and fury
that I was only barely able to match.

The voice from my dream rang in my head: *"Go back!
Go back! Go back!"*

Then it came toward me from out of the sky. A bird
the size of a condor.

Only it wasn't really a bird.

It was a bird-shaped thing.

It was all fire and static, and as it flashed toward me I
barely had time to brace my back against stone and heft
my climbing pick in my right hand, ready.

III

I sat in the small, dark room and watched the spinning,
colored lights. Ultrasonics were tickling my skull. I tried
to relax and give the man some Alpha rhythms. Somewhere a receiver was receiving, a computer was computing
and a recorder was recording.

It lasted perhaps twenty minutes.

When it was all over and they called me out, the doctor collared me. I beat him to the draw, though:

"Give me the tape and send me the bill in care of Henry Lanning at the Lodge."

"I want to discuss the reading," he said.

"I have my own brain-wave expert coming. Just give me the tape."

"Have you undergone any sort of traumatic experience recently?'

"You tell me. Is it indicated?"

"Well, yes and no," he said.

"That's what I like, a straight answer."

"I don't know what is normal for you, in the first place," he replied.

"Is there any indication of brain damage?"

"I don't read it that way. If you'd tell me what happened, and why you're suddenly concerned about your brain-waves, perhaps I'd be in a better position to. . . ."

"Cut," I said. "Just give me the tape and bill me."

"I'm concerned about you as a patient."

"But you don't think there were any pathological indications?'

"Not exactly. But tell me this, if you will: Have you had an epileptic seizure recently?"

"Not to my knowledge. Why?"

"You displayed a pattern similar to a residual subrhythm common in some forms of epilepsy for several days subsequent to a seizure."

"Could a bump on the head cause that pattern?"

"It's highly unlikely."

"What else *could* cause it?"

"Electrical shock, optical trauma—"

"Stop," I said, and I removed my glasses. "About the optical trauma. Look at my eyes."

"I'm not an ophtha—" he began, but I interrupted:

"Most normal light hurts my eyes. If I lost my glasses and was exposed to very bright light for three, four days, could that cause the pattern you spoke of?"

"Possibly. . . ." he said. "Yes, I'd say so."

"But there's more?"

"I'm not sure. We have to take more readings, and if I know the story behind this it will help a lot."

"Sorry," I said. "I need the tape now."

He sighed and made a small gesture with his left hand as he turned away.

"All right, Mister Smith."

Cursing the genius of the mountain, I left the General Hospital, carrying my tape like a talisman. In my mind I searched, through forests of memory, for a ghost-sword in a stone of smoke, I think.

Back at the Lodge, they were waiting. Lanning and the newsmen.

"What was it like?" asked one of the latter.

"What was what like?"

"The mountain. You were up on it, weren't you?"

"No comment."

"How high did you go?"

"No comment."

"How would you say it compares with Kasla?"

"No comment."

"Did you run into any complications?"

"Ditto. Excuse me, I want to take a shower."

Henry followed me into my room. The reporters tried to.

After I had shaved and washed up, mixed a drink and lit a cigarette, Lanning asked me his more general question:

"Well?" he said.

I nodded.

"Difficulties?"

I nodded again.

"Insurmountable?"

I hefted the tape and thought a moment.

"Maybe not."

He helped himself to the whiskey. The second time around, he asked:

"You going to try?"

I knew I was. I knew I'd try it all by myself if I had to.

"I really don't know," I said.

"Why not?"

"Because there's something up there," I said, "something that doesn't want us to do it."

"Something *lives* up there?"

"I'm not sure whether that's the right word."

He lowered the drink.

"What the hell happened?"

"I was threatened. I was attacked."

"Threatened? Verbally? In English?" He set his drink aside, which shows how serious his turn of mind had to be. "Attacked?" he added. "By what?"

"I've sent for Doc and Kelly and Stan and Mallardi and Vincent. I checked a little earlier. They've all replied. They're coming. Miguel and the Dutchman can't make it, and they send their regrets. When we're all together, I'll tell the story. But I want to talk to Doc first. So hold tight and worry and don't quote."

He finished his drink.

"When'll they be coming?"

"Four, five weeks," I said.

"That's a long wait."

"Under the circumstances," I said, "I can't think of any alternatives."

"What'll we do in the meantime?"

"Eat, drink and contemplate the mountain."

He lowered his eyelids a moment, then nodded, reached for his glass.

"Shall we begin?"

It was late, and I stood alone in the field with a bottle in one hand. Lanning had already turned in, and night's chimney was dark with cloud soot. Somewhere away from there, a storm was storming, and it was full of instant outlines. The wind came chill.

"Mountain," I said. "Mountain, you have told me to go away."

There was a rumble.

"But I cannot," I said, and I took a drink.

"I'm bringing you the best in the business," I said, "to go up on your slopes and to stand beneath the stars in your highest places. I must do this thing because you are there. No other reason. Nothing personal. . . ."

After a time, I said, "That's not true.

"I'm a man," I said, "and I need to break mountains to prove that I will not die even though I will die. I am less than I want to be, Sister, and you can make me more. So I guess it *is* personal.

"It's the only thing I know how to do, and you're the last one left—the last challenge to the skill I spent my life learning. Maybe it is that mortality is closest to immortality when it accepts a challenge to itself, when it survives a threat. The moment of triumph is the moment of salvation. I have needed many such moments, and the final one must be the longest, for it must last me the rest of my life.

"So you are there, Sister, and I am here and very mortal, and you have told me to go away. I cannot. I'm coming up, and if you throw death at me I will face it. It must be so."

I finished what remained in the bottle.

There were more flashes, more rumbles behind the mountain, more flashes.

"It is the closest thing to divine drunkenness," I said to the thunder.

And then she winked at me. It was a red star, so high upon her. Angel's sword. Phoenix' wing. Soul on fire. And it blazed at me, across the miles. Then the wind that blows between the worlds swept down over me. It was filled with tears and with crystals of ice. I stood there and felt it, then, "Don't go away," I said, and I watched until all was darkness once more and I was wet as an embryo waiting to cry out and breathe.

Most kids tell lies to their playmates—fictional autobiographies, if you like—which are either received with appropriate awe or countered with greater, more elaborate tellings. But little Jimmy, I've heard, always hearkened to his little buddies with wide, dark eyes, and near the endings of their stories the corners of his mouth would begin to twitch. By the time they were finished talking, his freckles would be mashed into a grin and his rusty head cocked to the side. His favorite expression, I understand, was "G'wan!" and his nose was broken twice before he was twelve. This was doubtless why he turned it toward books.

Thirty years and four formal degrees later, he sat across from me in my quarters in the Lodge, and I called him Doc because everyone did, because he had a license to cut people up and look inside them, as well as doctoring to their philosophy, so to speak, and because he looked as if he could be called Doc when he grinned and cocked his head to the side and said, "G'wan!"

I wanted to punch him in the nose.

"Damn it! It's true!" I told him. "I fought with a bird of fire!"

"We all hallucinated on Kasla," he said, raising one finger, "because of fatigue," two fingers, "because the altitude affected our circulatory systems and consequently our brains," three, "because of the emotional stimulation," four, "and because we were partly oxygen-drunk."

"You just ran out of fingers, if you'll sit on your other hand for a minute. So listen," I said, "it flew at me, and I swung at it, and it knocked me out and broke my goggles. When I woke up, it was gone and I was lying on the ledge. I think it was some sort of energy creature. You saw my EEG, and it wasn't normal. I think it shocked my nervous system when it touched me."

"You were knocked out because you hit your head against a rock—"

"It *caused* me to fall back against the rock!"

"I agree with that part. The rock was real. But nowhere in the universe has anyone ever discovered an 'energy creature.' "

"So? You probably would have said that about America a thousand years ago."

"Maybe I would have. But that neurologist explained your EEG to my satisfaction. Optical trauma. Why go out of your way to dream up an exotic explanation for events? Easy ones generally turn out better. You hallucinated and you stumbled."

"Okay," I said, "whenever I argue with you I generally need ammunition. Hold on a minute."

I went to my closet and fetched it down from the top shelf. I placed it on my bed and began unwrapping the blanket I had around it.

"I told you I took a swing at it," I said. "Well, I connected—right before I went under. Here!"

I held up my climbing pick—brown, yellow, black and pitted—looking as though it had fallen from outer space.

He took it into his hands and stared at it for a long time, then he started to say something about ball lightning,

changed his mind, shook his head and placed the thing
back on the blanket.

"I don't know," he finally said, and this time his freckles
remained unmashed, except for those at the edges of his
hands which got caught as he clenched them, slowly.

IV

We planned. We mapped and charted and studied the
photos. We plotted our ascent and we started a training
program.

While Doc and Stan had kept themselves in good shape,
neither had been climbing since Kasla. Kelly was in top
condition. Henry was on his way to fat. Mallardi and
Vince, as always, seemed capable of fantastic feats of en-
durance and virtuosity, had even climbed a couple times
during the past year, but had recently been living pretty
high on the tall hog, so to speak, and they wanted to get
some practice. So we picked a comfortable, decent-sized
mountain and gave it ten days to beat everyone back into
shape. After that, we stuck to vitamins, calisthenics and
square diets while we completed our preparations. During
this time, Doc came up with seven shiny, alloy boxes,
about six by four inches and thin as a first book of poems,
for us to carry on our persons to broadcast a defense
against the energy creature which he refused to admit
existed.

One fine, bitter-brisk morning we were ready. The newsmen liked me again. Much footage was taken of our gal-
lant assemblage as we packed ourselves into the fliers, to
be delivered at the foot of the lady mountain, there to
contend for what was doubtless the final time as the team
we had been for so many years, against the waiting gray
and the lavender beneath the sunwhite flame.

We approached the mountain, and I wondered how
much she weighed.

You know the way, for the first nine miles. So I'll skip
over that. It took us six days and part of a seventh. Nothing out of the ordinary occurred. Some fog there was, and
nasty winds, but once below, forgotten.

Stan and Mallardi and I stood where the bird had occurred, waiting for Doc and the others.

"So far, it's been a picnic," said Mallardi.

"Yeah," Stan acknowledged.

"No birds either."

"No," I agreed.

"Do you think Doc was right—about it being an hallucination?" Mallardi asked. "I remember seeing things on Kasla. . . ."

"As I recall," said Stan, "it was nymphs and an ocean of beer. Why would anyone want to see hot birds?"

"Damfino."

"Laugh, you hyenas," I said. "But just wait till a flock flies over."

Doc came up and looked around.

"This is the place?"

I nodded.

He tested the background radiation and half a dozen other things, found nothing untoward, grunted and looked upwards.

We all did. Then we went there.

It was very rough for three days, and we only made another five thousand feet during that time.

When we bedded down, we were bushed, and sleep came quickly. So did Nemesis.

He was there again, only not quite so near this time. He burned about twenty feet away, standing in the middle of the air, and the point of his blade indicated me.

"Go away," he said, three times, without inflection.

"Go to hell," I tried to say.

He made as if he wished to draw nearer. He failed.

"Go away yourself," I said.

"Climb back down. Depart. You may go no further."

"But I am going further. All the way to the top."

"No. You may not."

"Stick around and watch," I said.

"Go back."

"If you want to stand there and direct traffic, that's your business," I told him. "I'm going back to sleep."

I crawled over and shook Doc's shoulder, but when I looked back my flaming visitor had departed.

"What is it?"

"Too late," I said. "He's been here and gone."

Doc sat up.

"The bird?"

"No, the thing with the sword."

"Where was he?"

"Standing out there," I gestured.

Doc hauled out his instruments and did many things with them for ten minutes or so.

"Nothing," he finally said. "Maybe you were dreaming."

"Yeah, sure," I said. "Sleep tight," and I hit the sack again, and this time I made it through to daylight without further fire or ado.

It took us four days to reach sixty thousand feet. Rocks fell like occasional cannonballs past us, and the sky was a big pool, cool, where pale flowers floated. When we struck sixty-three thousand, the going got much better, and we made it up to seventy-five thousand in two and a half more days. No fiery things stopped by to tell me to turn back. Then came the unforeseeable, however, and we had enough in the way of natural troubles to keep us cursing.

We hit a big, level shelf.

It was perhaps four hundred feet wide. As we advanced across it, we realized that it did not strike the mountainside. It dropped off into an enormous gutter of a canyon. We would have to go down again, perhaps seven hundred feet, before we could proceed upward once more. Worse yet, it led to a featureless face which strove for and achieved perpendicularity for a deadly high distance: like miles. The top was still nowhere in sight.

"Where do we go now?" asked Kelly, moving to my side.

"Down," I decided, "and we split up. We'll follow the big ditch in both directions and see which way gives the better route up. We'll meet back at the midway point."

We descended. Then Doc and Kelly and I went left, and the others took the opposite way.

After an hour and a half, our trail came to an end. We stood looking at nothing over the edge of something. Nowhere, during the entire time, had we come upon a decent way up. I stretched out, my head and shoulders over the edge, Kelly holding onto my ankles, and I looked as far as I could to the right and up. There was nothing in sight that was worth a facing movement.

"Hope the others had better luck," I said, after they'd dragged me back.

"And if they haven't . . . ?" asked Kelly.

"Let's wait."

They had.

It was risky, though.

There was no good way straight up out of the gap. The trail had ended at a forty-foot wall which, when mounted, gave a clear view all the way down. Leaning out as I had done and looking about two hundred feet to the left and eighty feet higher, however, Mallardi had rested his eyes on a rough way, but a way, nevertheless, leading up and west and vanishing.

We camped in the gap that night. In the morning, I anchored my line to a rock, Doc tending, and went out with the pneumatic pistol. I fell twice, and made forty feet of trail by lunchtime.

I rubbed my bruises then, and Henry took over. After ten feet, Kelly got out to anchor a couple of body-lengths behind him, and we tended Kelly.

Then Stan blasted and Mallardi anchored. Then there had to be three on the face. Then four. By sundown, we'd made a hundred-fifty feet and were covered with white powder. A bath would have been nice. We settled for ultrasonic shakedowns.

By lunch the next day, we were all out there, roped together, hugging cold stone, moving slowly, painfully, slowly, not looking down much.

By day's end, we'd made it across, to the place where we could hold on and feel something—granted, not much —beneath our boots. It was inclined to be a trifle scant, however, to warrant less than a full daylight assault. So we returned once more to the gap.

In the morning, we crossed.

The way kept its winding angle. We headed west and up. We traveled a mile and made five hundred feet. We traveled another mile and made perhaps three hundred.

Then a ledge occurred, about forty feet overhead.

Stan went up the hard way, using the gun, to see what he could see.

He gestured, and we followed; and the view that broke upon us was good.

Down right, irregular but wide enough, was our new camp.

The way above it, ice cream and whiskey sours and morning coffee and a cigarette after dinner. It was beautiful and delicious: a seventy-degree slope full of ledges and projections and good clean stone.

"Hot damn!" said Kelly.

We all tended to agree.

We ate and we drank and we decided to rest our bruised selves that afternoon.

We were in the twilight world now, walking where no man had ever walked before, and we felt ourselves to be golden. It was good to stretch out and try to unache.

I slept away the day, and when I awakened the sky was a bed of glowing embers. I lay there too lazy to move, too full of sight to go back to sleep. A meteor burnt its way bluewhite across the heavens. After a time, there was another. I thought upon my position and decided that reaching it was worth the price. The cold, hard happiness of the heights filled me. I wiggled my toes.

After a few minutes, I stretched and sat up. I regarded the sleeping forms of my companions. I looked out across the night as far as I could see. Then I looked up at the mountain, then dropped my eyes slowly along tomorrow's trail.

There was movement within shadow.

Something was standing about fifty feet away and ten feet above.

I picked up my pick and stood.

I crossed the fifty and stared up.

She was smiling, not burning.

A woman, an impossible woman.

Absolutely impossible. For one thing, she would just have to freeze to death in a mini-skirt and a sleeveless shell-top. No alternative. For another, she had very little to breathe. Like, nothing.

But it didn't seem to bother her. She waved. Her hair was dark and long, and I couldn't see her eyes. The planes of her pale, high cheeks, wide forehead, small chin corresponded in an unsettling fashion with certain simple theorems which comprise the geometry of my heart. If all angles, planes, curves be correct, it skips a beat, then hurries to make up for it.

I worked it out, felt it do so, said, "Hello."

"Hello, Whitey," she replied.

"Come down," I said.

"No, you come up."

I swung my pick. When I reached the ledge she wasn't there. I looked around, then I saw her.

She was seated on a rock twelve feet above me.

"How it is that you know my name?" I asked.

"Anyone can see what your name must be."

"All right," I agreed. "What's yours?"

". . ." Her lips seemed to move, but I heard nothing.

"Come again?"

"I don't want a name," she said.

"Okay. I'll call you 'girl,' then."

She laughed, sort of.

"What are you doing here?" I asked.

"Watching you."

"Why?"

"To see whether you'll fall."

"I can save you the trouble," I said. "I won't."

"Perhaps," she said.

"Come down here."

"No, you come up here."

I climbed, but when I got there she was twenty feet higher.

"Girl, you climb well," I said, and she laughed and turned away.

I pursued her for five minutes and couldn't catch her. There was something unnatural about the way she moved.

I stopped climbing when she turned again. We were still about twenty feet apart.

"I take it you do not really wish me to join you," I said.

"Of course I do, but you must catch me first." And she turned once more, and I felt a certain fury within me.

It was written that no one could outclimb Mad Jack. I had written it.

I swung my pick and moved like a lizard.

I was near to her a couple of times, but never near enough.

The day's aches began again in my muscles, but I pulled my way up without slackening my pace. I realized, faintly, that the camp was far below me now, and that I was climbing alone through the dark up a strange slope. But I did not stop. Rather, I hurried, and my breath began to come hard in my lungs. I heard her laughter, and it was a goad. Then I came upon a two-inch ledge, and she was moving along it. I followed, around a big bulge of rock to where it ended. Then she was ninety feet above me, at the top of a smooth pinnacle. It was like a tapering, branchless tree. How she'd accomplished it, I didn't know. I was gasping by then, but I looped my line around it and began to climb. As I did this, she spoke:

"Don't you ever tire, Whitey? I thought you would have collapsed by now."

I hitched up the line and climbed further.

"You can't make it up here, you know."

"I don't know," I grunted.

"Why do you want so badly to climb here? There are other nice mountains."

"This is the biggest, girl. That's why."

"It can't be done."

"Then why all this bother to discourage me? Why not just let the mountain do it?"

As I neared her, she vanished. I made it to the top, where she had been standing, and I collapsed there.

Then I heard her voice again and turned my head. She was on a ledge, perhaps eighty feet away.

"I didn't think you'd make it this far," she said. "You are a fool. Good-by, Whitey." She was gone.

I sat there on the pinnacle's tiny top—perhaps four square feet of top—and I knew that I couldn't sleep there, because I'd fall. And I was tired.

I recalled my favorite curses and I said them all, but I didn't feel any better. I couldn't let myself go to sleep. I looked down. I knew the way was long. I knew she didn't think I could make it.

I began the descent.

The following morning when they shook me, I was still tired. I told them the last night's tale, and they didn't believe me. Not until later in the day, that is, when I detoured us around the bulge and showed them the pinnacle, standing there like a tapering, branchless tree, ninety feet in the middle of the air.

V

We went steadily upward for the next two days. We made slightly under ten thousand feet. Then we spent a day hammering and hacking our way up a great flat face. Six hundred feet of it. Then our way was to the right and upward. Before long we were ascending the western side of the mountain. When we broke ninety thousand feet, we stopped to congratulate ourselves that we had just surpassed the Kasla climb and to remind ourselves that we still had not hit the halfway mark. It took us another two and a half days to do that, and by then the land lay like a map beneath us.

And then, that night, we all saw the creature with the sword.

He came and stood near our camp, and he raised his sword above his head, and it blazed with such a terrible intensity that I slipped on my goggles. His voice was all thunder and lightning this time:

"Get off this mountain!" he said. *"Now! Turn back! Go down! Depart!"*

And then a shower of stones came down from above and rattled about us. Doc tossed his slim, shiny case, causing it to skim along the ground toward the creature.

The light went out, and we were alone.

Doc retrieved his case, took tests, met with the same success as before—*i.e.*, none. But now at least he didn't think I was some kind of balmy, unless of course he thought we all were.

"Not a very effective guardian," Henry suggested.

"We've a long way to go yet," said Vince, shying a stone through the space the creature had occupied. "I don't like it if the thing can cause a slide."

"That was just a few pebbles," said Stan.

"Yeah, but what if he decided to start them fifty thousand feet higher?"

"Shut up!" said Kelly. "Don't give him any ideas. He might be listening."

For some reason, we drew closer together. Doc made each of us describe what we had seen, and it appeared that we all had seen the same thing.

"All right," I said, after we'd finished. "Now you've all seen it, who wants to go back?"

There was silence.

After perhaps half a dozen heartbeats, Henry said, "I want the whole story. It looks like a good one. I'm willing to take my chances with angry energy creatures in order to get it."

"I don't know what the thing is," said Kelly. "Maybe it's no energy creature. Maybe it's something—supernatural—I know what you'll say, Doc. I'm just telling you how it struck me. If there are such things, this seems a good place for them. Point is—whatever it is, I don't care. I want this mountain. If it could have stopped us, I think it would've done it already. Maybe I'm wrong. Maybe it can. Maybe it's laid some trap for us higher up. But I want this mountain. Right now, it means more to me than anything. If I don't go up, I'll spend all my time wondering about it—and then I'll probably come back and try it again some day, when it gets so I can't stand thinking about it any more. Only then, maybe the rest of you won't be available. Let's face it, we're a good climbing team. Maybe the best in the business. Probably. If it can be done, I think we can do it."

"I'll second that," said Stan.

"What you said, Kelly," said Mallardi, "about it being supernatural—it's funny, because I felt the same thing for a minute when I was looking at it. It reminds me of something out of the *Divine Comedy*. If you recall, Purgatory was a mountain. And then I thought of the angel who guarded the eastern way to Eden. Eden had gotten moved to the top of Purgatory by Dante—and there was this angel. . . . Anyhow, I felt almost like I was committing some sin I didn't know about by being here. But now that I think it over, a man can't be guilty of something he doesn't know is wrong, can he? And I didn't see that thing flashing any angel ID card. So I'm willing to go up and see what's on top, unless he comes back with the Tablets of the Law, with a new one written in at the bottom."

"In Hebrew or Italian?" asked Doc.

"To satisfy you, I suppose they'd have to be drawn up in the form of equations."

"No," he said. "Kidding aside, I felt something funny too, when I saw it and heard it. And we didn't really hear it, you know. It skipped over the senses and got its message right into our brains. If you thing back over our descriptions of what we experienced, we each 'heard' different words telling us to go away. If it can communicate a meaning as well as a psychtranslator, I wonder if it can communicate an emotion, also. . . . You thought of an angel, too, didn't you, Whitey?"

"Yes," I said.

"That makes it almost unanimous then, doesn't it?"

Then we all turned to Vince, because he had no Christian background at all, having been raised as a Buddhist in Ceylon.

"What were your feelings concerning the thing?" Doc asked him.

"It was a Deva," he said, "which is sort of like an angel, I guess. I had the impression that every step I took up this mountain gave me enough bad karma to fill a lifetime. Except I haven't believed in it that way since I was a kid. I want to go ahead, up. Even if that feeling was correct, I want to see the top of this mountain."

"So do I," said Doc.

"That makes it unanimous," I said.

"Well, everybody hang onto his angel's-bane," said Stan, "and let's sack out."

"Good idea."

"Only let's spread out a bit," said Doc, "so that anything falling won't get all of us together."

We did that cheerful thing and slept untroubled by heaven.

Our way kept winding right, until we were at a hundred forty-four thousand feet and were mounting the southern slopes. Then it jogged back, and by a hundred fifty we were mounting to the west once more.

Then, during a devilish, dark and tricky piece of scaling, up a smooth, concave bulge ending in an overhang, the bird came down once again.

If we hadn't been roped together, Stan would have died. As it was, we almost all died.

Stan was lead man, as its wings splashed sudden flames against the violet sky. It came down from the overhang as though someone had kicked a bonfire over its edge, headed straight toward him and faded out at a distance of about twelve feet. He fell then, almost taking the rest of us with him.

We tensed our muscles and took the shock.

He was battered a bit, but unbroken. We made it up to the overhang, but went no further that day.

Rocks did fall, but we found another overhang and made camp beneath it.

The bird did not return that day, but the snakes came.

Big, shimmering scarlet serpents coiled about the crags, wound in and out of jagged fields of ice and gray stone. Sparks shot along their sinuous lengths. They coiled and unwound, stretched and turned, spat fires at us. It seemed they were trying to drive us from beneath the sheltering place to where the rocks could come down upon us.

Doc advanced upon the nearest one, and it vanished as it came within the field of his projector. He studied the place where it had lain, then hurried back.

"The fost is still on the punkin," he said.

"Huh?" said I.

"Not a bit of ice was melted beneath it."

"Indicating?"

"Illusion," said Vince, and he threw a stone at another and it passed through the thing.

"But you saw what happened to my pick," I said to Doc, "when I took a cut at that bird. The thing had to have been carrying some kind of charge."

"Maybe whatever has been sending them has cut that part out, as a waste of energy," he replied, "since the things can't get through to us anyhow."

We sat around and watched the snakes and falling rocks,

until Stan produced a deck of cards and suggested a better game.

The snakes stayed on through the night and followed us the next day. Rocks still fell periodically, but the boss seemed to be running low on them. The bird appeared, circled us and swooped on four different occasions. But this time we ignored it, and finally it went home to roost.

We made three thousand feet, could have gone more, but didn't want to press it past a cozy little ledge with a cave big enough for the whole party. Everything let up on us then. Everything visible, that is.

A before-the-storm feeling, a still, electrical tension, seemed to occur around us then, and we waited for whatever was going to happen to happen.

The worst possible thing happened: nothing.

This keyed-up feeling, this expectancy, stayed with us, was unsatisfied. I think it would actually have been a relief if some invisible orchestra had begun playing Wagner, or if the heavens had rolled aside like curtains and revealed a movie screen, and from the backward lettering we knew we were on the other side, or if we saw a high-flying dragon eating low-flying weather satellites. . . .

As it was, we just kept feeling that something was imminent, and it gave me insomnia.

During the night, she came again. The pinnacle girl.

She stood at the mouth of the cave, and when I advanced she retreated.

I stopped just inside and stood there myself, where she had been standing.

She said, "Hello, Whitey."

"No, I'm not going to follow you again," I said.

"I didn't ask you to."

"What's a girl like you doing in a place like this?"

"Watching," she said.

"I told you I won't fall."

"Your friend almost did."

" 'Almost' isn't good enough."

"You are the leader, aren't you?"

"That's right."

"If you were to die, the others would go back?"

"No," I said, "they'd go on without me."

I hit my camera then.

"What did you just do?" she asked.

"I took your picture—if you're really there."

"Why?"

"To look at after you go away. I like to look at pretty things."

". . ." She seemed to say something.

"What?"

"Nothing."

"Why not?"

". . . . die."

"Please speak up."

"She dies . . ." she said.

"Why? How?"

". . . . on mountain."

"I don't understand."

". . . . too."

"What's wrong?"

I took a step forward, and she retreated a step.

"Follow me?" she asked.

"No."

"Go back," she said.

"What's on the other side of that record?"

"You will continue to climb?"

"Yes."

Then, "Good!" she said suddenly. "I—" and her voice stopped again.

"Go back," she finally said, without emotion.

"Sorry."

And she was gone.

VI

Our trail took us slowly to the left once more. We crawled and sprawled and cut holes in the stone. Snakes sizzled in the distance. They were with us constantly now. The bird came again at crucial moments, to try to make us fall. A raging bull stood on a crag and bellowed down at us. Phantom archers loosed shafts of fire, which always faded right before they struck. Blazing blizzards swept at us, around us, were gone. We were back on the northern slopes and still heading west by the time we broke a hundred sixty thousand. The sky was deep and blue, and there were always stars. Why did the mountain hate us? I wondered. What was there about us to provoke this thing? I looked at the picture of the girl for the dozenth time and I wondered what she really was. Had she been picked from our minds and composed into girlform to lure us, to lead us, sirenlike, harpylike, to the place of the final fall? It was such a long way down. . . .

I thought back over my life. How does a man come to climb mountains? Is he drawn by the heights because he is afraid of the level land? Is he such a misfit in the society of men that he must flee and try to place himself above it? The way up is long and difficult, but if he succeeds they must grant him a garland of sorts. And if he falls, this too is a kind of glory. To end, hurled from the heights to the depths in hideous ruin and combustion down, is a fitting climax for the loser—for it, too, shakes mountains and minds, stirs things like thoughts below both, is a kind of blasted garland of victory in defeat, and cold, so cold that final action, that the movement is somewhere frozen forever into a statuelike rigidity of ultimate intent and purpose thwarted only by the universal malevolence we all fear exists. An aspirant saint or hero who lacks some necessary virtue may still qualify as a martyr, for the only thing that people will really remember in the end is the end. I had known that I'd had to climb Kasla, as I had climbed all the others, and I had known what the price would be. It had cost me my only home. But Kasla was there, and my boots cried out for my feet. I knew as I did so that somewhere I set them upon her summit, and below me a world was ending. What's a world if the moment of victory is at hand? And if truth, beauty and goodness be one, why is there always this conflict among them?

The phantom archers fired upon me and the bright bird swooped. I set my teeth, and my boots scarred rocks beneath me.

We saw the top.

At a hundred seventy-six thousand feet, making our way along a narrow ledge, clicking against rock, testing our way with our picks, we heard Vince say, "Look!"

We did.

Up and up, and again further, bluefrosted and sharp, deadly, and cold as Loki's dagger, slashing at the sky, it vibrated above us like electricity, hung like a piece of frozen thunder, and cut, cut, cut into the center of spirit that was desire, twisted, and became a fishhook to pull us on, to burn us with its barbs.

Vince was the first to look up and see the top, the first to die. It happened so quickly, and it was none of the terrors that achieved it.

He slipped.

That was all. It was a difficult piece of climbing. He was right behind me one second, was gone the next. There was no body to recover. He'd taken the long drop. The soundless blue was all around him and the great gray beneath. Then we were six. We shuddered, and I suppose we all prayed in our own ways.

—Gone Vince, may some good Deva lead you up the Path of Splendor. May you find whatever you wanted most at the other end, waiting there for you. If such a thing may be, remember those who say these words, oh strong intruder in the sky. . . .

No one spoke much for the rest of the day.

The fiery sword bearer came and stood above our camp the entire night. It did not speak.

In the morning, Stan was gone, and there was a note beneath my pack.

> *Don't hate me*, it said, *for running out, but I think it really is an angel. I'm scared of this mountain. I'll climb any pile of rocks, but I won't fight Heaven. The way down is easier than the way up, so don't worry about me. Good luck. Try to understand.*   S

So we were five—Doc and Kelly and Henry and Mallardi and me—and that day we hit a hundred eighty thousand and felt very alone.

The girl came again that night and spoke to me, black hair against black sky and eyes like points of blue fire, and she stood beside an icy pillar and said: "Two of you have gone."

"And the rest of us remain," I replied.

"For a time."

"We will climb to the top and then we will go away,"
I said. "How can that do you harm? Why do you hate us?"

"No hate, sir," she said.

"What, then?"

"I protect."

"What? What is it that you protect?"

"The dying, that she may live."

"What? Who is dying? How?"

But her words went away somewhere, and I did not
hear them. Then she went away too, and there was nothing
left but sleep for the rest of the night.

One hundred eighty-two thousand and three, and four, and
five. Then back down to four for the following night.

The creatures whined about us now, and the land pulsed
beneath us, and the mountain seemed sometimes to sway
as we climbed.

We carved a path to one eighty-six, and for three days
we fought to gain another thousand feet. Everything we
touched was cold and slick and slippery, sparkled, and
had a bluish haze about it.

When we hit one ninety, Henry looked back and
shuddered.

"I'm no longer worried about making it to the top," he
said. "It's the return trip that's bothering me now. The
clouds are like little wisps of cotton way down there."

"The sooner up, the sooner down," I said, and we began to climb once again.

It took us another week to cut our way to within a mile
of the top. All the creatures of fire had withdrawn, but
two ice avalanches showed us we were still unwanted. We
survived the first without mishap, but Kelly sprained his
right ankle during the second, and Doc thought he might
have cracked a couple of ribs, too.

We made a camp. Doc stayed there with him; Henry
and Mallardi and I pushed on up the last mile.

Now the going was beastly. It had become a mountain
of glass. We had to hammer out a hold for every foot we
made. We worked in shifts. We fought for everything we
gained. Our packs became monstrous loads and our fingers
grew numb. Our defense system—the projectors—seemed

to be wearing down, or else something was increasing its efforts to get us, because the snakes kept slithering closer, burning brighter. They hurt my eyes, and I cursed them.

When we were within a thousand feet of the top, we dug in and made another camp. The next couple hundred feet looked easier, then a rotten spot, and I couldn't tell what it was like above that.

When we awakened, there was just Henry and myself. There was no indication of where Mallardi had gotten to. Henry switched his communicator to Doc's letter and called below. I tuned in in time to hear him say, "Haven't seen him."

"How's Kelly?" I asked.

"Better," he replied. "Those ribs might not be cracked at that."

Then Mallardi called us.

"I'm four hundred feet above you, fellows," his voice came in. "It was easy up to here, but the going's just gotten rough again."

"Why'd you cut out on your own?" I asked.

"Because I think something's going to try to kill me before too long," he said. "It's up ahead, waiting at the top. You can probably even see it from here. It's a snake."

Henry and I used the binoculars.

Snake? A better word might be dragon—or maybe even Midgaard Serpent.

It was coiled around the peak, head upraised. It seemed to be several hundred feet in length, and it moved its head from side to side, and up and down, and it smoked solar coronas.

Then I spotted Mallardi climbing toward it.

"Don't go any further!" I called. "I don't know whether your unit will protect you against anything like that! Wait'll I call Doc—"

"Not a chance," he said. "This baby is mine."

"Listen! You can be first on the mountain, if that's what you want! But don't tackle that thing alone!"

A laugh was the only reply.

"All three units might hold it off," I said. "Wait for us."

There was no answer, and we began to climb.

I left Henry far below me. The creature was a moving

light in the sky. I made two hundred feet in a hurry, and when I looked up again, I saw that the creature had grown two more heads. Lightning bolts flashed from its nostrils, and its tail whipped around the mountain. I made another hundred feet, and I could see Mallardi clearly by then, climbing steadily, outlined against the brilliance. I swung my pick, gasping, and I fought the mountain, following the trail he had cut. I began to gain on him, because he was still pounding out his way and I didn't have that problem. Then I heard him talking:

"Not yet, big fella, not yet," he was saying, from behind a wall of static. "Here's a ledge. . . ."

I looked up, and he vanished.

Then that fiery tail came lashing down toward where I had last seen him, and I heard him curse and I felt the vibrations of his pneumatic gun. The tail snapped back again, and I heard another "Damn!"

I made haste, stretching and racking myself and grabbing at the holds he had cut, and then I heard him burst into song. Something from *Aida*, I think.

"Damn it! Wait up!" I said. "I'm only a few hundred feet behind."

He kept on singing.

I was beginning to get dizzy, but I couldn't let myself slow down. My right arm felt like a piece of wood, my left like a piece of ice. My feet were hooves, and my eyes burned in my head.

Then it happened.

Like a bomb, the snake and the swinging ended in a flash of brilliance that caused me to sway and almost lose my grip. I clung to the vibrating mountainside and squeezed my eyes against the light.

"Mallardi?" I said.

No answer. Nothing.

I looked down. Henry was still clinging. I continued to climb.

I reached the ledge Mallardi had mentioned, found him there.

His respirator was still working. His protective suit was blackened and scorched on the right side. Half of his pick had been melted away. I raised his shoulders.

I turned up the volume on the communicator and heard him breathing. His eyes opened, closed, opened.

"Okay. . . ." he said.

" 'Okay,' hell! Where do you hurt?"

"No place. . . . I feel jus' fine. . . . Listen! I think it's used up its juice for awhile. . . . Go plant the flag. Prop me up here first, though. I wanna watch. . . ."

I got him into a better position, squirted the water bulb, listened to him swallow. Then I waited for Henry to catch up. It took about six minutes.

"I'll stay here," said Henry, stooping beside him. "You go do it."

I started up the final slope.

VII

I swung and I cut and I blasted and I crawled. Some of the ice had been melted, the rocks scorched.

Nothing came to oppose me. The static had gone with the dragon. There was silence, and darkness between stars.

I climbed slowly, still tired from that last sprint, but determined not to stop.

All but sixty feet of the entire world lay beneath me, and heaven hung above me, and a rocket winked overhead. Perhaps it was the pressmen, with zoom cameras.

Fifty feet. . . .

No bird, no archer, no angel, no girl.

Forty feet. . . .

I started to shake. It was nervous tension. I steadied myself, went on.

Thirty feet . . . and the mountain seemed to be swaying now.

Twenty-five . . . and I grew dizzy, halted, took a drink. Then click, click, my pick again.

Twenty. . . .

Fifteen. . . .

Ten. . . .

I braced myself against the mountain's final assault, whatever it might be.

Five. . . .

Nothing happened as I arrived.

I stood up. I could go no higher.

I looked at the sky, I looked back down. I waved at the blazing rocket exhaust.

I extruded the pole and attached the flag.

I planted it, there where no breezes would ever stir it. I cut in my communicator, said, "I'm here."

No other words.

It was time to go back down and give Henry his chance, but I looked down the western slope before I turned to go.

The lady was winking again. Perhaps eight hundred feet below, the red light shone. Could that have been what I had seen from the town during the storm, on that night, so long ago?

I didn't know and I had to.

I spoke into the communicator.

"How's Mallardi doing?"

"I just stood up," he answered. "Give me another half hour, and I'm coming up myself."

"Henry," I said. "Should he?"

"Gotta take his word how he feels," said Lanning.

"Well," I said, "then take it easy. I'll be gone when you get here. I'm going a little way down the western side. Something I want to see."

"What?"

"I dunno. That's why I want to see."

"Take care."

"Check."

The western slope was an easy descent. As I went down it, I realized that the light was coming from an opening in the side of the mountain.

Half an hour later, I stood before it.

I stepped within and was dazzled.

I walked toward it and stopped. It pulsed and quivered and sang.

A vibrating wall of flame leapt from the floor of the cave, towered to the roof of the cave.

It blocked my way, when I wanted to go beyond it.

She was there, and I wanted to reach her.

I took a step forward, so that I was only inches away from it. My communicator was full of static and my arms of cold needles.

It did not bend toward me, as to attack. It cast no heat.

I stared through the veil of fires to where she reclined, her eyes closed, her breast unmoving.

I stared at the bank of machinery beside the far wall.

"I'm here," I said, and I raised my pick.

When its point touched the wall of flame someone took the lid off hell, and I staggered back, blinded. When my vision cleared, the angel stood before me.

"You may not pass here," he said.

"She is the reason you want me to go back?" I asked.

"Yes. Go back."

"Has she no say in the matter?"

"She sleeps. Go back."

"So I notice. Why?"

"She must. Go back."

"Why did she herself appear to me and lead me strangely?"

"I used up the fear-forms I knew. They did not work. I led you strangely because her sleeping mind touches upon my workings. It did so especially when I borrowed her form, so that it interfered with the directive. Go back."

"What is the directive?"

"She is to be guarded against all things coming up the mountain. Go back."

"Why? Why is she guarded?"

"She sleeps. Go back."

The conversation having become somewhat circular at that point, I reached into my pack and drew out the projector. I swung it forward and the angel melted. The flames bent away from my outstretched hand. I sought to open a doorway in the circle of fire.

It worked, sort of.

I pushed the projector forward, and the flames bent and bent and bent and finally broke. When they broke, I leaped forward. I made it through, but my protective suit was as scorched as Mallardi's.

I moved to the coffinlike locker within which she slept.

I rested my hands on its edge and looked down.

She was as fragile as ice.

In fact, she was ice. . . .

The machine came alive with lights then, and I felt her somber bedstead vibrate.

Then I saw the man.

He was half sprawled across a metal chair beside the machine.

He, too, was ice. Only his features were gray, were twisted. He wore black and he was dead and a statue, while she was sleeping and a statue.

She wore blue, and white. . . .

There was an empty casket in the far corner. . . .

But something was happening around me. There came a brightening of the air. Yes, it was air. It hissed upward from frosty jets in the floor, formed into great clouds. Then a feeling of heat occurred and the clouds began to fade and the brightening continued.

I returned to the casket and studied her features.

I wondered what her voice would sound like when/if she spoke. I wondered what lay within her mind. I wondered how her thinking worked, and what she liked and didn't like. I wondered what her eyes had looked upon, and when.

I wondered all these things, because I could see that whatever forces I had set into operation when I entered the circle of fire were causing her, slowly, to cease being a statue.

She was being awakened.

I waited. Over an hour went by, and still I waited, watching her. She began to breathe. Her eyes opened at last, and for a long time she did not see.

Then her bluefire fell upon me.

"Whitey," she said.

"Yes."

"Where am I . . . ?"

"In the damnedest place I could possibly have found anyone."

She frowned. "I remember," she said and tried to sit up. It didn't work. She fell back.

"What is your name?"

"Linda," she said. Then, "I dreamed of you, Whitey. Strange dreams. . . . How could that be?"

"It's tricky," I said.

"I knew you were coming," she said. "I saw you fighting monsters on a mountain as high as the sky."

"Yes, we're there now."

"H-have you the cure?"

"Cure? What cure?"

"Dawson's Plague," she said.

I felt sick. I felt sick because I realized that she did not sleep as a prisoner, but to postpone her death. She was sick.

"Did you come to live on this world in a ship that moved faster than light?" I asked.

"No," she said. "It took centuries to get here. We slept the cold sleep during the journey. This is one of the bunkers." She gestured toward the casket with her eyes. I noticed her cheeks had become bright red.

"They all began dying—of the plague," she said. "There was no cure. My husband—Carl—is a doctor. When he saw that I had it, he said he would keep me in extreme hypothermia until a cure was found. Otherwise, you only live for two days, you know."

Then she stared up at me, and I realized that her last two words had been a question.

I moved into a position to block her view of the dead man, who I feared must be her Carl. I tried to follow her husband's thinking. He'd had to hurry, as he was obviously further along than she had been. He knew the colony would be wiped out. He must have loved her and been awfully clever, both—awfully resourceful. Mostly, though, he must have loved her. Knowing that the colony would die, he knew it would be centuries before another ship arrived. He had nothing that could power a cold bunker for that long. But up here, on the top of this mountain, almost as cold as outer space itself, power wouldn't be necessary. Somehow, he had got Linda and the stuff up here. His machine cast a force field around the cave. Working in heat and atmoshpere, he had sent her deep into the cold sleep and then prepared his own bunker. When he dropped the wall of forces, no power would be necessary to guarantee the long, icy wait. They could sleep for centuries within the bosom of the Gray Sister, protected by a colony of defense-computer. This last had apparently been programmed quickly, for he was dying. He saw that it was too late to join her. He hurried to set the thing for basic defense, killed the force field, and then

went his way into that Dark and secret Place. Thus it
hurled its birds and its angels and its snakes, it raised its
walls of fire against me. He died, and it guarded her in
her near-death—against everything, including those who
would help. My coming to the mountain had activated it.
My passing of the defenses had caused her to be sum-
moned back to life.

"Go back!" I heard the machine say through its projected angel, for Henry had entered the cave.

"My God!" I heard him say. "Who's that?"

"Get Doc!" I said. "Hurry! I'll explain later. It's a
matter of life! Climb back to where your communicator
will work, and tell him it's Dawson's Plague—a bad local
bug! Hurry!"

"I'm on my way," he said and was.

"There *is* a doctor?" she asked.

"Yes. Only about two hours away. Don't worry. . . .
I still don't see how anyone could have gotten you up here
to the top of this mountain, let alone a load of machines."

"We're on the big mountain—the forty-miler?"

"Yes."

"How did *you* get up?" she asked.

"I climbed it."

"You really climbed Purgatorio? On the outside?"

"Purgatorio? That's what you call it? Yes, I climbed it,
that way."

"We didn't think it could be done."

"How else might one arrive at its top?"

"It's hollow inside," she said. "There are great caves
and massive passages. It's easy to fly up the inside in a
pressurized jet car. In fact, it was an amusement ride.
Two and a half dollars per person. An hour and a half
each way. A dollar to rent a pressurized suit and take an
hour's walk around the top. Nice way to spend an afternoon. Beautiful view . . . ?" She gasped deeply.

"I don't feel so good," she said. "Have you any water?"

"Yes," I said, and I gave her all I had.

As she sipped it, I prayed that Doc had the necessary
serum or else would be able to send her back to ice and
sleep until it could be gotten. I prayed that he would

make good time, for two hours seemed long when measured against her thirst and the red of her flesh.

"My fever is coming again," she said. "Talk to me,
Whitey, please. . . . Tell me things. Keep me with you till
he comes. I don't want my mind to turn back upon what
has happened. . . ."

"What would you like me to tell you about, Linda?"

"Tell me why you did it. Tell me what it was like, to
climb a mountain like this one. Why?"

I turned my mind back upon what had happened.

"There is a certain madness involved," I said, "a certain envy of great and powerful natural forces, that some
men have. Each mountain is a deity, you know. Each is
an immortal power. If you make sacrifices upon its slopes,
a mountain may grant you a certain grace, and for a
time you will share this power. Perhaps that is why they
call me. . . ."

Her hand rested in mine. I hoped that through it whatever power I might contain would hold all of her with me
for as long as ever possible.

"I remember the first time that I saw Purgatory, Linda,"
I told her. "I looked at it and I was sick. I wondered,
where did it lead . . . ?"

(Stars.

Oh let there be.

This once to end with.

Please.)

"Stars?"

8.

This Moment
of the Storm

BACK ON EARTH, my old philosophy prof—possibly because he'd misplaced his lecture notes—came into the classroom one day and scrutinized his sixteen victims for the space of half a minute. Satisfied then, that a sufficiently profound tone had been established, he asked:

"What is a man?"

He had known exactly what he was doing. He'd had an hour and a half to kill, and eleven of the sixteen were coeds (nine of them in liberal arts, and the other two stuck with an Area Requirement).

One of the other two, who was in the pre-med program, proceeded to provide a strict biological classification.

The prof (McNitt was his name, I suddenly recall) nodded then, and asked:

"Is that all?"

And there was his hour and a half.

I learned that Man is the Reasoning Animal, Man is the One Who Laughs, Man is greater than beasts but less than angels, Man is the one who watches himself watch himself doing things he knows are absurd (this from a Comparative Lit gal), Man is the culture-transmitting animal, Man is the spirit which aspires, affirms, loves, the one who uses tools, buries his dead, devises religions, and the one who tries to define himself. (That last from Paul

Schwartz, my roommate—which I thought pretty good, on the spur of the moment. Wonder whatever became of Paul?)

Anyhow, to most of these I say "perhaps" or "partly, but—" or just plain "crap!" I still think mine was the best, because I had a chance to try it out, on Tierra del Cygnus, Land of the Swan . . .

I'd said, "Man is the sum total of everything he has done, wishes to do or not to do, and wishes he had done, or hadn't."

Stop and think about it for a minute. It's purposely as general as the others, but it's got room in it for the biology and the laughing and the aspiring, as well as the culture-transmitting, the love, and the room full of mirrors, and the defining. I even left the door open for religion, you'll note. But it's limiting, too. Ever met an oyster to whom the final phrases apply?

Tierra del Cygnus, Land of the Swan—delightful name.

Delightful place too, for quite awhile . . .

It was there that I saw Man's definitions, one by one, wiped from off the big blackboard, until only mine was left.

. . . My radio had been playing more static than usual. That's all.

For several hours there was no other indication of what was to come.

My hundred-thirty eyes had watched Betty all morning, on that clear, cool spring day with the sun pouring down its honey and lightning upon the amber fields, flowing through the streets, invading western store-fronts, drying curbstones, and washing the olive and umber buds that spread the skin of the trees there by the roadway; and the light that wrung the blue from the flag before Town Hall made orange mirrors out of windows, chased purple and violet patches across the shoulders of Saint Stephen's Range, some thirty miles distant, and came down upon the forest at its feet like some supernatural madman with a million buckets of paint—each of a different shade of green, yellow, orange, blue and red—to daub with miles-wide brushes at its heaving sea of growth.

Mornings the sky is cobalt, midday is turquoise, and sunset is emeralds and rubies, hard and flashing. It was halfway between cobalt and seamist at 1100 hours, when I watched Betty with my hundred-thirty eyes and saw nothing to indicate what was about to be. There was only that persistent piece of static, accompanying the piano and strings within my portable.

It's funny how the mind personifies, engenders. Ships are always women: You say, "She's a good old tub," or, "She's a fast, tough number, this one," slapping a bulwark and feeling the aura of femininity that clings to the vessel's curves; or, conversely, "He's a bastard to start, that little Sam!" as you kick the auxiliary engine in an inland transport-vehicle; and hurricanes are always women, and moons, and seas. Cities, though, are different. Generally, they're neuter. Nobody calls New York or San Francisco "he" or "she". Usually, cities are just "it".

Sometimes, however, they do come to take on the attributes of sex. Usually, this is in the case of small cities near to the Mediterranean, back on Earth. Perhaps this is because of the sex-ridden nouns of the languages which prevail in that vicinity, in which case it tells us more about the inhabitants than it does about the habitations. But I feel that it goes deeper than that.

Betty was Beta Station for less than ten years. After two decades she was Betty officially, by act of Town Council. Why? Well, I felt at the time (ninety-some years ago), and still feel, that it was because she was what she was—a place of rest and repair, of surface-cooked meals and of new voices, new faces, of landscapes, weather, and natural light again, after that long haul through the big night, with its casting away of so much. She is not home, she is seldom destination, but she is like unto both. When you come upon light and warmth and music after darkness and cold silence, it is Woman. The oldtime Mediterranean sailor must have felt it when he first spied port at the end of a voyage. *I* felt it when I first saw Beta Station —Betty—and the second time I saw her, also.

I am her Hell Cop.

. . . When six or seven of my hundred-thirty eyes flickered, then saw again, and the music was suddenly washed away by a wave of static, it was then that I began to feel uneasy.

I called Weather Central for a report, and the recorded

girlvoice told me that seasonal rains were expected in the afternoon or early evening. I hung up and switched an eye from ventral to dorsal-vision.

Not a cloud. Not a ripple. Only a formation of green-winged skytoads, heading north, crossed the field of the lens.

I switched it back, and I watched the traffic flow, slowly, and without congestion, along Betty's prim, well-tended streets. Three men were leaving the bank and two more were entering. I recognized the three who were leaving, and in my mind I waved as I passed by. All was still at the post office, and patterns of normal activity lay upon the steel mills, the stockyard, the plast-synth plants, the airport, the spacer pads, and the surfaces of all the shopping complexes; vehicles came and went at the Inland Transport-Vehicle garages crawling from the rainbow forest and the mountains beyond like dark slugs, leaving tread-trails to mark their comings and goings through wilderness; and the fields of the countryside were still yellow and brown, with occasional patches of green and pink; the country houses, mainly simple. A-frame affairs, were chisel blade, spike-tooth, spire and steeple, each with a big lightning rod and dipped in many colors and scooped up in the cups of my seeing and dumped out again, as I sent my eyes on their rounds and tended my gallery of one hundred-thirty changing pictures, on the big wall of the Trouble Center, there atop the Watch Tower of Town Hall.

The static came and went until I had to shut off the radio. Fragments of music are worse than no music at all.

My eyes, coasting weightless along magnetic lines, began to blink.

I knew then that we were in for something.

I sent an eye scurrying off toward Saint Stephen's at full speed, which meant a wait of about twenty minutes until it topped the range. Another, I sent straight up, skywards, which meant perhaps ten minutes for a long shot of the same scene. Then I put the auto-scan in full charge of operations and went downstairs for a cup of coffee.

I entered the Mayor's outer office, winked at Lottie, the receptionist, and glanced at the inner door.

"Mayor in?" I asked.

I got an occasional smile from Lottie, a slightly heavy, but well-rounded girl of indeterminate age and intermittent acne, but this wasn't one of the occasions.

"Yes," she said, returning to the papers on her desk.

"Alone?"

She nodded, and her earrings danced. Dark eyes and dark complexion, she could have been kind of sharp, if only she'd fix her hair and use more makeup. Well . . .

I crossed to the door and knocked.

"Who?" asked the Mayor.

"Me," I said, opening it, "Godfrey Justin Holmes— 'God' for short. I want someone to drink coffee with, and you're elected."

She turned in her swivel chair, away from the window she had been studying, and her blonde-hair-white-hair-fused, short and parted in the middle, gave a little stir as she turned—like a sunshot snowdrift struck by sudden winds.

She smiled and said, "I'm busy."

'Eyes green, chin small, cute little ears—I love them all'—from an anonymous Valentine I'd sent her two months previous, and true.

". . . But not too busy to have coffee with God," she stated. "Have a throne, and I'll make us some instant."

I did, and she did.

While she was doing it, I leaned back, lit a cigarette I'd borrowed from her canister, and remarked, "Looks like rain."

"Uh-huh," she said.

"Not just making conversation" I told her "There's a bad storm brewing somewhere—over Saint Stephen's, I think. I'll know real soon."

"Yes, grandfather," she said, bringing me my coffee. "You old-timers with all your aches and pains are often better than Weather Central, it's an established fact. I won't argue."

She smiled, frowned, then smiled again.

I set my cup on the edge of her desk.

"Just wait and see," I said. "If it makes it over the mountains, it'll be a nasty high-voltage job. It's already jazzing up reception."

Big-bowed white blouse, and black skirt around a well-kept figure. She'd be forty in the fall, but she'd never completely tamed her facial reflexes—which was most engaging, so far as I was concerned. Spontaneity of expression so often vanishes so soon. I could see the sort of child she'd been by looking at her, listening to her now. The thought of being forty was bothering her again, too, I could tell. She always kids me about age when age is bothering her.

See, I'm around thirty-five, actually, which makes me her junior by a bit, but she'd heard her grandfather speak of me when she was a kid, before I came back again this last time. I'd filled out the balance of his two-year term, back when Betty-Beta's first mayor, Wyeth, had died after two months in office. I was born five hundred ninety-seven years ago, on Earth, but I spent about five hundred sixty-two of those years sleeping, during my long jaunts between the stars. I've made a few more trips than a few others; consequently, I am an anachronism. I am really, of course, only as old as I look—but still, people always seem to feel that I've cheated somehow, especially women in their middle years. Sometimes it is most disconcerting . . .

"Eleanor," said I, "your term will be up in November. Are you still thinking of running again?"

She took off her narrow, elegantly-trimmed glasses and brushed her eyelids with thumb and forefinger. Then she took a sip of coffee.

"I haven't made up my mind."

"I ask not for press-release purposes," I said, "but for my own."

"Really, I haven't decided," she told me. "I don't know . . ."

"Okay, just checking. Let me know if you do."

I drank some coffee.

After a time, she said, "Dinner Saturday? As usual?"

"Yes, good."

"I'll tell you then."

"Fine—capital."

As she looked down into her coffee, I saw a little girl staring into a pool, waiting for it to clear, to see her reflection or to see the bottom of the pool, or perhaps both.

She smiled at whatever it was she finally saw.

"A bad storm?" she asked me.

"Yep. Feel it in my bones."

"Tell it to go away?"

"Tried. Don't think it will, though."

"Better batten some hatches, then."

"It wouldn't hurt and it might help."

"The weather satellite will be overhead in another half hour. You'll have something sooner?"

"Think so. Probably any minute."

I finished my coffee, washed out the cup.

"Let me know right away what it is."

"Check. Thanks for the coffee."

Lottie was still working and did not look up as I passed.

Upstairs again, my highest eye was now high enough. I stood it on its tail and collected a view of the distance: Fleecy mobs of clouds boiled and frothed on the other side of Saint Stephen's. The mountain range seemed a breakwall, a dam, a ricky shoreline. Beyond it, the waters were troubled.

My other eye was almost in position. I waited the space of half a cigarette, then it delivered me a sight:

Gray, and wet and impenetrable, a curtain across the countryside, that's what I saw.

. . . And advancing.

I called Eleanor.

"It's gonna rain, chillun," I said.

"Worth some sandbags?"

"Possibly."

"Better be ready then. Okay. Thanks."

I returned to my watching.

Tierra del Cygnus, Land of the Swan—delightful name. It refers to both the planet and its sole continent.

How to describe the world, like quick? Well, roughly Earth-size; actually, a bit smaller, and more watery. —As for the main land-mass, first hold a mirror up to South America, to get the big bump from the right side over to the left, then rotate it ninety degrees in a counter-clock-wise direction and push it up into the northern hemisphere. Got that? Good. Now grab it by the tail and pull. Stretch it another six or seven hundred miles, slimming down

the middle as you do, and let the last five or six hundred
fall across the equator. There you have Cygnus, its big
gulf partly in the tropics, partly not. Just for the sake of
thoroughness, while you're about it, break Australia into
eight pieces and drop them about at random down in the
southern hemisphere, calling them after the first eight
letters in the Greek alphabet. Put a big scoop of vanilla
at each pole, and don't forget to tilt the globe about eighteen degrees before you leave. Thanks.

I recalled my wandering eyes, and I kept a few of the
others turned toward Saint Stephen's until the cloudbanks
breasted the range about an hour later. By then, though,
the weather satellite had passed over and picked the thing
up also. It reported quite an extensive cloud cover on the
other side. The storm had sprung up quickly, as they
often do here on Cygnus. Often, too, they disperse just as
quickly, after an hour or so of heaven's artillery. But then
there are the bad ones—sometimes lingering and lingering, and bearing more thunderbolts in their quivers than
any Earth storm.

Betty's position, too, is occasionally precarious, though
its advantages, in general, offset its liabilities. We are
located on the gulf about twenty miles inland, and are
approximately three miles removed (in the main) from a
major river, the Noble; part of Betty does extend down
to its banks, but this is a smaller part. We are almost a
strip city, falling mainly into an area some seven miles
in length and two miles wide, stretching inland, east from
the river, and running roughly parallel to the distant sea-
coast. Around eighty percent of the 100,000 population is
concentrated about the business district, five miles in from
the river.

We are not the lowest land about, but we are far from
being the highest. We are certainly the most level in the
area. This latter feature, as well as our nearness to the
equator, was a deciding factor in the establishment of Beta
Station. Some other things were our proximity both to
the ocean and to a large river. There are nine other cities
on the continent, all of them younger and smaller, and
three of them located upriver from us. We are the potential capital of a potential country.

We're a good, smooth, easy landing site for drop-boats

from orbiting interstellar vehicles, and we have major
assets for future growth and coordination when it comes
to expanding across the continent. Our original *raison
d'etre*, though, was Stopover, repair-point, supply depot,
and refreshment stand, physical and psychological, on the
way out to other, more settled worlds, further along the
line. Cyg was discovered later than many others—it just
happened that way—and the others got off to earlier starts.
Hence, the others generally attract more colonists. We are
still quite primitive. Self-sufficiency, in order to work on
our population:land scale, demanded a society on the
order of that of the mid-nineteenth century in the American southwest—at least for purposes of getting started.
Even now, Cyg is still partly on a natural economy system, although Earth Central technically determines the
coin of the realm.

Why Stopover, if you sleep most of the time between
the stars?

Think about it awhile, and I'll tell you later if you're
right.

The thunderheads rose in the east, sending billows and
streamers this way and that, until it seemed from the
formations that Saint Stephen's was a balcony full of monsters, leaning and craning their necks over the rail in the
direction of the stage, us. Cloud piled upon slate-colored
cloud, and then the wall slowly began to topple.

I heard the first rumbles of thunder almost half an hour
after lunch, so I knew it wasn't my stomach.

Despite all my eyes, I moved to a window to watch. It
was like a big, gray, aerial glacier plowing the sky.

There was a wind now, for I saw the trees suddenly
quiver and bow down. This would be our first storm of
the season. The turquoise fell back before it, and finally
it smothered the sun itself. Then there were drops upon
the windowpane, then rivulets.

Flint-like, the highest peaks of Saint Stephen's scraped
its belly and were showered with sparks. After a moment
it bumped into something with a terrible crash, and the
rivulets on the quartz panes turned into rivers.

I went back to my gallery, to smile at dozens of views
of people scurrying for shelter. A smart few had umbrellas

and raincoats. The rest ran like blazes. People never pay
attention to weather reports; this, I believe, is a constant
factor in man's psychological makeup, stemming probably
from an ancient tribal distrust of the shaman. You want
them to be wrong. If they're right, then they're somehow
superior, and this is even more uncomfortable than getting
wet.

I remembered then that I had forgotten my raincoat,
umbrella and rubbers. But it *had* been a beautiful morning, and W.C. *could* have been wrong . . .

Well, I had another cigarette and leaned back in my big
chair. No storm in the world could knock my eyes out of
the sky.

I switched on the filters and sat and watched the rain
pour past.

Five hours later it was still raining, and rumbling and
dark.

I'd had hopes that it would let up by quitting time, but
when Chuck Fuller came around the picture still hadn't
changed any. Chuck was my relief that night, the evening
Hell Cop.

He seated himself beside my desk.

"You're early," I said. "They don't start paying you for
another hour."

"Too wet to do anything but sit. Rather sit here than
at home."

"Leaky roof?"

He shook his head.

"Mother-in-law. Visiting again."

I nodded.

"One of the disadvantages of a small world."

He clasped his hands behind his neck and leaned back
in the chair, staring off in the direction of the window. I
could feel one of his outbursts coming.

"You know how old I am?" he asked, after awhile.

"No," I said, which was a lie. He was twenty-nine.

"Twenty-seven," he told me, "and going to be twenty-
eight soon. Know where I've been?"

"No."

"No place, that's where! I was born and raised on this
crummy world! And I married and I settled down here—

and I've never been off it! Never could afford it when I
was younger. Now I've got a family . . ."

He leaned forward again, rested his elbows on his knees,
like a kid. Chuck would look like a kid when he was fifty.
—Blond hair, close-cropped, pug nose, kind of scrawny,
takes a suntan quickly, and well. Maybe he'd act like a kid
at fifty, too. I'll never know.

I didn't say anything because I didn't have anything to
say.

He was quiet for a long while again.

Then he said, *"You've* been around."

After a minute, he went on:

"You were born on Earth. Earth! And you visited lots
of other worlds too, before I was even born. Earth is only
a name to me. And pictures. And all the others—they're
the same! Pictures. Names . . ."

I waited, then after I grew tired of waiting I said,
" 'Miniver Cheevy, child of scorn . . .' "

"What does that mean?"

"It's the beginning to an ancient poem. It's an ancient
poem now, but it wasn't really ancient when I was a boy.
Just old. *I* had friends, relatives, even in-laws, once myself. They are not just bones now. They are dust. Real
dust, not metaphorical dust. The past fifteen years seem
fifteen years to me, the same as to you, but they're not.
They are already many chapters back in the history books.
Whenever you travel between the stars you automatically
bury the past. The world you leave will be filled with
strangers if you ever return—or caricatures of your friends,
your relatives, even yourself. It's no great trick to be a
grandfather at sixty, a great-grandfather at seventy-five or
eighty—but go away for three hundred years, and then
come back and meet your great-great-great-great-great-
great-great-great-great-great-great-great-great-grandson, who happens to be fifty-five years old, and puzzled, when you look
him up. It shows you just how alone you really are. You
are not simply a man without a country or without a
world. You are a man without a time. You and the centuries do not belong to each other. You are like the
rubbish that drifts between the stars."

"It would be worth it," he said.

I laughed. I'd had to listen to his gripes every month or

two for over a year and a half. It had never bothered me
so much before, so I guess it was a cumulative effect that
day—the rain, and Saturday night next, and my recent
library visits, *and* his complaining, that had set me off.

His last comment had been too much. "It would be
worth it." What could I say to that?

I laughed.

He turned bright red.

"You're laughing at me!"

He stood up and glared down.

"No I'm not," I said, "I'm laughing at me. I shouldn't
have been bothered by what you said, but I was. That tells
me something funny about me."

"What?"

"I'm getting sentimental in my old age, and that's
funny."

"Oh." He turned his back on me and walked over to
the window and stared out. Then he jammed his hands
into his pockets and turned around and looked at me.

"Aren't you happy?" he asked. "Really, I mean? You've
got money, and no strings on you. You could pick up and
leave on the next I-V that passes, if you wanted to."

"Sure I'm happy," I told him. "My coffee was cold.
Forget it."

"Oh," again. He turned back to the window in time to
catch a bright flash full in the face, and to have to com-
pete with thunder to get his next words out. "I'm sorry,"
I heard him say, as in the distance. "It just seems to me
that you should be one of the happiest guys around . . ."

"I am. It's the weather today. It's got everybody down
in the mouth, yourself included."

"Yeah, you're right," he said. "Look at it rain, will you?
Haven't seen any rain in months . . ."

"They've been saving it all up for today."

He chuckled.

"I'm going down for a cup of coffee and a sandwich
before I sign on. Can I bring you anything?"

"No, thanks."

"Okay. See you in a little while."

He walked out whistling. He never stays depressed. Like
a kid's moods, his moods, up and down, up and down . . .
And he's a Hell Cop. Probably the worst possible job for

him, having to keep his attention in one place for so long. They say the job title comes from the name of an antique flying vehicle—a hellcopter, I think. We send our eyes on their appointed rounds, and they can hover or soar or back up, just like those old machines could. We patrol the city and the adjacent countryside. Law enforcement isn't much of a problem on Cyg. We never peek in windows or send an eye into a building without an invitation. Our testimony is admissible in court—or, if we're fast enough to press a couple buttons, the tape that we make does an even better job—and we can dispatch live or robot cops in a hurry, depending on which will do a better job.

There isn't much crime on Cyg, though, despite the fact that everybody carries a sidearm of some kind, even little kids. Everybody knows pretty much what their neighbors are up to, and there aren't too many places for a fugitive to run. We're mainly aerial traffic cops, with an eye out for local wildlife (which is the reason for all the sidearms).

S.P.C.U. is what we call the latter function—Society for the Prevention of Cruelty to Us—which is the reason each of my hundred-thirty eyes has six forty-five caliber eye-lashes.

There are things like the cute little panda-puppy—oh, about three feet high at the shoulder when it sits down on its rear like a teddy bear, and with big, square, silky ears, a curly pinto coat, large, limpid, brown eyes, pink tongue, button nose, powder puff tail, sharp little white teeth more poisonous than a Quemeda Island viper's, and possessed of a way with mammal entrails like unto the way of an imaginative cat with a rope of catnip.

Then there's a *snapper*, which *looks* as mean as it sounds: a feathered reptile, with three horns on its armored head—one beneath each eye, like a tusk, and one curving skyward from the top of its nose—legs about eighteen inches long, and a four-foot tail which it raises straight into the air whenever it jogs along at greyhound speed, and which it swings like a sandbag—and a mouth full of long, sharp teeth.

Also, there are amphibious things which come from the ocean by way of the river on occasion. I'd rather not speak of them. They're kind of ugly and vicious.

Anyway, those are some of the reasons why there are

Hell Cops—not just on Cyg, but on many, many frontier worlds. I've been employed in that capacity on several of them, and I've found that an experienced H.C. can always find a job Out Here. It's like being a professional clerk back home.

Chuck took longer than I thought he would, came back after I was technically off duty, looked happy though, so I didn't say anything. There was some pale lipstick on his collar and a grin on his face, so I bade him good morrow, picked up my cane, and departed in the direction of the big washing machine.

It was coming down too hard for me to go the two blocks to my car on foot.

I called a cab and waited another fifteen minutes. Eleanor had decided to keep Mayor's Hours, and she'd departed shortly after lunch; and almost the entire staff had been released an hour early because of the weather. Consequently, Town Hall was full of dark offices and echoes. I waited in the hallway behind the main door, listening to the purr of the rain as it fell, and hearing its gurgle as it found its way into the gutters. It beat the street and shook the windowpanes and made the windows cold to touch.

I'd planned on spending the evening at the library, but I changed my plans as I watched the weather happen. —Tomorrow, or the next day, I decided. It was an evening for a good meal, a hot bath, my own books and brandy, and early to bed. It was good sleeping weather, if nothing else. A cab pulled up in front of the Hall and blew its horn.

I ran.

The next day the rain let up for perhaps an hour in the morning. Then a slow drizzle began; and it did not stop again.

It went on to become a steady downpour by afternoon.

The following day was Friday, which I always have off, and I was glad that it was.

Put dittoes under Thursday's weather report. That's Friday.

But I decided to do something anyway.

I lived down in that section of town near the river. The

Noble was swollen, and the rains kept adding to it. Sewers had begun to clog and back up; water ran in the streets. The rain kept coming down and widening the puddles and lakelets, and it was accompanied by drum solos in the sky and the falling of bright forks and sawblades. Dead sky-toads were washed along the gutters, like burnt-out fire-works. Ball lightning drifted across Town Square; Saint Elmo's Fire clung to the flag pole, the Watch Tower, and the big statue of Wyeth trying to look heroic.

I headed uptown to the library, pushing my car slowly through the countless beaded curtains. The big furniture movers in the sky were obviously non-union, because they weren't taking any coffee breaks. Finally, I found a parking place and I umbrellaed my way to the library and entered.

I have become something of a bibliophile in recent years. It is not so much that I hunger and thirst after knowledge, but that I am news-starved.

It all goes back to my position in the big mixmaster. Admitted, there are *some* things faster than light, like the phase velocities of radio waves in ion plasma, or the tips of the ion-modulated light-beams of Duckbill, the comm-setup back in Sol System, whenever the hinges of the beak snap shut on Earth—but these are highly restricted in-stances, with no application whatsoever to the passage of shiploads of people and objects between the stars. You can't exceed lightspeed when it comes to the movement of matter. You can edge up pretty close, but that's about it.

Life can be suspended though, that's easy—it can be switched off and switched back on again with no trouble at all. This is why *I* have lasted so long. If we can't speed up the ships, we *can* slow down the people—slow them until they stop—and *let* the vessel, moving at near-light-speed, take half a century, or more if it needs it, to convey its passengers to where they are going. This is why I am very alone. Each little death means resurrection into both another land and another time. I have had several, and *this* is why I have become a bibliophile: news travels slowly, as slowly as the ships and the people. Buy a news-paper before you hop aboard ship and it will still be a newspaper when you reach your destination—but back where you bought it, it would be considered an historical document. Send a letter back to Earth and your correspondent's grandson may be able to get an answer back to your great-grandson, if the message makes real good connections and both kids live long enough.

All the little libraries Out Here are full of rare books—first editions of best sellers which people pick up before they leave Someplace Else, and which they often donate after they've finished. We assume that these books have entered the public domain by the time they reach here, and we reproduce them and circulate our own editions. No author has ever sued, and no reproducer has ever been around to *be* sued by representatives, designates, or assigns.

We are completely autonomous and are always behind the times, because there is a transit-lag which cannot be overcome. Earth Central, therefore, exercises about as much control over us as a boy jiggling a broken string while looking up at his kite.

Perhaps Yeats had something like this in mind when he wrote that fine line, "Things fall apart; the center cannot hold". I doubt it, but I still have to go to the library to read the news.

The day melted around me.

The words flowed across the screen in my booth as I read newspapers and magazines, untouched by human hands, and the waters flowed across Betty's acres, pouring down from the mountains now, washing the floors of the forest, churning our fields to peanut-butter, flooding basements, soaking its way through everything, and tracking our streets with mud.

I hit the library cafeteria for lunch, where I learned from a girl in a green apron and yellow skirts (which swished pleasantly) that the sandbag crews were now hard at work and that there was no eastbound traffic past Town Square.

After lunch I put on my slicker and boots and walked up that way.

Sure enough, the sandbag wall was already waist high across Main Street; but then, the water *was* swirling around at ankle level, and more of it falling every minute.

I looked up at old Wyeth's statue. His halo had gone

away now, which was sort of to be expected. It had made an honest mistake and realized it after a short time.

He was holding a pair of glasses in his left hand and sort of glancing down at me, as though a bit apprehensive, wondering perhaps, there inside all that bronze, if I would tell on him now and ruin his hard, wet, greenish splendor. Tell . . . ? I guess I was the only one left around who really remembered the man. He had wanted to be the father of this great new country, literally, and he'd tried awfully hard. Three months in office and I'd had to fill out the rest of the two-year term. The death certificate gave the cause as "heart stoppage," but it didn't mention the piece of lead which had helped slow things down a bit. Everybody involved is gone now: the irate husband, the frightened wife, the coroner. All but me. And I won't tell anybody if Wyeth's statue won't, because he's a hero now, and we need heroes' statues Out Here even more than we do heroes. He *did* engineer a nice piece of relief work during the Butler Township floods, and he may as well be remembered for that.

I winked at my old boss, and the rain dripped from his nose and fell into the puddle at my feet.

I walked back to the library through loud sounds and bright flashes, hearing the splashing and the curses of the work crew as the men began to block off another street. Black, overhead, an eye drifted past. I waved, and the filter snapped up and back down again. I think H.C. John Keams was tending shop that afternoon, but I'm not sure.

Suddenly the heavens opened up and it was like standing under a waterfall.

I reached for a wall and there wasn't one, slipped then, and managed to catch myself with my cane before I flopped. I found a doorway and huddled.

Ten minutes of lightning and thunder followed. Then, after the blindness and the deafness passed away and the rains had eased a bit, I saw that the street (Second Avenue) had become a river. Bearing all sorts of garbage, papers, hats, sticks, mud, it sloshed past my niche, gurgling nastily. It looked to be over my boot tops, so I waited for it to subside.

It didn't.

It got right up in there with me and started to play footsie.

So, then seemed as good a time as any. Things certainly weren't getting any better.

I tried to run, but with filled boots the best you can manage is a fast wade, and my boots were filled after three steps.

That shot the afternoon. How can you concentrate on anything with wet feet? I made it back to the parking lot, then churned my way homeward, feeling like a riverboat captain who really wanted to be a camel driver.

It seemed more like evening than afternoon when I pulled up into my damp but unflooded garage. It seemed more like night than evening in the alley I cut through on the way to my apartment's back entrance. I hadn't seen the sun for several days, and it's funny how much you can miss it when it takes a vacation. The sky was a sable dome, and the high brick walls of the alley were cleaner than I'd ever seen them, despite the shadows.

I stayed close to the lefthand wall, in order to miss some of the rain. As I had driven along the river I'd noticed that it was already reaching after the high water marks on the sides of the piers. The Noble was a big, spoiled, blood sausage, ready to burst its skin. A lightning flash showed me the whole alley, and I slowed in order to avoid puddles.

I moved ahead, thinking of dry socks and dry martinis, turned a corner to the right, and it struck at me: an org.

Half of its segmented body was reared at a forty-five-degree angle above the pavement, which placed its wide head with the traffic-signal eyes saying "Stop," about three and a half feet off the ground, as it rolled toward me on all its pale little legs, with its mouthful of death aimed at my middle.

I pause now in my narrative for a long digression concerning my childhood, which, if you will but consider the circumstances, I was obviously quite fresh on in an instant:

Born, raised, educated on Earth, I had worked two summers in a stockyard while going to college. I still remember the smells and the noises of the cattle; I used to prod them out of the pens and on their way up the last mile. And I remember the smells and noises of the university: the formaldehyde in the Bio labs, the sounds of

Freshmen slaughtering French verbs, the overpowering aroma of coffee mixed with cigarette smoke in the Student Union, the splash of the newly-pinned frat man as his brothers tossed him into the lagoon down in front of the Art Museum, the sounds of ignored chapel bells and class bells, the smell of the lawn after the year's first mowing (with big, black Andy perched on his grass-chewing monster, baseball cap down to his eyebrows, cigarette somehow not burning his left cheek), and always, always, the *tick-tick-snick-stamp!* as I moved up or down the strip. I had not wanted to take General Physical Education, but four semesters of it were required. The only out was to take a class in a special sport. I picked fencing because tennis, basketball, boxing, wrestling, handball, judo, all sounded too strenuous, and I couldn't afford a set of golf clubs. Little did I suspect what would follow this choice. It was as strenuous as any of the others, and more than several. But I liked it. So I tried out for the team in my Sophomore year, made it on the épée squad, and picked up three varsity letters, because I stuck with it through my Senior year. Which all goes to show: Cattle who persevere in looking for an easy way out still wind up in the abattoir, but they may enjoy the trip a little more.

When I came out here on the raw frontier where people all carry weapons, I had my cane made. It combines the better features of the épée and the cattle prod. Only, it is the kind of prod which, if you were to prod cattle with, they would never move again.

Over eight hundred volts, max, when the tip touches, if the stud in the handle is depressed properly . . .

My arm shot out and up and my fingers depressed the stud properly as it moved.

That was it for the org.

A noise came from between the rows of razor blades in its mouth as I scored a touch on its soft underbelly and whipped my arm away to the side—a noise halfway between an exhalation and "peep"—and that was it for the org (short for "organism-with-a-long-name-which-I-can't-remember").

I switched off my cane and walked around it. It was one of those things which sometimes come out of the river. I remember that I looked back at it three times, then I switched the cane on again at max and kept it that way till I was inside my apartment with the door locked behind me and all the lights burning.

Then I permitted myself to tremble, and after awhile I changed my socks and mixed my drink.

May your alleys be safe from orgs.

Saturday.

More rain.

Wetness was all.

The entire east side had been shored with sand bags. In some places they served only to create sandy waterfalls, where otherwise the streams would have flowed more evenly and perhaps a trifle more clearly. In other places they held it back, for awhile.

By then, there were six deaths as a direct result of the rains.

By then, there had been fires caused by the lightning, accidents by the water, sicknesses by the dampness, the cold.

By then, property damages were beginning to mount pretty high.

Everyone was tired and angry and miserable and wet, by then. This included me.

Though Saturday was Saturday, I went to work. I worked in Eleanor's office, with her. We had the big relief map spread on a table, and six mobile eyescreens were lined against one wall. Six eyes hovered above the half-dozen emergency points and kept us abreast of the actions taken upon them. Several new telephones and a big radio set stood on the desk. Five ashtrays looked as if they wanted to be empty, and the coffeepot chuckled cynically at human activity.

The Noble had almost reached its high water mark. We were not an isolated storm center by any means. Upriver, Butler Township was hurting, Swan's Nest was adrip, Laurie was weeping into the river, and the wilderness in between was shaking and streaming.

Even though we were in direct contact we went into the field on three occasions that morning—once, when the north-south bridge over the Lance River collapsed and was washed down toward the Noble as far as the bend by the

Mack steel mill; again, when the Wildwood Cemetery, set up on a storm-gouged hill to the east, was plowed deeply, graves opened, and several coffins set awash; and finally, when three houses full of people toppled, far to the east. Eleanor's small flyer was buffeted by the winds as we fought our way through to these sites for on-the-spot supervision; I navigated almost completely by instruments. Downtown proper was accommodating evacuees left and right by then. I took three showers that morning and changed clothes twice.

Things slowed down a bit in the afternoon, including the rain. The cloud cover didn't break, but a drizzle-point was reached which permitted us to gain a little on the waters. Retaining walls were reinforced, evacuees were fed and dried, some of the rubbish was cleaned up. Four of the six eyes were returned to their patrols, because four of the emergency points were no longer emergency points.

. . . And we wanted all of the eyes for the org patrol.

Inhabitants of the drenched forest were also on the move. Seven *snappers* and a horde of panda-puppies were shot that day, as well as a few crawly things from the troubled waters of the Noble—not to mention assorted branch-snakes, stingbats, borers, and land-eels.

By 1900 hours it seemed that a stalemate had been achieved. Eleanor and I climbed into her flyer and drifted skyward.

We kept rising. Finally, there was a hiss as the cabin began to pressurize itself. The night was all around us. Eleanor's face, in the light from the instrument panel, was a mask of weariness. She raised her hands to her temples as if to remove it, and then when I looked back again it appeared that she had. A faint smile lay across her lips now and her eyes sparkled. A stray strand of hair shadowed her brow.

"Where are you taking me?" she asked.

"Up, high," said I, "above the storm."

"Why?"

"It's been many days," I said, "since we have seen an uncluttered sky."

"True," she agreed, and as she leaned forward to light a cigarette I noticed that the part in her hair had gone all askew. I wanted to reach out and straighten it for her, but I didn't.

We plunged into the sea of clouds.

Dark was the sky, moonless. The stars shone like broken diamonds. The clouds were a floor of lava.

We drifted. We stared up into the heavens. I "anchored" the flyer, like an eye set to hover, and lit a cigarette myself.

"You are older than I am,'" she finally said, "really. You know?"

"No."

"There is a certain wisdom, a certain strength, something like the essence of the time that passes—that seeps into a man as he sleeps between the stars. I know, because I can feel it when I'm around you."

"No," I said.

"Then maybe it's people expecting you to have the strength of centuries that gives you something like it. It was probably there to begin with."

"No."

She chuckled.

"It isn't exactly a positive sort of thing either."

I laughed.

"You asked me if I was going to run for office again this fall. The answer is 'no'. I'm planning on retiring. I want to settle down."

"With anyone special?"

"Yes, very special, Juss," she said, and she smiled at me and I kissed her, but not for too long, because the ash was about to fall off her cigarette and down the back of my neck.

So we put both cigarettes out and drifted above the invisible city, beneath a sky without a moon.

I mentioned earlier that I would tell you about Stopovers. If you are going a distance of a hundred forty-five light years and are taking maybe a hundred-fifty actual years to do it, why stop and stretch your legs?

Well, first of all and mainly, almost nobody sleeps out the whole jaunt. There are lots of little gadgets which require human monitoring at all times. No one is going to sit there for a hundred-fifty years and watch them, all by himself. So everyone takes a turn or two, passengers included. They are all briefed on what to do till the doctor comes, and who to awaken and how to go about it, should troubles crop up. Then everyone takes a turn at guard mount for a month or so, along with a few companions. There are always hundreds of people aboard, and after you've worked down through the role you take it again from the top. All sorts of mechanical agents are backing them up, many of which they are unaware of (to protect *against* them, as well as *with* them—in the improbable instance of several oddballs getting together and deciding to open a window, change course, murder passengers, or things like that), and the people are well-screened and carefully matched up, so as to check and balance each other as well as the machinery. All of this because gadgets and people both bear watching.

After several turns at ship's guard, interspersed with periods of cold sleep, you tend to grow claustrophobic and somewhat depressed. Hence, when there is an available Stopover, it is utilized to restore mental equilibrium and to rearouse flagging animal spirits. This also serves the purpose of enriching the life and economy of the Stopover world, by whatever information and activities you may have in you.

Stopover, therefore, has become a traditional holiday on many worlds, characterized by festivals and celebrations on some of the smaller ones, and aften by parades and world-wide broadcast interviews and press conferences on those with greater populations. I understand that it is now pretty much the same on Earth, too, whenever colonial visitors stop by. In fact, one fairly unsuccessful young starlet, Marilyn Austin, made a long voyage Out, stayed a few months, and returned on the next vessel headed back. After appearing on tri-dee a couple times, sounding off about interstellar culture, and flashing her white, white teeth, she picked up a flush contract, a third husband, and her first big part in tapes. All of which goes to show the value of Stopovers.

I landed us atop Helix, Betty's largest apartment-complex, wherein Eleanor had her double-balconied corner suite, affording views both of the distant Noble and of the lights of Posh Valley, Betty's residential section.

Eleanor prepared steaks, with baked potato, cooked corn, beer—everything I liked. I was happy and sated and such, and I stayed till around midnight, making plans for our future. Then I took a cab back to Town Square, where I was parked.

When I arrived, I thought I'd check with the Trouble Center just to see how things were going. So I entered the Hall, stamped my feet, brushed off excess waters, hung my coat, and proceeded up the empty hallway to the elevator.

The elevator was too quiet. They're supposed to rattle, you know? They shouldn't sigh softly and have doors that open and close without a sound. So I walked around an embarrassing corner on my way to the Trouble Center.

It was a pose Rodin might have enjoyed working with. All I can say is that it's a good thing I stopped by when I did, rather than five or ten minutes later.

Chuck Fuller and Lottie, Eleanor's secretary, were practicing mouth to mouth resuscitation and keeping the victim warm techniques, there on the couch in the little alcove off to the side of the big door to T.C.

Chuck's back was to me, but Lottie spotted me over his shoulder, and her eyes widened and she pushed him away. He turned his head quickly.

"Juss . . ." he said.

I nodded.

"Just passing by," I told him. "Thought I'd stop in to say hello and take a look at the eyes."

"Uh—everything's going real well," he said, stepping back into the hallway. "It's on auto right now, and I'm on my—uh, coffee break. Lottie is on night duty, and she came by to—to see if we had any reports we needed typed. She had a dizzy spell, so we came out here where the couch . . ."

"Yeah, she looks a little—peaked," I said. "There are smelling salts and aspirins in the medicine chest."

I walked on by into the Center, feeling awkward.

Chuck followed me after a couple of minutes. I was watching the screens when he came up beside me. Things appeared to be somewhat in hand, though the rains were still moistening the one hundred thirty views of Betty.

"Uh, Juss," he said, "I didn't know you were coming by . . ."

"Obviously."

"What I'm getting at is—you won't report me, will you?"

"No, I won't report you."

". . . And you wouldn't mention it to Cynthia, would you?"

"Your extracurricular activities," I said, "are your own business. As a friend, I suggest you do them on your own time and in a more propitious location. But it's already beginning to slip my mind. I'm sure I'll forget the whole thing in another minute."

"Thanks, Juss," he said.

I nodded.

"What's Weather Central have to say these days?" I asked, raising the phone.

He shook his head, so I dialed and listened.

"Bad," I said, hanging up. "More wet to come."

"Damn," he announced and lit a cigarette, his hands shaking. "This weather's getting me down."

"Me too," said I. "I'm going to run now, because I want to get home before it starts in bad again. I'll probably be around tomorrow. See you."

"Night."

I elevated back down, fetched my coat, and left. I didn't see Lottie anywhere about, but she probably was, waiting for me to go.

I got to my car and was halfway home before the faucets came on full again. The sky was torn open with lightnings, and a sizzlecloud stalked the city like a long-legged arachnid, forking down bright limbs and leaving tracks of fire where it went. I made it home in another fifteen minutes, and the phenomenon was still in progress as I entered the garage. As I walked up the alley (cane switched on) I could hear the distant sizzle and the rum-ble, and a steady half-light filled the spaces between the buildings, from its *flash-burn-flash-burn* striding.

Inside, I listened to the thunder and the rain, and I watched the apocalypse off in the distance.

Delirium of a city under storm—

The buildings across the way were quite clear in the pulsing light of the thing. The lamps were turned off in my apartment so that I could better appreciate the vision. All of the shadows seemed incredibly black and inky, lying right beside glowing stairways, pediments, windowsills, balconies; and all of that which was illuminated seemed to burn as though with an internal light. Overhead, the living/not living insect-thing of fire stalked, and an eye wearing a blue halo was moving across the tops of nearby buildings. The fires pulsed and the clouds burnt like the hills of Gehenna; the thunders burbled and banged; and the white rain drilled into the roadway which had erupted into a steaming lather. Then a *snapper,* tri-horned, wet-feathered, demon-faced, sword-tailed, and green, raced from around a corner, a moment after I'd heard a sound which I had thought to be a part of the thunder. The creature ran, at an incredible speed, along the smoky pavement. The eye swooped after it, adding a hail of lead to the falling raindrops. Both vanished up another street. It had taken but an instant, but in that instant it had resolved a question in my mind as to whom should do the painting. Not El Greco, not Blake; no: Bosch. Without any question, Bosch—with his nightmare visions of the streets of Hell. He would be the one to do justice to this moment of the storm.

I watched until the sizzlecloud drew its legs up into itself, hung like a burning cocoon, then died like an ember retreating into ash. Suddenly, it was very dark and there was only the rain.

Sunday was the day of chaos.

Candles burned, churches burned, people drowned, beasts ran wild in the streets (or swam there), houses were torn up by the roots and bounced like paper boats along the waterways, the great wind came down upon us, and after that the madness.

I was not able to drive to Town Hall, so Eleanor sent her flyer after me.

The basement was filled with water, and the ground floor was like Neptune's waiting room. All previous high water marks had been passed.

We were in the middle of the worst storm in Betty's history.

Operations had been transferred up onto the third floor. There was no way to stop things now. It was just a matter of riding it out and giving what relief we could. I sat before my gallery and watched.

It rained buckets, it rained vats; it rained swimming pools and lakes and rivers. For awhile it seemed that it rained oceans upon us. This was partly because of the wind which came in from the gulf and suddenly made it seem to rain sideways with the force of its blasts. It began at about noon and was gone in a few hours, but when it left our town was broken and bleeding. Wyeth lay on his bronze side, the flagpole was gone, there was no building without broken windows and water inside, we were suddenly suffering lapses of electrical power, and one of my eyes showed three panda-puppies devouring a dead child. Cursing, I killed them across the rain and the distance. Eleanor wept at my side. There was a report later of a pregnant woman who could only deliver by Caesarean section, trapped on a hilltop with her family, and in labor. We were still trying to get through to her with a flyer, but the winds . . . I saw burning buildings and the corpses of people and animals. I saw half-buried cars and splintered homes. I saw waterfalls where there had been no waterfalls before. I fired many rounds that day, and not just at beasts from the forest. Sixteen of my eyes had been shot out by looters. I hope that I never again see some of the films I made that day.

When the worst Sunday night in my life began, and the rains did not cease, I knew the meaning of despair for the third time in my life.

Eleanor and I were in the Trouble Center. The lights had just gone out for the eighth time. The rest of the staff was down on the third floor. We sat there in the dark without moving, without being able to do a single thing to halt the course of chaos. We couldn't even watch it until the power came back on.

So we talked.

Whether it was for five minutes or an hour, I don't really know. I remember telling her, though, about the girl buried on another world, whose death had set me to running. Two trips to two worlds and I had broken my bond with the times. But a hundred years of travel do not bring a century of forgetfulness—not when you cheat time with the *petite mort* of the cold sleep. Time's vengeance is memory, and though for an age you plunder the eye of seeing and empty the ear of sound, when you awaken your past is still with you. The worst thing to do then is to return to visit your wife's nameless grave in a changed land, to come back as a stranger to the place you had made your home. You run again then, and after a time you *do* forget, some, because a certain amount of actual time must pass for you also. But by then you are alone, all by yourself: completely alone. That was the *first* time in my life that I knew the meaning of despair. I read, I worked, I drank, I whored, but came the morning after and I was always me, by myself. I jumped from world to world, hoping things would be different, but with each change I was further away from all the things I had known.

Then another feeling gradually came upon me, and a really terrible feeling it was: There *must* be a time and a place best suited for each person who has ever lived. After the worst of my grief had left me and I had come to terms with the vanished past, I wondered about a man's place in time and in space. Where, and *when* in the cosmos would I most like to live out the balance of my days? —To live at my fullest potential? The past *was* dead, but perhaps a better time waited on some as yet undiscovered world, waited at one yet-to-be-recorded moment in its history. How could I *ever* know? How could I ever be sure that my Golden Age did not lay but one more world away, and that I might be struggling in a Dark Era while the Renaissance of my days was but a ticket, a visa and a diary-page removed? That was my *second* despair. I did not know the answer until I came to the Land of the Swan. I do not know why I loved you, Eleanor, but I did, and that was my answer. Then the rains came.

When the lights returned we sat there and smoked. She had told me of her husband, who had died a hero's death in time to save him from the delirium tremors which would have ended his days. Died as the bravest die—not knowing why—because of a reflex, which after all had been a part of him, a reflex which had made him cast himself into the path of a pack of wolf-like creatures attacking the exploring party he was with—off in that forest at the foot of Saint Stephen's—to fight them with a machete and to be torn apart by them while his companions fled to the camp, where they made a stand and saved themselves. Such is the essence of valor: an unthinking moment, a spark along the spinal nerves, predetermined by the sum total of everything you have ever done, wished to do or not to do, and wish you had done, or hadn't, and then comes the pain.

We watched the gallery on the wall. Man is the reasoning animal? Greater than beasts but less than angels? Not the murderer I shot that night. He wasn't even the one who uses tools or buries his dead. —Laughs, aspires, affirms? I didn't see any of those going on. —Watches himself watch himself doing what he knows is absurd? Too sophisticated. He just did the absurd without watching. Like running back into a burning house after his favorite pipe and a can of tobacco. —Devises religions? I saw people praying, but they weren't devising. They were making last-ditch efforts at saving themselves, after they'd exhausted everything else they knew to do. Reflex.

The creature who loves?

That's the only one I might not be able to gainsay.

I saw a mother holding her daughter up on her shoulders while the water swirled about her armpits, and the little girl was holding her doll up above *her* shoulders, in the same way. But isn't that—the love—a part of the total? Of everything you have ever done, or wished? Positive or neg? I know that it is what made me leave my post, running, and what made me climb into Eleanor's flyer and what made me fight my way through the storm and out to that particular scene.

I didn't get there in time.

I shall never forget how glad I was that someone else did. Johnny Keams blinked his lights above me as he rose, and he radioed down:

"It's all right. They're okay. Even the doll."

"Good," I said, and headed back.

As I set the ship down on its balcony landing, one figure came toward me. As I stepped down, a gun appeared in Chuck's hand.

"I wouldn't kill you, Juss," he began, "but I'd wound you. Face that wall. I'm taking the flyer."

"Are you crazy?" I asked him.

"I know what I'm doing. I need it, Juss."

"Well, if you need it, there it is. You don't have to point a gun at me. I just got through needing it myself. Take it."

"Lottie and I both need it," he said. "Turn around!"

I turned toward the wall.

"What do you mean?" I asked.

"We're going away, together—now!"

"You *are* crazy," I said. "This is no time . . ."

"C'mon, Lottie," he called, and there was a rush of feet behind me and I heard the flyer's door open.

"Chuck!" I said. "We need you now! You can settle this thing peacefully, in a week, in a month, after some order has been restored. There *are* such things as divorces, you know."

"That won't get me off this world, Juss."

"So how is *this* going to?"

I turned, and I saw that he had picked up a large canvas bag from somewhere and had it slung over his left shoulder, like Santa Claus.

"Turn back around! I don't want to shoot you," he warned.

The suspicion came, grew stronger.

"Chuck, have you been looting?" I asked him.

"Turn around!"

"All right, I'll turn around. How far do you think you'll get?"

"Far enough," he said. "Far enough so that no one will find us—and when the time comes, we'll leave this world."

"No," I said. "I don't think you will, because I know you."

"We'll see." His voice was further away then.

I heard three rapid footsteps and the slamming of a door. I turned then, in time to see the flyer rising from the balcony.

I watched it go. I never saw either of them again.

Inside, two men were unconscious on the floor. It turned out that they were not seriously hurt. After I saw them cared for, I rejoined Eleanor in the Tower.

All that night did we wait, emptied, for morning.

Somehow, it came.

We sat and watched the light flow through the rain. So much had happened so quickly. So many things had occurred during the past week that we were unprepared for morning.

It brought an end to the rains.

A good wind came from out of the north and fought with the clouds, like En-ki with the serpent Tiamat. Suddenly, there was a canyon of cobalt.

A cloudquake shook the heavens and chasms of light opened across its dark landscape.

It was coming apart as we watched.

I heard a cheer, and I croaked in unison with it as the sun appeared.

The good, warm, drying, beneficent sun drew the highest peak of Saint Stephen's to its face and kissed both its cheeks.

There was a crowd before each window. I joined one and stared, perhaps for ten minutes.

When you awaken from a nightmare you do not normally find its ruins lying about your bedroom. This is one way of telling whether or not something was only a bad dream, or whether or not you are really awake.

We walked the streets in great boots. Mud was everywhere. It was in basements and in machinery and in sewers and in living room clothes closets. It was on buildings and on cars and on people and on the branches of trees. It was broken brown blisters drying and waiting to be peeled off from clean tissue. Swarms of skytoads rose into the air when we approached, hovered like dragonflies, returned to spoiling food stores after we had passed. Insects were having a heyday, too. Betty would have to be deloused. So many things were overturned or fallen down, and half-buried in the brown Sargassos of the streets. The dead had not yet been numbered. The water still ran by, but sluggish and foul. A stench was beginning to rise across the city. There were smashed-in store fronts and there was glass everywhere, and bridges fallen down and holes in the streets . . . But why go on? If you don't get the picture by now, you never will. It was the big morning after, following a drunken party by the gods. It is the lot of mortal man always to clean up their leavings or to be buried beneath them.

So clean we did, but by noon Eleanor could no longer

stand. So I took her home with me, because we were working down near the harbor section and my place was nearer.

That's almost the whole story—light to darkness to light—except for the end, which I don't really know. I'll tell you of its beginning, though . . .

I dropped her off at the head of the alleyway, and she went on toward my apartment while I parked the car. Why didn't I keep her with me? I don't know. Unless it was because the morning sun made the world seem at peace, despite its filth. Unless it was because I was in love and the darkness was over, and the spirit of the night had surely departed.

I parked the car and started up the alley. I was halfway before the corner where I had met the org when I heard her cry out.

I ran. Fear gave me speed and strength and I ran to the corner and turned it.

The man had a bag, not unlike the one Chuck had carried away with him, lying beside the puddle in which he stood. He was going through Eleanor's purse, and she lay on the ground—so still!—with blood on the side of her head.

I cursed him and ran toward him, switching on my cane as I went. He turned, dropped her purse, and reached for the gun in his belt.

We were about thirty feet apart, so I threw my cane.

He drew his gun, pointed it at me, and my cane fell into the puddle in which he stood.

Flights of angels sang him to his rest, perhaps.

She was breathing, so I got her inside and got hold of a doctor—I don't remember how, not too clearly, anyway—and I waited and waited.

She lived for another twelve hours and then she died. She recovered consciousness twice before they operated on her, and not again after. She didn't say anything. She smiled at me once, and went to sleep again.

I don't know.

Anything, really.

It happened again that I became Betty's mayor, to fill in until November, to oversee the rebuilding. I worked, I worked my head off, and I left her bright and shiny, as I had found her. I think I could have won if I had run for the job that fall, but I did not want it.

The Town Council overrode my objections and voted to erect a statue of Godfrey Justin Holmes beside the statue of Eleanor Schirrer which was to stand in the Square across from cleaned-up Wyeth. I guess it's out there now.

I said that I would never return, but who knows? In a couple of years, after some more history has passed, I may revisit a Betty full of strangers, if only to place a wreath at the foot of the one statue. Who knows but that the entire continent may be steaming and clanking and whirring with automation by then, and filled with people from shore to shining shore?

There was a Stopover at the end of the year and I waved good-bye and climbed aboard and went away, anywhere.

I went aboard and went away, to sleep again the cold sleep.

Delirium of ship among stars—

Years have passed, I suppose. I'm not really counting them any more. But I think of this thing often: Perhaps there *is* a Golden Age someplace, a Renaissance for me sometime, a special time somewhere, somewhere but a ticket, a visa, a diary-page away. I don't know where or when. Who does? Where are all the rains of yesterday?

In the invisible city?

Inside me?

It is cold and quiet outside and the horizon is infinity. There is no sense of movement.

There is no moon, and the stars are very bright, like broken diamonds, all.

9.

The Great
Slow Kings

DRAX AND DRAN sat in the great Throne Hall of Glan, discussing life. Monarchs by virtue of superior intellect and physique—and the fact that they were the last two survivors of the race of Glan—theirs was a divided rule over the planet and their one subject, Zindrome, the palace robot.

Drax had been musing for the past four centuries (theirs was a sluggish sort) over the possibility of life on other planets in the galaxy.

Accordingly, "Dran," said he, addressing the other (who was becoming mildly curious as to his thoughts), "Dran, I've been thinking: There may be life on other planets in the galaxy."

Dran considered his reply to this, as the world wheeled several times about its sun.

"True," he finally agreed, "there may."

After several months Drax shot back, "If there is, we ought to find out."

"Why?" asked Dran with equal promptness, which caused the other to suspect that he, too, had been thinking along these lines.

So he measured his next statement out cautiously, first testing each word within the plated retort of his reptilian skull.

"Our kingdom is rather underpopulated at present," he observed. "It would be good to have many subjects once more."

Dran regarded him askance, then slowly turned his head. He closed one eye and half-closed the other, taking full stock of his co-ruler, whose appearance, as he suspected, was unchanged since the last time he had looked. "That, also, is true," he noted. "What do you suggest we do?"

This time Drax turned, reappraising him, eye to eye.

"I think we ought to find out if there is life on other planets in the galaxy."

"Hmm."

Two quick roundings of the seasons went unnoticed, then, "Let me think about it," he said, and turned away.

After what he deemed a polite period of time, Drax coughed.

"Have you thought sufficiently?"

"No."

Drax struggled to focus his eyes on the near-subliminal streak of bluish light which traversed, re-traversed and re-re-traversed the Hall as he waited.

"Zindrome!" he finally called out.

The robot slowed his movements to a statue-like immobility to accommodate his master. A feather duster protruded from his right limb.

"You called, great Lord of Glan?"

"Yes, Zindrome, worthy subject. Those old spaceships which we constructed in happier days, and never got around to using. Are any of them still capable of operation?"

"I'll check, great Lord."

He seemed to change position slightly.

"There are three hundred eighty-two," he announced, "of which four are in functioning condition, great Lord. I've checked all the operating circuits."

"Drax," warned Dran, "you are arrogating unauthorized powers to yourself once more. You should have conferred with me before issuing that order."

"I apologize," stated the other. "I simply wanted to

expedite matters, should your decision be that we conduct a survey."

"You have anticipated my decision correctly," nodded Dran, "but your eagerness seems to bespeak a hidden purpose."

"No purpose but the good of the realm," smiled the other.

"That may be, but the last time you spoke of 'the good of the realm' the civil strife which ensued cost us our other robot."

"I have learned my lesson and profited thereby. I shall be more judicious in the future."

"I hope so. Now, about this expedition—which part of the galaxy do you intend to investigate first?"

A tension-filled pause ensued.

"I had assumed," murmured Drax, "that you would conduct the expedition. Being the more mature monarch, yours should be a more adequate decision as to whether or not a particular species is worthy of our enlightened rule."

"Yes, but your youth tends to make you more active than I. The journey should be more expeditiously conducted by you." He emphasized the word "expeditiously."

"We could both go, in separate ships," offered Drax. "That would be truly expeditious—"

Their heated debating was cut short by a metallic coughequivalent.

"Masters," suggested Zindrome, "the half-life of radioactive materials being as ephemeral as it is, I regret to report that only one spaceship is now in operational condition."

"That settles it, Drax. *You* go. It will require a steadier *rrand* to manage an underpowered ship."

"And leave you to foment civil strife and usurp unfranchised powers? No, you go!"

"I suppose we could *both* go," sighed Drax.

"Fine! Leave the kingdom leaderless! *That* is the kind of muddleheaded thinking which brought about our present political embarrassment."

"Masters," said Zindrome, "if *someone* doesn't go soon the ship will be useless."

They both studied their servant, approving the rapid chain of logic forged by his simple statement.

"Very well," they smiled in unison, *"you* go."

Zindrome bowed quite obsequiously and departed from the great Throne Hall of Glan.

"Perhaps we should authorize Zindrome to construct facsimiles of himself," stated Dran, tentatively. "If we had more subjects we could accomplish more."

"Are you forgetting our most recent agreement?" asked Drax. "A superfluity of robots tended to stimulate factionalism last time—and certain people grew ambitious . . ." He let his voice trail off over the years, for emphasis.

"I am not certain as to whether your last allusion contains a hidden accusation," began the other carefully. "If so, permit me to caution you concerning rashness—and to remind you who it was who engineered the Mono-Robot Protection Pact."

"Do you believe things will be different in the case of a multitude of organic subjects?" inquired the other.

"Definitely," said Dran. "There is a certain irrational element in the rationale of the organic being, making it less amenable to direct orders than a machine would be. Our robots, at least, were faithful when we ordered them to destroy one another. Irresponsible organic subjects either do it without being told, which is boorish, or refuse to do it when you order them, which in insubordination."

"True," smiled Drax, unearthing a gem he had preserved for milennia against this occasion. "Concerning organic life the only statement which can be made with certainty is that life is uncertain."

"Hmm." Dran narrowed his eyes to slits. "Let me ponder that a moment. Like much of your thinking it seems to smack of a concealed sophistry."

"It contains none, I assure you. It is the fruit of much meditation."

"Hmm."

Dran's pondering was cut short, by the arrival of Zindrome who clutched two brownish blurs beneath his metal arms.

"Back already, Zindrome? What have you there? Slow them down so we can see them."

"They are under sedation at present, great Masters. It is the movements caused by their breathing which produce the unpleasant vibration pattern on your retinas. To subject them to more narcosis could prove deleterious."

"Nevertheless," maintained Dran, "we must appraise our new subjects carefully, which requires that we see them. Slow them down some more."

"You gave that order without—" began Drax, but was distracted by the sudden appearance of the two hairy bipeds.

"Warm-blooded?" he asked.

"Yes, Lord."

"That bespeaks a very brief life-span."

"True," offered Dran, "but that kind tends to reproduce quite rapidly."

"That observation tends to be correct," nodded Drax. "Tell me, Zindrome, do they represent the sexes necessary for reproduction?"

"Yes, Master. There are two sexes among these anthropoids, so I brought one of each."

"That was very wise. Where did you find them?"

"Several billion light years from here."

"Turn these two loose outside and go fetch us some more."

The creatures vanished. Zindrome appeared not to have moved.

"Have you the fuel necessary for another such journey?"

"Yes, my Lord. More of it has evolved recently."

"Excellent."

The robot departed.

"What sort of governmental setup should we inaugurate this time?" asked Drax.

"Let us review the arguments for the various types."

"A good idea."

In the midst of their discussion Zindrome returned and stood waiting to be recognized.

"What is it, Zindrome? Did you forget something?"

"No, great Lords. When I returned to the world from which I obtained the samples I discovered that the race had progressed to the point where it developed fission processes, engaged in an atomic war and annihilated itself."

"That was extremely inconsiderate—typical, however, I should say, of warm-blooded instability."

Zindrome continued to shift.

"Have you something else to report?"

"Yes, great Masters. The two specimens I released have multiplied and are now spread over the entire planet of Glan."

"We should have been advised!"

"Yes, great Lords, but I was absent and—"

"They themselves should have reported this action!"

"Masters, I am afraid they are unaware of your existence."

"How could that have happened?" asked Dran.

"We are presently buried beneath several thousand layers of alluvial rock. The geological shifts—"

"You have your orders to maintain the place and clean the grounds," glowered Dran. "Have you been frittering away your time again?"

"No, great Lords! It all occurred during my absence. I shall attend to it immediately."

"First," ordered Drax, "tell us what else our subjects have been up to, that they saw fit to conceal from us."

"Recently," observed the robot, "they have discovered how to forge and temper metals. Upon landing, I observed that they had developed many ingenious instruments of a cutting variety. Unfortunately they were using them to cut one another."

"Do you mean," roared Dran, "that there is strife in the kingdom?"

"Uh, yes, my Lord."

"I will not brook unauthorized violence among my subjects!"

"Our subjects," added Drax, with a meaningful glare.

"Our subjects," amended Dran. "We must take immediate action."

"Agreed."

"Agreed."

"I shall issue orders forbidding their engagement in activities leading to bloodshed."

"I presume that you mean a joint proclamation," stated Drax.

"Of course. I was not slighting you, I was simply shaken by the civil emergency. We shall draft an official proclamation. Let Zindrome fetch us writing instruments."

"Zindrome, fetch—"

"I have them here, my Lords."

"Now, let me see. How shall we phrase it . . . ?"

"Perhaps I should clean the palace while your Excellencies—"

"No! Wait right here! This will be very brief and to the point."

"Mm. 'We hereby proclaim . . .'"

"Don't forget our titles."

"True. 'We, the imperial monarchs of Glan, herebeneath undersigned, do hereby . . .'"

A feeble pulse of gamma rays passed unnoticed by the two rulers. The faithful Zindrome diagnosed its nature, however, and tried unsuccessfully to obtain his monarchs' attention. Finally, he dismissed the project with a stoical gesture typical of his kind. He waited.

"There!" they agreed, flourishing the document. "Now you can tell us what you have been trying to say, Zindrome. But make it brief, you must deliver this soon."

"It is already too late, great Lords. This race, also, progressed into civilized states, developed nuclear energy and eradicated itself while you were writing."

"Barbarous!"

"Warm-blooded irresponsibility!"

"May I go clean up now, great Masters?"

"Soon, Zindrome, soon. First, though, I move that we file the proclamation in the Archives for future use, in the event of similar occurrences."

Dran nodded.

"I agree. *We* so order."

The robot accepted the crumbling proclamation and vanished from sight.

"You know," Drax mused, "there must be lots of radioactive material lying about now . . ."

"There probably is."

"It could be used to fuel a ship for another expedition."

"Perhaps."

"This time we could instruct Zindrome to bring back something with a longer life-span and more deliberate habits—somewhat nearer our own."

"That would have its dangers. But perhaps we could

junk the Mono-Robot Protection Pact and order Zindrome to manufacture extras of himself. Under strict supervision."

"That would have its dangers too."

"At any rate, I should have to ponder your suggestion carefully."

"And I yours."

"It's been a busy day," nodded Dran. "Let's sleep on it."

"A good idea."

Sounds of saurian snoring emerged from the great Throne Hall of Glan.

10.

A Museum Piece

FORCED TO ADMIT that his art was going unnoticed in a frivolous world, Jay Smith decided to get out of that world. The four dollars and ninety-eight cents he spent for a mail order course entitled *Yoga—The Path to Freedom* did not, however, help to free him. Rather, it served to accentuate his humanity, in that it reduced his ability to purchase food by four dollars and ninety-eight cents.

Seated in a padmasana, Smith contemplated little but the fact that his navel drew slightly closer to his backbone with each day that passed. While nirvana is a reasonably esthetic concept, suicide assuredly is not, particularly if you haven't the stomach for it. So he dismissed the fatalistic notion quite reasonably:

"How simply one could take one's own life in ideal surroundings!" he sighed (tossing his golden locks which, for obvious reasons, had achieved classically impressive lengths). "The fat stoic in his bath, fanned by slave girls and sipping his wine, as a faithful Greek leech opens his veins, eyes downcast! One delicate Circassian," he sighed again, *"there* perhaps, plucking upon a lyre as he dictates his funeral oration—the latter to be read by a faithful countryman, eyes all a-blink. How easily *he* might do it! But the fallen artist—nay! Born yesterday and scorned today he goes, like the elephant to his graveyard, alone and secret!"

He rose to his full height of six feet, one and a half inches, and swung to face the mirror. Regarding his skin, pallid as marble, and his straight nose, broad forehead, and wide-spaced eyes, he decided that if one could not live by creating art, then one might do worse than turn the thing the other way about, so to speak.

He flexed those thews which had earned him half-tuition as a halfback for the four years in which he had stoked the stithy of his soul to the forging out of a movement all his own: two-dimensional painted sculpture.

"Viewed in the round," one crabbed critic had noted, "Mister Smith's offerings are either frescoes without walls or vertical lines. The Etruscans excelled in the former form because they knew where it belonged; kindergartens inculcate a mastery of the latter in all five-year-olds."

Cleverness! Mere cleverness! Bah! He was sick of those Johnsons who laid down the law at someone else's dinner table!

He noted with satisfaction that his month-long ascetic regime had reduced his weight by thirty pounds to a mere two twenty-five. He decided that he could pass as a Beaten Gladiator, post-Hellenic.

"It is settled," he pronounced. "I'll *be* art."

Later that afternoon a lone figure entered the Museum of Art, a bundle beneath his arm.

Spiritually haggard (although clean-shaven to the armpits), Smith loitered about the Greek Period until it was emptied of all but himself and marble.

He selected a dark corner and unwrapped his pedestal. He secreted the various personal items necessary for a showcase existence, including most of his clothing, in its hollow bottom.

"Good-bye, world," he renounced, "you should treat your artists better," and mounted the pedestal.

His food money had not been completely wasted, for the techniques he had mastered for four ninety-eight while on the Path to Freedom, had given him a muscular control such as allowed him perfect, motionless statuity whenever the wispy, middle-aged woman followed by forty-four children under age nine, left her chartered bus at the curb and passed through the Greek Period, as she did every Tuesday and Thursday between 9:35 and 9:40 in the morning. Fortunately, he had selected a seated posture.

Before the week passed he had also timed the watchman's movements to an alternate *tick* of the huge clock in the adjacent gallery (a delicate Eighteenth Century timepiece, all of gold leaf, enamel, and small angels who chased one another in circles). He should have hated being reported stolen during the first week of his career, with nothing to face then but the pospect of second-rate galleries or an uneasy role in the cheerless private collections of cheerless and private collectors. Therefore, he moved judiciously when raiding staples from the stores in the downstairs lunch room, and strove to work out a sympathetic bond with the racing angels. The directors had never seen fit to secure the refrigerator or pantry from depredations by the exhibits, and he applauded their lack of imagination. He nibbled at boiled ham and pumpernickel (light), and munched ice cream bars by the dozen. After a month he was forced to take calisthenics (heavy) in the Bronze Age.

"Oh, lost!" he reflected amidst the Neos, surveying the kingdom he had once staked out as his own. He wept over the statue of Achilles Fallen as though it were his own. It was.

As in a mirror, he regarded himself in a handy collage of bolts and nutshells. "If you had not sold out," he accused, "if *you* had hung on a little longer—like these, the simplest of Art's creatures . . . But no! It could not be!

"Could it?" he addressed a particularly symmetrical mobile overhead. *"Could* it?"

"Perhaps," came an answer from somewhere, which sent him flying back to his pedestal.

But little came of it. The watchman had been taking guilty delight in a buxom Rubens on the other side of the building and had not overheard the colloquy. Smith decided that the reply signified his accidental nearing of Dharana. He returned to the Path, re-doubling his efforts toward negation and looking Beaten.

In the days that followed he heard occasional chuckling

and whispering, which he at first dismissed as the chort-
lings of the children of Mara and Maya, intent upon his
distraction. Later, he was less certain, but by then he had
decided upon a classical attitude of passive inquisitiveness.

And one spring day, as green and golden as a poem by
Dylan Thomas, a girl entered the Greek Period and looked
about, furtively. He found it difficult to maintain his
marbly placidity, for lo! she began to disrobe!

And a square parcel on the floor, in a plain wrapper.
It could only mean . . .

Competition!

He coughed politely, softly, classically . . .

She jerked to an amazing attention, reminding him of
a women's underwear ad having to do with Thermopylae.
Her hair was the correct color for the undertaking—that
palest shade of Parian manageable—and her gray eyes
glittered with the icy-orbed intentness of Athene.

She surveyed the room minutely, guiltily, attractively . . .

"Surely stone is not susceptible to virus infections," she
decided. " 'Tis but my guilty conscience that cleared its
throat. Conscience, thus do I cast thee off!"

And she proceeded to become Hecuba Lamenting, di-
agonally across from the Beaten Gladiator and, fortunately,
not facing in his direction. She handled it pretty well, too,
he grudgingly admitted. Soon she achieved an esthetic immobility. After a professional appraisal he decided that
Athens was indeed mother of all the arts; she simply could
not have carried it as Renaissance nor Romanesque. This
made him feel rather good.

When the great doors finally swung shut and the alarms
had been set she heaved a sigh and sprang to the floor.

"Not yet," he cautioned, "the watchman will pass
through in ninety-three seconds."

She had presence of mind sufficient to stifle her scream,
a delicate hand with which to do it, and eighty-seven
seconds in which to become Hecuba Lamenting once more.
This she did, and he admired her delicate hand and her
presence of mind for the next eighty-seven seconds.

The watchman came, was nigh, was gone, flashlight and
beard bobbing in musty will o' the-wispfulness through the
gloom.

"Goodness!" she expelled her breath. "I had thought I was alone!"

"And correctly so," he replied. " 'Naked and alone we come into exile . . . Among brights stars on this most weary unbright cinder, lost . . . Oh, lost—' "

"Thomas Wolfe," she stated.

"Yes," he sulked. "Let's go have supper."

"Supper?" she inquired, arching her eyebrows. "Where? I had brought some K-Rations, which I purchased at an Army Surplus Store—"

"Obviously," he retorted, "you have a short-timer's attitude. I believe that chicken figured prominently on the menu for today. Follow me!"

They made their way through the T'ang Dynasty, to the stairs.

"Others might find it chilly in here after hours," he began, "but I daresay you have thoroughly mastered the techniques of breath control?"

"Indeed," she replied, "my fiancé was no mere Zen faddist. He followed the more rugged path of Lhasa. Once he wrote a modern version of the Ramayana, full of topical allusions and advice to modern society."

"And what did modern society think of it?"

"Alas! Modern society never saw it. My parents brought him a one-way ticket to Rome, first-class, and several hundred dollars' worth of Travellers' Checks. He has been gone ever since. That is why I have retired from the world."

"I take it your parents did not approve of Art?"

"No, and I believe they must have threatened him also." He nodded.

"Such is the way of society with genius. I, too, in my small way, have worked for its betterment and received but scorn for my labors."

"Really?"

"Yes. If we stop in the Modern Period on the way back, you can see my Achilles Fallen."

A very dry chuckle halted them.

"Who is there?" he inquired, cautiously.

No reply. They stood in the Glory of Rome, and the stone senators were still.

"*Someone* laughed," she observed.

"We are not alone," he stated, shrugging. "There've been other indications of such, but whoever they are, they're as talkative as Trappists—which is good.

"Remember, thou art but stone," he called gaily, and they continued on to the cafeteria.

One night they sat together at dinner in the Modern Period.

"Had you a name, in life?" he asked.

"Gloria," she whispered. "And yours?"

"Smith, Jay."

"What prompted you to become a statue, Smith, if it is not too bold of me to ask?"

"Not at all," he smiled, invisibly. "Some are born to obscurity and others only achieve it through diligent effort. I am one of the latter. Being an artistic failure, and broke, I decided to become my own monument. It's warm in here, and there's food below. The environment is congenial, and I'll never be found out because no one ever looks at anything standing around museums."

"No one?"

"Not a soul, as you must have noticed. Children come here against their wills, young people come to flirt with one another, and when one develops sufficient sensibility to look at anything," he lectured bitterly, "he is either myopic or subject to hallucinations. In the former case he would not notice, in the latter he would not talk. The parade passes."

"Then what good are museums?"

"My dear girl! That the former affianced of a true artist should speak in such a manner indicates that your relationship was but brief—"

"Really!" she interrupted. "The proper word is 'companionship'."

"Very well," he amended, " 'companionship'. But museums mirror the past, which is dead, the present, which never notices, and transmit the race's cultural heritage to the future, which is not yet born. In this, they are near to being temples of religion."

"I never thought of it that way," she mused. "Rather a beautiful thought, too. You should really be a teacher."

"It doesn't pay well enough, but the thought consoles me. Come, let us raid the icebox again."

They nibbled their final ice cream bars and discussed Achilles Fallen, seated beneath the great mobile which resembled a starved octopus. He told her of his other great projects and of the nasty reviewers, crabbed and bloodless, who lurked in Sunday editions and hated life. She, in turn, told him of her parents, who knew Art and also knew why she shouldn't like him, and of her parents' vast fortunes, equally distributed in timber, real estate, and petroleum. He, in turn, patted her arm and she, in turn, blinked heavily and smiled Hellenically.

"You know," he said, finally, "as I sat upon my pedestal, day after day, I often thought to myself: Perhaps I should return and make one more effort to pierce the cataract in the eye of the public—perhaps if I were secure and at ease in all things material—perhaps, if I could find the proper woman—but nay! There is no such a one!"

"Continue! Pray continue!" cried she. "I, too, have, over the past days, thought that, perhaps, another artist could remove the sting. Perhaps the poison of loneliness could be drawn by a creator of beauty— If we—"

At this point a small and ugly man in a toga cleared his throat.

"It is as I feared," he announced.

Lean, wrinkled, and grubby was he; a man of ulcerous bowel and much spleen. He pointed an accusing finger.

"It is as I feared," he repeated.

"Wh-who are you?" asked Gloria.

"Cassius," he replied, "Cassius Fitzmullen—art critic, retired, for the Dalton *Times*. You are planning to defect."

"And what concern is it of yours if we leave?" asked Smith, flexing his Beaten Gladiator halfback muscles.

Cassius shook his head.

"Concern? It would threaten a way of life for you to leave now. If you go, you will doubtless become an artist or a teacher of art—and sooner or later, by word or by gesture, by sign or by unconscious indication, you will communicate what you have suspected all along. I have listened to your conversations over the past weeks. You know, for certain now, that this is where all art critics finally come, to spend their remaining days mocking the things they have hated. It accounts for the increase of Roman Senators in recent years."

"I have often suspected it, but never was certain."

"The suspicion is enough. It is lethal. You must be judged."

He clapped his hands.

"Judgment!" he called.

Other ancient Romans entered slowly, a procession of bent candles. They encircled the two lovers. Smelling of dust and yellow newsprint and bile and time, the old reviewers hovered.

"They wish to return to humanity," announced Cassius. "They wish to leave and take their knowledge with them."

"We would not tell," said Gloria, tearfully.

"It is too late," replied one dark figure. "You are already entered into the Catalog. See here!" He produced a copy and read: " 'Number 28, Hecuba Lamenting. Number 32, The Beaten Gladiator.' No! It is too late. There would be an investigation."

"Judgment!" repeated Cassius.

Slowly, the Senators turned their thumbs down.

"You *cannot* leave."

Smith chuckled and seized Cassius' tunic in a powerful sculptor's grip.

"Little man," he said, "how do you propose stopping us? One scream by Gloria would bring the watchman, who would sound an alarm. One blow by me would render you unconscious for a week."

"We shut off the guard's hearing aid as he slept," smiled Cassius. "Critics are not without imagination, I assure you. Release me, or you will suffer."

Smith tightened his grip.

"Try *anything*."

"Judgment," smiled Cassius.

"He is modern," said one.

"Therefore, his tastes are catholic," said another.

"To the lions with the Christians!" announced a third, clapping his hands.

And Smith sprang back in panic at what he thought he saw moving in the shadows. Cassius pulled free.

"You cannot do this!" cried Gloria, covering her face. "We are from the Greek Period!"

"When in Greece, do as the Romans do," chuckled Cassius.

The odor of cats came to their nostrils.

"How could you—here . . . ? A lion . . . ?" asked Smith.

"A form of hypnosis privy to the profession," observed Cassius. "We keep the beast paralyzed most of the time. Have you not wondered why there has never been a theft from this museum? Oh, it has been tried, all right! We protect our interests."

The lean, albino lion which generally slept beside the main entrance padded slowly from the shadows and growled—once, and loudly.

Smith pushed Gloria behind him as the cat began its stalking. He glanced toward the Forum, which proved to be vacant. A sound, like the flapping of wings by a flock of leather pigeons, diminished in the distance.

"We are alone," noted Gloria.

"Run," ordered Smith, "and I'll try to delay him. Get out, if you can."

"And desert you? Never, my dear! Together! Now, and always!"

"Gloria!"

"Jay Smith!"

At that moment the beast conceived the notion to launch into a spring, which it promptly did.

"Good-bye, my lovely."

"Farewell. One kiss before dying, pray."

The lion was high in the air, uttering healthy coughs, eyes greenly aglow.

"Very well."

They embraced.

Moon hacked in the shape of cat, that palest of beasts hung overhead—hung high, hung menacingly, hung long . . .

It began to writhe and claw about wildly in that middle space between floor and ceiling for which architecture possesses no specific noun.

"Mm! Another kiss?"

"Why not? Life is sweet."

A minute ran by on noiseless feet; another pursued it.

"I say, what's holding up that lion?"

"I am," answered the mobile. "You humans aren't the only ones to seek umbrage amidst the relics of your dead past."

The voice was thin, fragile, like that of a particularly busy Aeolian Harp.

"I do not wish to seem inquisitive," said Smith, "but who are you?"

"I am an alien life form," it tinkled back, digesting the lion. "My ship suffered an accident on the way to Arcturus. I soon discovered that my appearance was against me on your planet, except in the museums, where I am greatly admired. Being a member of a rather delicate and, if I do say it, somewhat narcissistic race—" He paused to belch daintily, and continued, "—I rather enjoy it here—'among bright stars on this most weary unbright cinder [belch], lost.'"

"I see," said Smith. "Thanks for eating the lion."

"Don't mention it—but it wasn't *wholly* advisable. You see, I'm going to have to divide now. Can the other me go with you?"

"Of course. You saved our lives, and we're going to need something to hang in the living room, when we have one."

"Good."

He divided, in a flurry of hemidemisemiquavers, and dropped to the floor beside them.

"Good-bye, me," he called upward.

"Good-bye," from above.

They walked proudly from the Modern, through the Greek, and past the Roman Period, with much hauteur and a wholly quiet dignity. Beaten Gladiator, Hecuba Lamenting, and Xena ex Machina no longer, they lifted the sleeping watchman's key and walked out the door, down the stairs, and into the night, on youthful legs and drop-lines.

11.
Divine Madness

"... I IS THIS *?hearers wounded-wonder like stand them makes and stars wandering the conjures sorrow of phrase Whose ...*"

He blew smoke through the cigarette and it grew longer.

He glanced at the clock and realized that its hands were moving backwards.

The clock told him that it was 10:33, going on 10:32 in the P.M.

Then came the thing like despair, for he knew there was not a thing he could do about it. He was trapped, moving in reverse through the sequence of actions past. Somehow, he had missed the warning.

Usually, there was a prism-effect, a flash of pink static, a drowsiness, then a moment of heightened perception ...

He turned the pages, from left to right, his eyes retracing their path back along the lines.

"*?emphasis an such bears grief whose he is What*"

Helpless, there behind his eyes, he watched his body perform.

The cigarette had reached its full length. He clicked on the lighter, which sucked away its glowing point, and then he shook the cigarette back into the pack.

He yawned in reverse: first an exhalation, then an inhalation.

It wasn't real—the doctor had told him. It was grief and epilepsy, meeting to form an unusual syndrome.

"He'd already had the seizure. The dialantin wasn't helping. This was a post-traumatic locomotor hallucination, elicited by anxiety, precipitated by the attack.

But he did not believe it, could not believe it—not after twenty minutes had gone by, in the other direction—not after he had placed the book upon the reading stand, stood, walked backward across the room to his closet, hung up his robe, redressed himself in the same shirt and slacks he had worn all day, backed over to the bar and regurgitated a Martini, sip by cooling sip, until the glass was filled to the brim and not a drop spilled.

There was an impending taste of olive, and then everything was changed again.

The second-hand was sweeping around his wristwatch in the proper direction.

The time was 10:07.

He felt free to move as he wished.

He redrank his Martini.

Now, if he would be true to the pattern, he would change into his robe and try to read. Instead, he mixed another drink.

Now the sequence would not occur.

Now the things would not happen as he thought they had happened, and un-happened.

Now everything was different.

All of which went to prove it had been an hallucination.

Even the notion that it had taken twenty-six minutes each way was an attempted rationalization.

Nothing had happened.

. . . Shouldn't be drinking, he decided. It might bring on a seizure.

He laughed.

Crazy, though, the whole thing . . .

Remembering, he drank.

In the morning he skipped breakfast, as usual, noted that it would soon stop being morning, took two aspirins, a lukewarm shower, a cup of coffee, and a walk.

The park, the fountain, the children with their boats,

the grass, the pond, he hated them; and the morning, and the sunlight, and the blue moats around the towering clouds.

Hating, he sat there. And remembering.

If he was on the verge of a crackup, he decided, then the thing he wanted most was to plunge ahead into it, not to totter halfway out, halfway in.

He remembered why.

But it was clear, so clear, the morning, and everything crisp and distinct and burning with the green fires of spring, there in the sign of the Ram, April.

He watched the winds pile up the remains of winter against the far gray fence, and he saw them push the boats across the pond, to come to rest in shallow mud the children tracked.

The fountain jetted its cold umbrella above the green-tinged copper dolphins. The sun ignited it whenever he moved his head. The wind rumpled it.

Clustered on the concrete, birds pecked at part of a candy bar stuck to a red wrapper.

Kites swayed on their tails, nosed downward, rose again, as youngsters tugged at invisible strings. Telephone lines were tangled with wooden frames and torn paper, like broken G clefs and smeared glissandos.

He hated the telephone lines, the kites, the children, the birds.

Most of all, though, he hated himself.

How does a man undo that which has been done? He doesn't. There is no way under the sun. He may suffer, remember, repent, curse, or forget. Nothing else. The past, in this sense, is inevitable.

A woman walked past. He did not look up in time to see her face, but the dusky blonde fall of her hair to her collar and the swell of her sure, sheer-netted legs below the black hem of her coat and above the matching click of her heels heigh-ho, stopped his breath behind his stomach and snared his eyes in the wizard-weft of her walking and her posture and some more, like a rhyme to the last of his thoughts.

He half-rose from the bench when the pink static struck his eyeballs, and the fountain became a volcano spouting rainbows.

The world was frozen and served up to him under glass.
. . . The woman passed back before him and he looked down too soon to see her face.

The hell was beginning once more, he realized, as the backward-flying birds passed before.

He gave himself to it. Let it keep him until he broke, until he was all used up and there was nothing left.

He waited, there on the beach, watching the slithey toves be brillig, as the fountain sucked its waters back within itself, drawing them up in a great arc above the unmoving dolphins, and the boats raced backward across the pond, and the fence divested itself of stray scraps of paper, as the birds replaced the candy bar within the red wrapper, bit by crunchy bit.

His thoughts only were inviolate, his body belonged to the retreating tide.

Eventually, he rose and strolled backwards out of the park.

On the street a boy backed past him, unwhistling snatches of a popular song.

He backed up the stairs to his apartment, his hangover growing worse again, undrank his coffee, unshowered, unswallowed his aspirins, and got into bed, feeling awful.

Let this be it, he decided.

A faintly-remembered nightmare ran in reverse through his mind, giving it an undeserved happy ending.

It was dark when he awakened.

He was very drunk.

He backed over to the bar and began spitting out his drinks, one by one into the same glass he had used the night before, and pouring them from the glass back into the bottles again. Separating the gin and vermouth was no trick at all. The proper liquids leapt into the air as he held the uncorked bottles above the bar.

And he grew less and less drunk as this went on.

Then he stood before an early Martini and it was 10:07 in the P.M. There, within the hallucination, he wondered about another hallucination. Would time loop-the-loop, forward and then backward again, through his previous seizure?

No.

It was as though it had not happened, had never been.

He continued on back through the evening, undoing things.

He raised the telephone, said "good-bye," untold Murray that he would not be coming to work again tomorrow, listened a moment, recradled the phone and looked at it as it rang.

The sun came up in the west and people were backing their cars to work.

He read the weather report and the headlines, folded the evening paper and placed it out in the hall.

It was the longest seizure he had ever had, but he did not really care. He settled himself down within it and watched as the day unwound itself back to morning.

His hangover returned as the day grew smaller, and it was terrible when he got into bed again.

When he awakened the previous evening the drunkenness was high upon him. Two of the bottles he refilled, recorked, resealed. He knew he would take them to the liquor store soon and get his money back.

As he sat there that day, his mouth uncursing and un-drinking and his eyes unreading, he knew that new cars were being shipped back to Detroit and disassembled, that corpses were awakening into their death-throes, and that priests the world over were saying black mass, unknowing.

He wanted to chuckle, but he could not tell his mouth to do it.

He unsmoked two and a half packs of cigarettes.

Then came another hangover and he went to bed. Later, the sun set in the east.

Time's winged chariot fled before him as he opened the door and said "good-bye" to his comforters and they came in and sat down and told him not to grieve overmuch.

And he wept without tears as he realized what was to come.

Despite his madness, he hurt.

. . . Hurt, as the days rolled backward.

. . . Backward, inexorably.

. . . Inexorably, until he knew the time was near at hand.

He gnashed the teeth of his mind.

Great was his grief and his hate and his love.

He was wearing his black suit and undrinking drink after drink, while somewhere the men were scraping the clay back onto the shovels which would be used to undig the grave.

He backed his car to the funeral parlor, parked it, and climbed into the limousine.

They backed all the way to the graveyard.

He stood among his friends and listened to the preacher.

".dust to dust; ashes to Ashes," the man said, which is pretty much the same whichever way you say it.

The casket was taken back to the hearse and returned to the funeral parlor.

He sat through the service and went home and un-shaved and unbrushed his teeth and went to bed.

He awakened and dressed again in black and returned to the parlor.

The flowers were all back in place.

Solemn-faced friends unsigned the Sympathy Book and unshook his hand. Then they went inside to sit awhile and stare at the closed casket. Then they left, until he was alone with the funeral director.

Then he was alone with himself.

The tears ran up his cheeks.

His suit and shirt were crisp and unwrinkled again.

He backed home, undressed, uncombed his hair. The day collapsed around him into morning, and he returned to bed to unsleep another night.

The previous evening, when he awakened, he realized where he was headed.

Twice, he exerted all of his will power in an attempt to interrupt the sequence of events. He failed.

He wanted to die. If he had killed himself that day, he would not be headed back toward it now.

There were tears within his mind as he realized the past which lay less than twenty-four hours before him.

The past stalked him that day as he unnegotiated the purchase of the casket, the vault, the accessories.

Then he headed home into the biggest hangover of all and slept until he was awakened to undrink drink after drink and then return to the morgue and come back in

time to hang up the telephone on that call, that call
which had come to break . . .

. . . The silence of his anger with its ringing.

She was dead.

She was lying somewhere in the fragments of her car
on Interstate 90 now.

As he paced, unsmoking, he knew she was lying there
bleeding.

. . . Then dying, after that crash at 80 miles an hour.

. . . Then alive?

Then re-formed, along with the car, and alive again,
arisen? Even now backing home at a terrible speed, to
re-slam the door on their final argument? To unscream
at him and to be unscreamed at?

He cried out within his mind. He wrung the hands of
his spirit.

It couldn't stop at this point. No. Not now.

All his grief and his love and his self-hate had brought
him back this far, this near to the moment . . .

It *couldn't* end now.

After a time, he moved to the living room, his legs
pacing, his lips cursing, himself waiting.

The door slammed open.

She stared in at him, her mascara smeared, tears upon
her cheeks.

"!hell to go Then," he said.

"!going I'm," she said.

She stepped back inside, closed the door.

She hung her coat hurriedly in the hall closet.

".it about feel you way the that's If," he said, shrugging.

"!yourself but anybody about care don't You," she said.

"!child a like behaving You're," he said.

"!sorry you're say least at could You"

Her eyes flashed like emeralds through the pink static,
and she was lovely and alive again. In his mind he was
dancing.

The change came.

"You could at least say you're sorry!"

"I am," he said, taking her hand in a grip that she
could not break. "How much, you'll never know."

"Come here," and she did.

12.

Corrida

HE AWOKE TO an ultrasonic wailing. It was a thing that tortured his eardrums while remaining just beyond the threshhold of the audible.

He scrambled to his feet in the darkness.

He bumped against the walls several times. Dully, he realized that his arms were sore, as though many needles had entered there.

The sound maddened him . . .

Escape! He had to get away!

A tiny patch of light occurred to his left.

He turned and raced toward it and it grew into a doorway.

He dashed through and stood blinking in the glare that assailed his eyes.

He was naked, he was sweating. His mind was full of fog and the rag-ends of dreams.

He heard a roar, as of a crowd, ad he blinked against the brightness.

Towering, a dark figure stood before him in the distance. Overcome by rage, he raced toward it, not quite certain why.

His bare feet trod hot sand, but he ignored the pain as he ran to attack.

Some portion of his mind framed the question "Why?" but he ignored it.

Then he stopped.

A nude woman stood before him, beckoning, inviting, and there came a sudden surge of fire within his loins.

He turned slightly to his left and headed toward her.

She danced away.

He increased his speed. But as he was about to embrace her, there came a surge of fire in his right shoulder and she was gone.

He looked at his shoulder and an aluminum rod protruded from it, and the blood ran down along his arm. There arose another roar.

. . . And she appeared again.

He pursued her once more and his left shoulder burned with sudden fires. She was gone and he stood shaking and sweating, blinking against the glare.

"It's a trick," he decided. "Don't play the game!"

She appeared again and he stood stock still, ignoring her.

He was assailed by fires, but he refused to move, striving to clear his head.

The dark figure appeared once more, about seven feet tall and possessing two pairs of arms.

It held something in one of its hands. If only the lightning weren't so crazy, perhaps he . . .

But he hated that dark figure and he charged it.

Pain lashed his side.

Wait a minute! Wait a minute!

Crazy! It's all crazy! he told himself, recalling his identity. *This is a bullring and I'm a man, and that dark thing isn't. Something's wrong.*

He dropped to his hands and knees, buying time. He scooped up a double fistful of sand while he was down.

There came proddings, electric and painful. He ignored them for as long as he could, then stood.

The dark figure waved something at him and he felt himself hating it.

He ran toward it and stopped before it. He knew it was a game now. His name was Michael Cassidy. He was an attorney. New York. Of Johnson, Weems, Daugherty and Cassidy. A man had stopped him, asking for a light. On a street corner. Late at night. That he remembered.

He threw sand at the creature's head.

It swayed momentarily, and its arms were raised toward what might have been its face.

Gritting his teeth, he tore the aluminum rod from his shoulder and drove its sharpened end into the creature's middle.

Something touched the back of his neck, and there was darkness and he lay still for a long time.

When he could move again, he saw the dark figure and he tried to tackle it.

He missed, and there was pain across his back and something wet.

When he stood once more, he bellowed, "You can't do this to me! I'm a man! Not a bull!"

There came a sound of applause.

He raced toward the dark thing six times, trying to grapple with it, hold it, hurt it. Each time, he hurt himself.

Then he stood, panting and gasping, and his shoulders ached and his back ached, and his mind cleared a moment and he said, "You're God, aren't you? And this is the way You play the game . . ."

The creature did not answer him and he lunged.

He stopped short, then dropped to one knee and dove against its legs.

He felt a terrible fiery pain within his side as he brought the dark one to earth. He struck at it twice with his fists, then the pain entered his breast and he felt himself grow numb.

"Or are you?" he asked, thick-lipped. "No, you're not . . . Where am I?"

His last memory was of something cutting away at his ears.

13.

Love Is
an Imaginary Number

THEY SHOULD HAVE known that they could not keep me bound forever. Probably they did, which is why there was always Stella.

I lay there staring over at her, arm outstretched above her head, masses of messed blond hair framing her sleeping face. She was more than wife to me: she was warden. How blind of me not to have realized it sooner!

But then, what else had they done to me?

They had made me to forget what I was.

Because I was like them but not of them they had bound me to this time and this place.

They had made me to forget. They had nailed me with love.

I stood up and the last chains fell away.

A single bar of moonlight lay upon the floor of the bedchamber. I passed through it to where my clothing was hung.

There was a faint music playing in the distance. That was what had done it. It had been so long since I had heard that music . . .

How had they trapped me?

That little kingdom, ages ago, some Other, where I had introduced gunpowder— Yes! That was the place! They

232

had trapped me there with my Other-made monk's hood and my classical Latin.

Then brainmash and binding to this Otherwhen.

I chuckled softly as I finished dressing. How long had I lived in this place? Forty-five years of memory—but how much of it counterfeit?

The hall mirror showed me a middle-aged man, slightly obese, hair thinning, wearing a red sport shirt and black slacks.

The music was growing louder, the music only I could hear: guitars, and the steady *thump* of a leather drum.

My different drummer, aye! Mate me with an angel and you still do not make me a saint, my comrades!

I made myself young and strong again.

Then I descended the stair to the living room, moved to the bar, poured out a glass of wine, sipped it until the music reached its fullest intensity, then gulped the remainder and dashed the glass to the floor. I was free!

I turned to go, and there was a sound overhead.

Stella had awakened.

The telephone rang. It hung there on the wall and rang and rang until I could stand it no longer.

I raised the receiver.

"You have done it again," said that old, familiar voice.

"Do not go hard with the woman," said I. "She could not watch me always."

"It will be better if you stay right where you are," said the voice. "It will save us both much trouble."

"Good night," I said, and hung up.

The receiver snapped itself around my wrist and the cord became a chain fastened to a ring-bolt in the wall. How childish of them!

I heard Stella dressing upstairs. I moved eighteen steps sidewise from There, to the place where my scaled limb slid easily from out the vines looped about it.

Then, back again to the living room and out the front door. I needed a mount.

I backed the convertible out of the garage. It was the faster of the two cars. Then out onto the nighted highway, and then a sound of thunder overhead.

It was a Piper Cub, sweeping in low, out of control. I slammed on the brakes and it came on, shearing treetops

and snapping telephone lines, to crash in the middle of
the street half a block ahead of me. I took a sharp left
turn into an alley, and then onto the next street paralleling
my own.

If they wanted to play it that way, well—I am not
exactly without resources along those lines myself. I was
pleased that they had done it first, though.

I headed out into the country, to where I could build
up a head of steam.

Lights appeared in my rear-view mirror.

Them?

Too soon.

It was either just another car headed this way, or it was
Stella.

Prudence, as the Greek Chorus says, is better than
imprudence.

I shifted, not gears.

I was whipping along in a lower, more powerful car.

Again, I shifted.

I was driving from the wrong side of the vehicle and
headed up the wrong side of the highway.

Again.

No wheels. My car sped forward on a cushion of air,
above a beaten and dilapidated highway. All the buildings
I passed were of metal. No wood or stone or brick had
gone into the construction of anything I saw.

On the long curve behind me, a pair of headlights
appeared.

I killed my own lights and shifted, again and again, and
again.

I shot through the air, high above a great swampland,
stringing sonic booms like beads along the thread of my
trail. Then another shift, and I shot low over the steaming land where great reptiles raised their heads like bean-
stalks from out their wallows. The sun stood high in this
world, like an acetylene torch in the heavens. I held the
struggling vehicle together by an act of will and waited for
pursuit. There was none.

I shifted again . . .

There was a black forest reaching almost to the foot of
the high hill upon which the ancient castle stood. I was
mounted on a hippogriff, flying, and garbed in the manner

of a warrior-image. I steered my mount to a landing within the forest.

"Become a horse," I ordered, giving the proper guide-word.

Then I was mounted upon a black stallion, trotting along the trail which twisted through the dark forest.

Should I remain here and fight them with magic, or move on and meet them in a world where science prevailed?

Or should I beat a circuitous route from here to some distant Other, hoping to elude them completely?

My questions answered themselves.

There came a clatter of hoofs at my back, and a knight appeared: he was mounted upon a tall, proud steed; he wore burnished armor; upon his shield was set a cross of red.

"You have come far enough," he said. "Draw rein!"

The blade he bore upraised was a wicked and gleaming weapon, until I transformed it into a serpent. He dropped it then, and it slithered off into the underbrush.

"You were saying . . . ?"

"Why don't you give up?" he asked. "Join us, or quit trying?"

"Why don't *you* give up? Quit them and join with me? We could change many times and places together. You have the ability, and the training . . ."

By then he was close enough to lunge, in an attempt to unhorse me with the edge of his shield.

I gestured and his horse stumbled, casting him to the ground.

"Everywhere you go, plagues and wars follow at your heels!" he gasped.

"All progress demands payment. These are the growing pains of which you speak, not the final results."

"Fool! There is no such thing as progress! Not as you see it! What good are all the machines and ideas you un-loose in their cultures, if you do not change the men themselves?"

"Thought and mechanism advances; men follow slowly," I said, and I dismounted and moved to his side. "All that your kind seek is a perpetual Dark Age on all planes of existence. Still, I am sorry for what I must do."

I unsheathed the knife at my belt and slipped it through his visor, but the helm was empty. He had escaped into another Place, teaching me once again the futility of arguing with an ethical evolutionary.

I remounted and rode on.

After a time, there came again the sound of hoofs at my back.

I spoke another word, which mounted me upon a sleek unicorn, to move at a blinding speed through the dark wood. The pursuit continued, however.

Finally, I came upon a small clearing, a cairn piled high in its center. I recognized it as a place of power, so I dismounted and freed the unicorn, which promptly vanished.

I climbed the cairn and sat at its top. I lit a cigar and waited. I had not expected to be located so soon, and it irritated me. I would confront this pursuer here.

A sleep gray mare entered the clearing.

"Stella!"

"Get down from there!" she cried. "They are preparing to unleash an assault any moment now!"

"Amen," I said. "I am ready for it."

"They outnumber you! They always have! You will lose to them again, and again and again, so long as you persist in fighting. Come down and come away with me. It may not be too late!"

"Me, retire?" I asked. "I'm an institution. They would soon be out of crusades without me. Think of the boredom—"

A bolt of lightning dropped from the sky, but it veered away from my cairn and fried a nearby tree.

"They've started!"

"Then get out of here, girl. This isn't your fight."

"You're mine!"

"I'm my own! Nobody else's! Don't forget it!"

"I love you!"

"You betrayed me!"

"No. You say that you love humanity . . ."

"I do."

"I don't believe you! You couldn't, after all you've done to it!"

I raised my hand. "I banish thee from this Now and Here," I said, and I was alone again.

More lightnings descended, charring the ground about me.

I shook my fist.

"Don't you *ever* give up? Give me a century of peace to work with them, and I'll show you a world that you don't believe could exist!" I cried.

In answer, the ground began to tremble.

I fought them. I hurled their lightnings back in their faces. When the winds arose, I bent them inside-out. But the earth continued to shake, and cracks appeared at the foot of the cairn.

"Show yourselves!" I cried. "Come at me one at a time, and I'll teach you of the power I wield!"

But the ground opened up and the cairn came apart.

I fell into darkness.

I was running. I had shifted three times, and I was a furred creature now with a pack howling at my heels, eyes like fiery headlights, fangs like swords.

I was slithering among the dark roots of the banyan, and the long-billed criers were probing after my scaly body . . .

I was darting on the wings of a hummingbird and I heard the cry of a hawk . . .

I was swimming through blackness and there came a tentacle . . .

I broadcast away, peaking and troughing at a high frequency.

I met with static.

I was falling and they were all around me.

I was taken, as a fish is taken in a net. I was snared, bound . . .

I heard her weeping somewhere.

"Why do you try, again and ever again?" she asked. "Why can you not be content with me, with a life of peace and leisure? Do you not remember what they have done to you in the past? Were not your days with me infinitely better?"

"No!" I cried.

"I love you," she said.

"Such love is an imaginary number," I told her, and I was raised from where I lay and borne away.

She followed behind, weeping.

"I pleaded with them to give you a chance at peace, but you threw that gift in my face."

"The peace of the eunuch; the peace of lobotomy, lotus and Thorazine," I said. "No, better they work their wills upon me and let their truth give forth its lie as they do."

"Can you really say that and mean it?" she asked. "Have you already forgotten the sun of the Caucasus—the vulture tearing at your side, day after red hot day?"

"I do not forget," I said, "but I curse them. I will oppose them until the ends of When and Wherever, and someday I shall win."

"I love you," she said.

"How can you say that and mean it?"

"Fool!" came a chorus of voices, as I was laid upon this rock in their cavern and chained.

All day long a bound serpent spits venom into my face, and she holds a pan to catch it. It is only when the woman who betrayed me must empty that pan that its spits into my eyes and I scream.

But I *will* come free again, to aid long-suffering mankind with my many gifts, and there will be a trembling on high that day I end my bondage. Until then, I can only watch the delicate, unbearable bars of her fingers across the bottom of that pan, and scream each time she takes them away.

14.

The Man
Who Loved the Faioli

IT IS THE story of John Auden and the Faioli, and no one
knows it better than I. Listen—

It happened on that evening, as he strolled (for there
was no reason not to stroll) in his favorite places in the
whole world, that he saw the Faioli near the Canyon of
the Dead, seated on a rock, her wings of light flickering,
flickering, flickering and then gone, until it appeared that
a human girl was sitting there, dressed all in white and
weeping, with long black tresses coiled about her waist.

He approached her through the terrible light from the
dying, half-dead sun, in which human eyes could not
distinguish distances nor grasp perspectives properly
(though his could), and he lay his right hand upon her
shoulder and spoke a word of greeting and of comfort.

It was as if he did not exist, however. She continued to
weep, streaking with silver her cheeks the color of snow
or a bone. Her almond eyes looked forward as though
they saw through him, and her long fingernails dug into
the flesh of her palms, though no blood was drawn.

Then he knew that it was true, the things that are said
of the Faioli—that they see only the living and never the
dead, and that they are formed into the loveliest women in
the entire universe. Being dead himself, John Austen de-

239

bated the consequences of becoming a living man once
again, for a time.

The Faioli were known to come to a man the month
before his death—those rare men who still died—and to
live with such a man for that final month of his existence,
rendering to him every pleasure that it is possible for a
human being to know, so that on the day when the kiss of
death is delivered, which sucks the remaining life from his
body, that man accepts it—no, seeks it—with desire and
with grace, for such is the power of the Faioli among all
creatures that there is nothing more to be desired after
such knowledge.

John Auden considered his life and his death, the conditions of the world upon which he stood, the nature of his
stewardship and his curse and the Faioli—who was the
loveliest creature he had seen in all of his four hundred
thousand days of existence—and he touched the place
beneath his left armpit which activated the necessary
mechanism to make him live again.

The creature stiffened beneath his touch, for suddenly
it was flesh, his touch, and flesh, warm and woman-filled,
that he was touching, now that the sensations of life had
returned to him. He knew that his touch had become the
touch of a man once more.

"I said 'hello, and don't cry,' " he said, and her voice
was like the breezes he had forgotten through all the trees
that he had forgotten, with their moisture and their odors
and their colors all brought back to him thus, "From
where do you come, man? You were not here a moment
ago."

"From the Canyon of the Dead," he said.

"Let me touch your face," and he did, and she did.

"It is strange that I did not feel you approach."

"This is a strange world," he replied.

"That is true," she said. "You are the only living thing
upon it."

And he said, "What is your name?"

She said, "Call me Sythia," and he did.

"My name is John," he told her, "John Auden."

"I have come to be with you, to give you comfort and
pleasure," she said, and he knew that the ritual was
beginning.

"Why were you weeping when I found you?" he asked.

"Because I thought there was nothing upon this world, and I was so tired from my travels," she told him. "Do you live near here?"

"Not far away," he answered. "Not far away at all."

"Will you take me there? To the place where you live?"

"Yes."

And she rose and followed him into the Canyon of the Dead, where he made his home.

They descended and they descended, and all about them were the remains of people who once had lived. She did not seem to see these things, however, but kept her eyes fixed upon John's face and her hand upon his arm.

"Why do you call this place the Canyon of the Dead?" she asked him.

"Because they are all about us here, the dead," he replied.

"I feel nothing."

"I know."

They crossed through the Valley of the Bones, where millions of the dead from many races and worlds lay stacked all about them, and she did not see these things. She had come to the graveyard of all the worlds, but she did not realize this thing. She had encountered its tender, its keeper, and she did not know what he was, he who staggered beside her like a man drunken.

John Auden took her to his home—not really the place where he lived, but it would be now—and there he activated ancient circuits within the building within the mountain, and in response light leaped forth from the walls, light he had never needed before but now required.

The door slid shut behind them and the temperature built up to a normal warmth. Fresh air circulated and he took it into his lungs and expelled it, glorying in the forgotten sensation. His heart beat within his breast, a red warm thing that reminded him of the pain and of the pleasure. For the first time in ages, he prepared a meal and fetched a bottle of wine from one of the deep, sealed lockers. How many others could have borne what he had borne?

None, perhaps.

She dined with him, toying with the food, sampling a

bit of everything, eating very little. He, on the other hand, glutted himself fantastically, and they drank of the wine and were happy.

"This place is so strange," she said. "Where do you sleep?"

"I used to sleep in there," he told her, indicating a room he had almost forgotten; and they entered and he showed it to her, and she beckoned him toward the bed and the pleasures of her body.

That night he loved her, many times, with a desperation that burnt away the alcohol and pushed all of his life forward with something like a hunger, but more.

The following day, when the dying sun had splashed the Valley of the Bones with its pale, moonlike light, he awakened and she drew his head to her breast, not having slept herself, and she asked him, "What is the thing that moves you, John Auden? You are not like one of the men who live and who die, but you take life almost like one of the Faioli, squeezing from it everything that you can and pacing it at a tempo that bespeaks a sense of time no man should know. What are you?"

"I am one who knows," he said. "I am one who knows that the days of a man are numbered and one who covets their dispositions as he feels them draw to a close."

"You are strange," said Sythia. "Have I pleased you?"

"More than anything else I have ever known," he said. And she sighed, and he found her lips once again.

They breakfasted, and that day they walked in the Valley of the Bones. He could not distinguish distances nor grasp perspectives properly, and she could not see anything that had been living and now was dead. So, of course, as they sat there on a shelf of stone, his arm about her shoulders, he pointed out to her the rocket which had just come down from out of the sky, and she squinted after his gesture. He indicated the robots, which had begun unloading the remains of the dead of many worlds from the hold of the ship, and she cocked her head to one side and stared ahead, but she did not really see what he was talking about.

Even when one of the robots lumbered up to him and held out the board containing the receipt and the stylus, and as he signed the receipt for the bodies received, she did not see or understand what it was that was occurring.

In the days that followed, his life took upon it a dream-like quality, filled with the pleasure of Sythia and shot through with certain inevitable streaks of pain. Often, she saw him wince, and she asked him concerning his expressions.

And always he would laugh and say, "Pleasure and pain are near to one another," or some thing such as that.

And as the days wore on, she came to prepare the meals and to rub his shoulders and mix his drinks and to recite to him certain pieces of poetry he had somehow once come to love.

A month. A month, he knew, and it would come to an end. The Faioli, whatever they were, paid for the life that they took with the pleasures of the flesh. They always knew when a man's death was near at hand. And in this sense, they always gave more than they received. The life was fleeing anyway, and they enhanced it before they took it away with them, to nourish themselves most likely, price of the things that they'd given.

John Auden knew that no Faioli in the entire universe had ever met a man such as himself.

Sythia was mother-of-pearl, and her body was alternately cold and warm to his caresses, and her mouth was a tiny flame, igniting wherever it touched, with its teeth like needles and its tongue like the heart of a flower. And so he came to know the thing called love for the Faioli called Sythia.

Nothing much really happened beyond the loving. He knew that she wanted him, to use him ultimately, and he was perhaps the only man in the universe able to gull one of her kind. His was the perfect defense against life and against death. Now that he was human and alive, he often wept when he considered it.

He had more than a month to live.

He had maybe three or four.

This month, therefore, was a price he'd willingly pay for what it was that the Faioli offered.

Sythia racked his body and drained from it every drop of pleasure contained within his tired nerve cells. She turned him into a flame, an iceberg, a little boy, an old man. When they were together, his feelings were such that he considered the *consolamentum* as a thing he might really accept at the end of the month, which was drawing near. Why not? He knew she had filled his mind with her presence, on purpose. But what more did existence hold for him? This creature from beyond the stars had brought him every single thing a man could desire. She had baptized him with passion and confirmed him with the quietude which follows after. Perhaps the final oblivion of her final kiss was best after all.

He seized her and drew her to him. She did not understand him, but she responded.

He loved her for it, and this was almost his end.

There is a thing called disease that battens upon all living things, and he had known it beyond the scope of all living men. She could not understand, woman-thing who had known only life.

So he never tried to tell her, though with each day the taste of her kisses grew stronger and saltier and each seemed to him a strengthening shadow, darker and darker, stronger and heavier, of that one thing which he now knew he desired most.

And the day would come. And come it did.

He held her and caressed her, and the calendars of all his days fell about them.

He knew, as he abandoned himself to her ploys and the glories of her mouth, her breasts, that he had been ensnared, as had all men who had known them, by the power of the Faioli. Their strength was their weakness. They were the ultimate in Woman. By their frailty they begat the desire to please. He wanted to merge himself with the pale landscape of her body, to pass within the circles of her eyes and never depart.

He had lost, he knew. For as the days had vanished about him, he had weakened. He was barely able to scrawl his name upon the receipt proffered him by the robot who had lumbered toward him, crushing rib cages and cracking skulls with each terrific step. Briefly, he envied the thing. Sexless, passionless, totally devoted to duty. Before he dismissed it, he asked it, "What would you do if you had desire and you met with a thing that gave you all things you wished for in the world?"

"I would—try to—keep it," it said, red lights blinking

about its dome, before it turned and lumbered off, across the Great Graveyard.

"Yes," said John Auden aloud, "but this thing cannot be done."

Sythia did not understand him, and on that thirty-first day they returned to that place where he had lived for a month and he felt the fear of death, strong, so strong, come upon him.

She was more exquisite than ever before, but he feared this final encounter.

"I love you," he said finally, for it was a thing he had never said before, and she stroked his brow and kissed it.

"I know," she told him, "and your time is almost at hand, to love me completely. Before the final act of love, my John Auden, tell me a thing: What is it that sets you apart? Why is it that you know so much more of things-that-are-not-life than mortal man should know? How was it that you approached me on that first night without my knowing it?"

"It is because I am already dead," he told her. "Can't you see it when you look into my eyes? Do you not feel it, as a certain special chill, whenever I touch you? I came here rather than sleep the cold sleep, which would have me to be in a thing like death anyhow, an oblivion wherein I would not even know I was waiting, waiting for the cure which might never happen, the cure for one of the very last fatal diseases remaining in the universe, the disease which now leaves me only small time of life."

"I do not understand," she said.

"Kiss me and forget it," he told her. "It is better this way. There will doubtless never be a cure, for some things remain always dark, and I have surely been forgotten. You must have sensed the death upon me, when I restored my humanity, for such is the nature of your kind. I did it to enjoy you, knowing you to be of the Faioli. So have your pleasure of me now, and know that I share it. I welcome thee. I have courted thee all the days of my life, unknowing."

But she was curious and asked him (using the familiar for the first time), "How then dost thou achieve this balance between life and that-which-is-not-life, this thing which keeps thee conscious yet unalive?"

"There are controls set within this body I happen, unfortunately, to occupy. To touch this place beneath my armpit will cause my lungs to cease their breathing and my heart to stop its beating. It will set into effect an installed electrochemical system, like those my robots (invisible to you, I know) possess. This is my life within death. I asked for it because I feared oblivion. I volunteered to be gravekeeper to the universe, because in this place there are none to look upon me and be repelled by my deathlike appearance. This is why I am what I am. Kiss me and end it."

But having taken the form of woman, or perhaps being woman all along, the Faioli who was called Sythia was curious, and she said, "This place?" and she touched the spot beneath his left armpit.

With this he vanished from her sight, and with this also, he knew once again the icy logic that stood apart from emotion. Because of this, he did not touch upon the critical spot once again.

Instead, he watched her as she sought for him about the place where he once had lived.

She checked into every closet and adytum, and when she could not discover a living man, she sobbed once, horribly, as she had on that night when first he had seen her. Then the wings flickered, flickered, weakly flickered, back into existence upon her back, and her face dissolved and her body slowly melted. The tower of sparks that stood before him then vanished, and later on that crazy night during which he could distinguish distances and grasp perspectives once again he began looking for her.

And that is the story of John Auden, the only man who ever loved a Faioli and lived (if you could call it that) to tell of it. No one knows it better than I.

No cure has ever been found. And I know that he walks the Canyon of the Dead and considers the bones, sometimes stops by the rock where he met her, blinks after the moist things that are not there, wonders at the judgment that he gave.

It is that way, and the moral may be that life (and perhaps love also) is stronger than that which it contains, but never that which contains it. But only a Faioli could tell you for sure, and they never come here any more.

15.

Lucifer

CARLSON STOOD ON the hill in the silent center of the city whose people had died.

He stared up at the Building—the one structure that dwarfed every hotel-grid, skyscraper-needle, or apartment-cheesebox packed into all the miles that lay about him. Tall as a mountain, it caught the rays of the bloody sun. Somehow it turned their red into golden halfway up its height.

Carlson suddenly felt that he should not have come back.

It had been over two years, as he figured it, since last he had been here. He wanted to return to the mountains now. One look was enough. Yet still he stood before it, transfixed by the huge Building, by the long shadow that bridged the entire valley. He shrugged his thick shoulders then, in an unsuccessful attempt to shake off memories of the days, five (or was it six?) years ago, when he had worked within the giant unit.

Then he climbed the rest of the way up the hill and entered the high, wide doorway.

His fiber sandals cast a variety of echoes as he passed through the deserted offices and into the long hallway that led to the belts.

The belts, of course, were still. There were no thousands

247

riding them. There was no one alive to ride. Their deep belly-rumble was only a noisy phantom in his mind as he climbed onto the one nearest him and walked ahead into the pitchy insides of the place.

It was like a mausoleum. There seemed no ceiling, no walls, only the soft *pat-pat* of his soles on the flexible fabric of the belt.

He reached a junction and mounted a cross-belt, instinctively standing still for a moment and waiting for the forward lurch as it sensed his weight.

Then he chuckled silently and began walking again.

When he reached the lift, he set off to the right of it until his memory led him to the maintenance stairs. Shouldering his bundle, he began the long, groping ascent.

He blinked at the light when he came into the Power Room. Filtered through its hundred high windows, the sunlight trickled across the dusty acres of machinery.

Carlson sagged against the wall, breathing heavily from the climb. After awhile he wiped a workbench clean and set down his parcel.

Then he removed his faded shirt, for the place would soon be stifling. He brushed his hair from his eyes and advanced down the narrow metal stair to where the generators stood, row on row, like an army of dead, black beetles. It took him six hours to give them all a cursory check.

He selected three in the second row and systematically began tearing them down, cleaning them, soldering their loose connections with the auto-iron, greasing them, oiling them and sweeping away all the dust, cobwebs, and pieces of cracked insulation that lay at their bases.

Great rivulets of perspiration ran into his eyes and down along his sides and thighs, spilling in little droplets onto the hot flooring and vanishing quickly.

Finally, he put down his broom, remounted the stair and returned to his parcel. He removed one of the water bottles and drank off half its contents. He ate a piece of dried meat and finished the bottle. He allowed himself one cigarette then, and returned to work.

He was forced to stop when it grew dark. He had planned on sleeping right there, but the room was too oppressive.

So he departed the way he had come and slept beneath the stars, on the roof of a low building at the foot of the hill.

It took him two more days to get the generators ready. Then he began work on the huge Broadcast Panel. It was in better condition than the generators, because it had last been used two years ago. Whereas the generators, save for the three he had burned out last time, had slept for over five (or was it six?) years.

He soldered and wiped and inspected until he was satisfied. Then only one task remained.

All the maintenance robots stood frozen in mid-gesture. Carlson would have to wrestle a three hundred pound power cube without assistance. If he could get one down from the rack and onto a cart without breaking a wrist he would probably be able to convey it to the Igniter without much difficulty. Then he would have to place it within the oven. He had almost ruptured himself when he did it two years ago, but he hoped that he was somewhat stronger —and luckier—this time.

It took him ten minutes to clean the Igniter oven. Then he located a cart and pushed it back to the rack.

One cube was resting at just the right height, approximately eight inches above the level of the cart's bed. He kicked down the anchor chocks and moved around to study the rack. The cube lay on a downward-slanting shelf, restrained by a two-inch metal guard. He pushed at the guard. It was bolted to the shelf.

Returning to the work area, he searched the tool boxes for a wrench. Then he moved back to the rack and set to work on the nuts.

The guard came loose as he was working on the fourth nut. He heard a dangerous creak and threw himself back out of the way, dropping the wrench on his toes.

The cube slid forward, crushed the loosened rail, teetered a bare moment, then dropped with a resounding crash onto the heavy bed of the cart. The bed surface bent and began to crease beneath its weight; the cart swayed toward the outside. The cube continued to slide until over half a foot projected beyond the edge. Then the cart righted itself and shivered into steadiness.

Carlson sighed and kicked loose the chocks, ready to

jump back should it suddenly give way in his direction.
It held.

Gingerly, he guided it up the aisle and between the
rows of generators, until he stood before the Igniter. He
anchored the cart again, stopped for water and a cigarette,
then searched up a pinch bar, a small jack and a long,
flat metal plate.

He laid the plate to bridge the front end of the cart
and the opening to the oven. He wedged the far end in
beneath the Igniter's doorframe.

Unlocking the rear chocks, he inserted the jack and
began to raise the back end of the wagon, slowly, working
with one hand and holding the bar ready in the other.

The cart groaned as it moved higher. Then a sliding,
grating sound began and he raised it faster.

With a sound like the stroke of a cracked bell the cube
tumbled onto the bridgeway; it slid forward and to the left.
He struck at it with the bar, bearing to the right with all
his strength. About half an inch of it caught against the
left edge of the oven frame. The gap between the cube
and the frame was widest at the bottom.

He inserted the bar and heaved his weight against it—
three times.

Then it moved forward and came to rest within the
Igniter.

He began to laugh. He laughed until he felt weak. He
sat on the broken cart, swinging his legs and chuckling to
himself, until the sounds coming from his throat seemed
alien and out of place. He stopped abruptly and slammed
the door.

The Broadcast Panel had a thousand eyes, but none of
them winked back at him. He made the final adjustments
for Transmit, then gave the generators their last checkout.

After that, he mounted a catwalk and moved to a
window.

There was still some daylight to spend, so he moved
from window to window pressing the "Open" button set
below each sill.

He ate the rest of his food then, and drank a whole bottle
of water and smoked two cigarettes. Sitting on the stair,
he thought of the days when he had worked with Kelly

and Murchison and Djizinsky, twisting the tails of electrons until they wailed and leapt out over the walls and fled down into the city.

The clock! He remembered it suddenly—set high on the wall, to the left of the doorway, frozen at 9:33 (and forty-eight seconds).

He moved a ladder through the twilight and mounted it to the clock. He wiped the dust from its greasy face with a sweeping, circular movement. Then he was ready.

He crossed to the Igniter and turned it on. Somewhere the ever-batteries came alive, and he heard a click as a thin, sharp shaft was driven into the wall of the cube. He raced back up the stairs and sped hand-over-hand up to the catwalk. He moved to a window and waited.

"God," he murmured, "don't let them blow! Please don't—"

Across an eternity of darkness the generators began humming. He heard a crackle of static from the Broadcast Panel and he closed his eyes. The sound died.

He opened his eyes as he heard the window slide upward. All around him the hundred high windows opened. A small light came on above the bench in the work area below him, but he did not see it.

He was staring out beyond the wide drop of the acropolis and down into the city. His city.

The lights were not like the stars. They beat the stars all to hell. They were the gay, regularized constellation of a city where men made their homes: even rows of streetlamps, advertisements, lighted windows in the cheesebox-apartments, a random solitaire of bright squares running up the sides of skyscraper-needles, a searchlight swivelling its luminous antenna through cloudbanks that hung over the city.

He dashed to another window, feeling the high night breezes comb at his beard. Belts were humming below; he heard their wry monologues rattling through the city's deepest canyons. He pictured the people in their homes, in theaters, in bars—talking to each other, sharing a common amusement, playing clarinets, holding hands, eating an evening snack. Sleeping ro-cars awakened and rushed past each other on the levels above the belts; the background hum of the city told him its story of production, of function, of movement and service to its inhabitants. The sky seemed to wheel overhead, as though the city were its turning hub and the universe its outer rim.

Then the lights dimmed from white to yellow and he hurried, with desperate steps, to another window.

"No! Not so soon! Don't leave me yet!" he sobbed.

The windows closed themselves and the lights went out. He stood on the walk for a long time, staring at the dead embers. A smell of ozone reached his nostrils. He was aware of a blue halo about the dying generators.

He descended and crossed the work area to the ladder he had set against the wall.

Pressing his face against the glass and squinting for a long time he could make out the position of the hands.

"Nine thirty-five, and twenty-one seconds," Carlson read.

"Do you hear that?" he called out, shaking his fist at anything. "Ninety-three seconds! I made you live for ninety-three seconds!"

Then he covered his face against the darkness and was silent.

After a long while he descended the stairway, walked the belt, and moved through the long hallway and out of the Building. As he headed back toward the mountains he promised himself—again—that he would never return.